PRAISE FOR JESSICA WARMAN

 the last good day of the year

"Engrossing. . . . A suspenseful and haunting look at the uncertainty of memory." —*Booklist*

"Hauntingly written." —*Kirkus Reviews*

 beautiful Lies

★ "Warman seems to specialize in intimacy made urgent by grief, and it's that as much as the thriller plot that readers will be left remembering." —*BCCB*, starred review

 Between

A YALSA-ALA Best Fiction for Young Adults Pick

★ "Compelling." —*BCCB*, starred review

★ "A perfect read for teens who like complex characters." —*Booklist*, starred review

Books by Jessica Warman

Breathless
Where the Truth Lies
Between
Beautiful Lies
The Last Good Day of the Year

the last good day of the year

jessica warman

BLOOMSBURY
NEW YORK LONDON OXFORD NEW DELHI SYDNEY

First published in the United States of America in May 2015
by Bloomsbury Children's Books
Paperback edition published in May 2016
www.bloomsbury.com

Bloomsbury is a registered trademark of Bloomsbury Publishing Plc

For information about permission to reproduce selections from this book, write to
Permissions, Bloomsbury Children's Books, 1385 Broadway, New York, New York 10018
Bloomsbury books may be purchased for business or promotional use. For information on bulk
purchases please contact Macmillan Corporate and Premium Sales Department at
specialmarkets@macmillan.com

The Library of Congress has cataloged the hardcover edition as follows:
Warman, Jessica.
The last good day of the year / by Jessica Warman.
pages   cm
Summary: Ten years after Samantha and her next door neighbor Remy watched as a man broke into
Sam's home and lifted her younger sister, Turtle, from her sleeping bag, Sam's shattered family
returns to her childhood home in an effort to heal, and the more they re-examine the events of that
fateful night, the more questions they discover about what really happened to Turtle.
ISBN 978-0-8027-3662-8 (hardcover) • ISBN 978-0-8027-3664-2 (e-book)
[1. Kidnapping—Fiction. 2. Sisters—Fiction. 3. Family problems—Fiction.
4. Psychic trauma—Fiction.] I. Title.
PZ7.W2374Las 2015   [Fic]—dc23   2014021230

ISBN 978-0-8027-3663-5 (paperback)

Book design by Amanda Bartlett
Typeset by Westchester Book Composition
Printed and bound in the U.S.A. by Berryville Graphics Inc, Berryville, Virginia
2 4 6 8 10 9 7 5 3 1

All papers used by Bloomsbury Publishing, Inc., are natural, recyclable products
made from wood grown in well-managed forests. The manufacturing processes
conform to the environmental regulations of the country of origin.

For Colin, of course.
And for my father, William Bush. Thank you for teaching me how
to keep a promise—and for teaching me that it matters.

Hiraeth: *n*: homesickness for a home to which you cannot return, a home that maybe never was; nostalgia, yearning, grief for the lost places of your past

chapter one

New Year's Day, 1986

Midnight had come and gone, but Remy and I were still awake. How could anyone expect us to sleep with all the activity going on above us? Our mothers had tucked us into our sleeping bags hours ago, but the adults had continued their party upstairs. Through the thin basement ceiling above our heads, we felt the constant, dull tremble of the music playing on the living room stereo. If we paid close enough attention, we could track the path of every footstep right down to its owner—my mom's light gait, my dad's clumsy plodding that sent occasional sprinkles of drywall from the seams of the recently finished basement walls. We heard their countdown to midnight, followed by the *pop-pop-pop* of corks from champagne bottles. We listened to Ed Tickle and Darla—whom we all knew as Darla Tickle, even though she and Abby's dad were never married—saying their good-nights. Remy's mom played a tinny version of "Auld Lang Syne" on the electric keyboard I'd gotten for Christmas a few days earlier. We smelled the cigars that our dads had lit up the second us kids had been banished to the game room, the smoke spilling downstairs and permeating every surface, souring the warm basement air almost instantly. We heard Remy's dad tell a dirty joke, and I thought I'd never be able to look him straight in the eye again. We heard our mothers screeching with laughter at the punch line, and I think we both felt horrified by this quick glimpse behind the curtain of adulthood, which brought with it the creeping realization that our parents, when they weren't being our parents, did all kinds of things we didn't understand or expect.

Beside me on the floor, Turtle slept through all of it. My sister—whose real name was Tabitha, but nobody ever called her that—was four years old. Remy and I were seven. The three of us were resting side by side on the carpet, with Remy nearest the stairs, me in the middle, and Turtle cocooned next to me in her Disney Princess sleeping bag, Boris, her tattered stuffed bear, in her arms. Her wavy blond hair almost glowed in the moonlight that shined through the sliding glass door at our backs. I'd always been jealous of her hair, which was thick and dense but soft as silk. My own hair was coarse and wavy, full of cowlicks that kept it looking unkempt, and my mother forced me to wear a bob cut even though I wanted to grow it long; but my little sister's hair hung almost to her waist in smooth tendrils that sometimes seemed to sigh with the weight of their own beauty. Turtle's small body took up less than half of the length of her sleeping bag. She was sucking her right thumb, like babies do, and pulling in slow, even breaths as she remained unconscious despite all the noise coming from upstairs.

It was well known in my family that Turtle could sleep through just about anything. A few months earlier, our dad had fallen asleep on the sofa late at night, forgetting he'd left the oven on with a frozen pizza baking inside. The sound of the smoke alarm was so loud and piercing that my eyes watered; if it had gone on too much longer, I might have thrown up. On my way back to bed, I found my mother standing in the doorway to the room I shared with Turtle, staring at her. My sister was still dead asleep, Boris nestled beside her with his head peeking out from under the blanket. Turtle's thumb was planted securely in her mouth as she dreamed of rainbows or puppies, or whatever four-year-olds dream about. Her blanket was still smooth across her body, the top folded down and tucked beneath her chin, just the way our mother had left it hours ago. Turtle hadn't moved.

According to Channel 4 meteorologist Mike Schmitt, that year's winter was our area's coldest in decades. Shelocta, the little town where I lived, was situated in a valley in the mountains of southeastern Pennsylvania. Lousy winter weather was nothing new, but that season was so cold and hostile to life that I remember wondering whether nature was deliberately trying to harm us. By early December, school had already been canceled a handful of times due to the temperature alone. There was a ten-day stretch where it didn't even manage to climb into the single digits. People had trouble starting their cars in the morning. Some of the moms in our neighborhood put together a list of all the elderly residents and took turns checking up on them, making sure they hadn't frozen to death. Leo and Milly Souza, the elderly Portuguese couple who lived down the street, started dressing their beloved German shepherds in thick sweaters and booties that Milly had knitted herself. Some mornings we'd wake up to find that, while we slept, slivers of frost had grown through the seams around the light switch beside our kitchen sink. It was a mean kind of cold. My dad called it "suicide weather."

The game room was toasty, though, with all three baseboard radiators purring along at full blast. Combined with the heat coming from the space heater that my dad had left running in the bathroom a few feet away—he spent a lot of time that year fretting over the possibility of a burst pipe—it was almost too warm; I was sweating inside my sleeping bag. Remy was still awake, but I was starting to fade. I tried to fight it. Remy thought he was so tough, being a boy and all, even though I was taller and could run faster. He'd bet me a dollar that I couldn't stay up until midnight. I'd already won, but I wanted to be the last to fall asleep. I knew I wasn't going to be able to hold out much longer.

Our moms had ushered us downstairs at ten o'clock sharp that evening—a full hour past our normal bedtimes, but still disappointingly early for New Year's Eve. They'd pulled the standard bedtime scam that parents shamelessly use on holidays and special occasions: "You don't have to go to sleep yet, but you have to stay in bed." Once we were downstairs, Turtle threw a temper tantrum when I wouldn't let her share my sleeping bag. She had a pitchy, shrill way of crying that could drive anyone crazy, and anytime she was overtired, her collapse into sleep was always preceded by a meltdown. The adults were having none of it that night: my mom ignored Turtle while she put our copy of *Sleeping Beauty* in the VCR and turned it down so low that we couldn't hear a thing over the crying, kissed our foreheads, zipped up our sleeping bags, switched off the lights, marched upstairs, and shut the basement door behind her. She managed to do all of this while still holding on to her drink, a red plastic cup filled with foamy champagne that splashed onto my nightgown when she bent over to kiss me good night.

"I think your mom is drunk," Remy said.

"What's 'drunk'?" Turtle asked. She had finished crying, and would be asleep any second.

Remy and I exchanged an annoyed look, as though it were such an awful drag to be down here with someone so intellectually inferior to us, a couple of real mental giants. Turtle and I were like most sisters in the sense that we loved each other fiercely but fought almost nonstop. I didn't like having a little sister. There were so many things I wasn't allowed to do because *she* was too little, and our parents didn't want her to feel left out. I'd wasted countless pennies already in my short life, tossing them into fountains and wishing she would disappear. "Don't you know anything, Turtle? You're so dumb sometimes." I pinched her on the arm, harder than I should have. Even once I knew it was too hard—after she yelped and tried to pull her arm away—I held on for two or three more seconds. Even then, I couldn't have told you why I did it.

Turtle's chin trembled, and her eyes filled up again. "I'm not dumb. I'm four."

"Go to sleep. We don't want to play with you."

"Remy does." And she looked at him for confirmation, but all he did was turn away and focus his gaze on the television screen. While lonely Aurora sang of her yearning for the one true love who would come into her life and make everything okay, I saw the pain I'd caused Turtle for no good reason and thought, *Good.*

My sister shut her eyes, wringing tears from her lashes. She held on tightly to Boris. She never went to bed without him. His white fur was matted and dirty because Turtle refused to let our mother put him through the wash. She was afraid his ear would fall off, and she was probably right to be. Caligula (one of the Souzas' dogs) had torn it off months earlier during an ill-conceived game of tug-of-war. Mrs. Souza had sewn it back on with purple thread, creating a crooked scar along the seam.

"I'm going to tell Momma you won't play with me."

"You'll get punished. We aren't supposed to go upstairs."

"You're being too mean."

"I hate you."

I was only seven, and we were siblings. Siblings fight. It's not like we were heading into Cain and Abel territory quite yet. But when she put her head onto her pillow and closed her eyes, she balled her hands into little fists and cried without making any noise, and I knew I'd gone too far. I told her I was sorry. I think I even told her I loved her. She asked me to snuggle with her while we watched the movie—that was her big thing, always wanting to snuggle with everybody—and I did, until she fell asleep a few minutes later. I pulled her sleeping bag up to her chin and brushed a few stray hairs from her face. I kissed her cheek and whispered, "Good night."

Remy and I practiced cartwheels and headstands while the

movie played. We started a game of Bloody Mary in the bathroom, but got too scared to finish. We took turns seeing how long we could stand being outside without a coat or shoes. Neither of us made it past twenty seconds.

Remy was like a brother to me. His family had lived next door my whole life. Our mothers were best friends who had been pregnant with us at the same time; I'd seen tons of photos taken throughout their pregnancies, their arms around each other's waists, big bellies nearly touching. We even shared the same birthday—August 25—and had joint parties every year. Each July, our families piled into Mr. Mitchell's old conversion van and drove eight hours to a rented beach bungalow in Ocean City. Those were the days I like to mull over now, when I need something happy to remember. Neither of our families had much money, but that fact didn't make the stars above the ocean shine any less at night.

For the first seven years of our lives, I spent almost as much time at Remy's house as I did at mine, and vice versa. I had two sisters—Turtle and Gretchen, who was seventeen—but Remy was an only child, and I think he and I gave each other something we otherwise would have missed. Having Remy next door meant that I always had somewhere to go when I'd had enough of my own sisters. For Remy, having me meant having someone like a sibling, even if that someone was a girl.

By the time the movie ended, we were both in our sleeping bags again. "I don't think I'll go to sleep at all tonight," Remy said. "I'm not tired." He was out by the time I bothered to respond. Without him to keep me company, there wasn't much to do besides listen to our parents as they goofed around above us. I heard Remy's dad shouting from the kitchen: "Sharon, can I eat this cookie dough? You sure? Awesome."

The one-sided exchange filled me with enough fury to sit up and silently freak out at the ceiling, waving my arms and mouthing my outrage. My mother had clearly forgotten that it was my cookie dough she was so thoughtlessly giving away. I thought about stomping upstairs to remind her, but knew it would get me nowhere. I lay on my side and pouted while I stared into our yard through the sliding glass doors. It was a clear night with a full moon, and it had started to snow a little bit, the flakes swirling in the wind, the cold air whipping past with what felt like purpose, its singular goal to destroy even the tiniest pocket of warmth.

My eyes were shut when I heard the *click* of the backyard floodlight turning on. It had a motion sensor, and I turned my head to look outside, expecting to see a deer. Instead I saw Santa Claus. He was just standing there in the snow, his body so still and calm that I could have mistaken him for a statue if he hadn't begun to sway ever so slightly. He was thinner than any self-respecting Santa ought to be. His wig and beard, which were one piece, rested crookedly on his head.

As I watched him, I felt more curious than anything else. I wasn't scared, not at first. We were safely on the other side of the sliding glass door, and our parents were only a few steps away. Nobody was going to hurt us, especially not this guy. I mean, I knew he wasn't the real Santa. I wasn't even sure Santa existed at all. But a seven-year-old's grasp on reality is fluid at best. *Santa's skinny now? And he's in my yard? That doesn't seem right, but I'll accept it.*

All that time he kept staring at the ground, swaying a little but otherwise not moving. If I had to guess, I'd say he stood there for a full minute like that before he started opening and closing his fists like someone getting himself ready for a fight, the same as I'd seen my dad do only the day before. The stranger in my yard raised his face and started strolling toward my house. I closed my eyes and held them shut for as long as I could stand it, and then took a peek.

He stood with his nose pressed against the sliding glass door, his gloved hands cupped around his eyes as he peered inside.

The fear was swift and crippling, in the sense that I had no control over it whatsoever. Have you ever had a dream or a nightmare in which you're trying to scream but can't force your body to make any sound? It was like that. I felt as if I had no mouth at all, like I was suffocating with fear. I kept my eyes shut, hoping I'd only imagined Santa, but when I opened them he was still there. His hand was on the door handle now, and I knew the door was not locked. I knew he was coming in. I closed my eyes again. I wanted to scream so badly, but I could barely breathe. I couldn't move. All I felt was the cold rattle of panic in my gut and the hard beat of blood in my ears.

The party upstairs suddenly seemed very far away. I heard the door slide open and felt the freezing air rush into the basement, and I knew it was too late to run; he was right here, inside, standing above us. I could hear him breathing. The sound seemed to fill the room, drowning out all other noise. I could smell tobacco on his clothing. He stood there for what felt like forever, although in reality it was probably less than a minute. Then he knelt down behind us, and I felt the warmth of his breath on my face and heard his clothing moving against his body. I heard him slowly unzip Turtle's sleeping bag and lift her small, sleeping form into his arms, but I still could not force myself to move or scream. I wanted to more than anything, but I couldn't.

I kept my eyes shut as I sensed him carrying her away. She was wearing shoes with her nightgown; she'd gotten a pair of red slip-ons covered in sequins, like Dorothy's in *The Wizard of Oz*, for Christmas and had been wearing them nonstop for the past week. When I was finally able to open my eyes, the first thing I saw was the sliding glass door, which he'd closed, and the dark backyard lit only by the moon. I thought maybe it had all been a terrible nightmare. I reached for my sister, but she wasn't there. Turtle was gone. I didn't know it yet, but she was never coming home.

chapter two

Summer 1996

I didn't realize how poor we were, not until the fact became an important plot point in the media's approach to my family's narrative. People say the news doesn't care about missing kids unless they're rich, white, and cute. I guess even if you can't claim all three of those, having one of them in spades can still be enough to hold people's attention. When a journalist from National Public Radio did a story on Turtle and our family back in 1990, he described our appearance for listeners by observing that if Hollywood ever made a movie based on us, they'd have a tough time finding actors good-looking enough to play our parts with any accuracy.

But we were poor back then, whether I knew it or not, and we're still poor today. I've been holding on to all these memories of home for ten years, clinging to the version of my childhood that's easiest to manage. Everything about our old house is *sort* of the same as I remember it, but it's different in a million little ways that add up quick: the ceilings are lower, the windows and rooms are smaller, the kitchen linoleum is a seamy array of ugly black and white squares instead of the shiny checkerboard floor of my memories. It was a dump back then, and it's still a dump now; the only real difference is that it's older. My mind has done its best to Photoshop those early years, to make what was dull and bleak more shiny and hopeful by polishing the memories with so much nostalgic wax.

Our place in Shelocta was at the end of a cul-de-sac. We were the last of a four-unit block of town houses. The Mitchells lived next door; the Souzas were on their other side, followed by Ed Tickle and his daughter, Abby, and Ed's girlfriend, Darla. If Remy was like my brother, then Abby Tickle was Gretchen's sister. They were best friends.

We moved almost a year to the day after my sister was taken, and it always seemed to me that the idea was to never, ever return. I guess plans change. When my dad lost his job in Virginia last winter, my parents couldn't afford to pay our rent anymore. They've never been great with money.

The move back here is supposed to be temporary. It was the only choice we had; we couldn't afford to go anywhere else. Since my parents couldn't manage to sell the house on Taylor Street, even at a steep discount, they've been renting it out for the past nine years. But the last tenant disappeared in January after failing to pay his rent for the third month in a row. On February 1, I woke before dawn to the sounds of my mom's Toyota getting towed away by a repo company. Two weeks later, on Valentine's Day, my father fell asleep in our old station wagon while it was parked in our garage with the engine still running. The doctor at the emergency room told us he'd nearly died from asphyxiation. My dad insists the whole thing was an accident. Nobody believes him.

So here we are, once again. It's the last place any of us wants to be, and the only place left for us to go.

Mike Mitchell taps on our kitchen window with his beer can while I'm unpacking a box of silverware. The clock on our stove reads 11:39 a.m. I wave him inside and call downstairs to the basement for my parents.

"Look at you, Sammie. All grown up." His mustache is foamy with Michelob.

"How old are you now?" he asks.

"I'm the same age as Remy."

"They have the same birthday, you dolt!" My mother gives him a hug; he wraps his arms around her and leans back, lifting her entire body a few inches off the floor. "It's so good to see you." She looks around. "Where's your beautiful wife?"

"Susie's on her way over—here she comes." Mike looks disappointed by his wife's arrival at the back door.

"I told you to leave them alone until this afternoon, Mike. I *told* him to leave you alone until later," Susan explains, giving my mom a quick half hug.

"Don't worry about it. We know how excited he gets." My mom winks. I wonder if she realizes how awkward other women feel when she starts oozing charm. Even Susan probably doesn't appreciate it.

Susan was always pretty—not beautiful—and I know my mom

will say later that her old friend has "let herself go," as though it's the worst thing a woman can do. Today, Susan wears a shapeless yellow dress that's seen the inside of a washing machine a few dozen times too many. Her brown hair is starting to turn gray. She's tried to cover it up with a bad dye job—she probably does it herself in front of the bathroom mirror—and there are narrow bands of color starting at her scalp that vary slightly in shade and intensity, like a tree's rings. She still teaches music at the local high school, and looks every bit the part.

If you look at them side by side, my mom and Susan don't seem like they could ever be friends. My mom has always been a high-maintenance kind of woman when it comes to her looks. She was an honest-to-goodness beauty queen in her younger days. She won the title of Little Miss Pittsburgh at age twelve; at seventeen she was Miss Pennsylvania; and by nineteen she was a top-ten finalist at the Miss America pageant. She went right from appearing at local supermarket openings and corporate ribbon-cutting ceremonies to marrying my dad. That wasn't the order in which she'd planned to do things—she'd wanted to go to college, then get married, and then have kids, which was the way everyone was supposed to do it. But things don't always go according to plan; crazy how that works, isn't it? She got pregnant, got married, and had Gretchen three months later. She liked being a mom so much that she hung up her sash and tiara for good, but her looks stuck around. Even now, she's a knockout at forty-eight, prettier than I could ever dream of being. Men still stop her on the street sometimes and say, "Has anyone ever told you that you look just like Christie Brinkley?" She loves the attention. She'll bat her eyelashes and pretend to get flustered, but she doesn't let them get the wrong impression: "That's so sweet. My husband says the same thing all the time."

"Oh. My. God. This cannot be Sam," Susan says, clapping a hand to her mouth. "Little Samantha? Is that really you?" When she goes to smooth my hair with her fingers, I instinctively duck away.

"Sam, honey, don't be shy." My mom then talks about me as if I'm not even in the same room. "Samantha is our little misfit right now. She's very underwhelmed by adolescence. She was such an early bloomer—"

"*Mom!*"

"Ha! And she's so shy! I don't know where she gets it from. She spent the entire car ride with her nose buried in a book. She loves to read. Don't you, Sam?"

"Sharon. You're embarrassing her." My dad gets it. He never does much about it, but he gets it.

"Aw, relax, Sam." Mike Mitchell slings an arm around my shoulders. "You can't be shy around us! Hell, I've seen you naked!"

"*Michael.* Jesus. Could you not?"

"Susie-Q. Gimme a break. She's a gorgeous young woman." He takes a step back to get a better look at me. "We all get older, Sam, but not everyone gets better. You've got yourself a winning lottery ticket when it comes to looks, though."

"Ha, ha, ha!" My mom actually tosses her head back as she laughs, showing everyone her mouth full of silver fillings. "You're so bad!"

"Mike, you're acting like an ass." Susan rolls her eyes, but it's

all for show; she knows it, Mike knows it, and my parents and I
know it. Mr. Mitchell has always been this way—loud, inappropriate, goofy—and Susan has always pretended to be *this close* to
fed up with him.

"Is Remy home?" I ask, trying to change the subject.

"Remy?" Mike shakes his head. "Who the hell knows what he's
doing? Probably knocking off a 7-Eleven right about now."

"He's out with friends," Susan says, "but he'll be home soon.
He's excited to see you, Sam."

I'm sure he can't wait.

From her place beneath the kitchen table, my little sister,
Hannah, taps my leg. I kneel down to meet her at eye level. "What
are you doing down here?"

"Hiding." Hannah is five. She's charming and beautiful, my
mother's new everything. Next January, Hannah will compete in
her first beauty pageant. We may not have money to pay our rent
every month, but somehow my mother finds room in our budget
for as many dance lessons and sequined costumes as Hannah's
pursuits require.

My parents call her their miracle baby. That's one way of putting it, I guess. They've always used little euphemisms to explain the
wide age gaps between some of their children: Gretchen was their
"oops" baby; I was their "pleasant surprise." Out of their four children, only Turtle was planned. Hannah wasn't an accident, but I
wouldn't call her "planned" as much as I'd call her . . . I don't
know. Something else.

"Come on up. Everybody is nice, I promise."

She pops a thumb into her mouth and shakes her head. She's

not supposed to be sucking her thumb. Mom has tried to break her of the habit by wiping her nail with acetone to make it taste bad.

"Why are you being shy?"

She shrugs and removes her thumb just enough to speak clearly. "I want to go home."

"We are home. Come on, you'll be fine." Before I have a chance to stand up, she scoots past me and goes running down the hallway. The Mitchells barely get a glimpse of her ruffled yellow dress and black patent leather mini-heels before she disappears into the dining room. For the briefest moment, I catch a look of horror on Susan Mitchell's face, and I know exactly what she's thinking. I mean, she knew my parents had another child after Turtle disappeared, but I guess seeing her in the flesh really drives home the point: Hannah is their do-over.

"Is she okay upstairs by herself?" Susan's gaze lingers on the empty hallway as Hannah's footsteps fade above us.

"She's not by herself," I say. "Gretchen is up there, too, but I think she's in the shower."

My mom's smile always seems genuine, even when it's not. It's a skill she picked up as a teenage beauty queen. "Why don't you go check on her?" She beams at me. Her eyes sparkle, but her jaw is clenched.

"Okay." I pause. "Do you mean Hannah? Or Gretchen?"

"She means Gretchen." Mike winks at me. "Go make sure she doesn't already have a boy up there in her bedroom." He winces as the words are still leaving his mouth. "Christ, that's not what I meant. I'm sorry."

My mom pretends he didn't say anything that would require an apology. "You've been getting some sun, Mike. You look great."

My dad hands him a fresh beer. "Have something to wash your foot down." Beads of sweat are gathered along his hairline, even though the house is cool. A fat vein pulses on the side of his neck. "Drink up, buddy. It's five o'clock somewhere, right?"

Gretchen is on the floor in our parents' bedroom. Her hair is wrapped in a towel, and she's wearing a ratty old bathrobe that used to belong to our mother. She holds a red plastic Solo cup between her knees, silently running an index finger along the rim.

I don't know my sister that well. Once she left for college in Texas, she rarely came home to visit. We weren't even invited to her wedding. I remember overhearing lots of heated phone calls as a kid, my mom crying and begging her to come home. My parents were more worried about her than angry or upset. They worried when she dropped out of college and moved in with one of her professors, a Dr. M. Paul Culangelo. They worried when she called to inform us she'd eloped in Maui. They worried when she finally brought him home to meet us, because he was kind and seemed to genuinely adore her. His first name, we learned, was Michael. Think about it for a second. I didn't expect to like him, but I did. He was only six years older than Gretchen, so not quite the middle-aged predator my parents had expected. It was nice for a while, but their visits—three of them in the space of four months, which was more than I'd seen my sister in the past ten years—always had a twinge of desperation, as though they were an attempt to paste together a family from scraps. We hoped the sense of togetherness would last, but knew it wouldn't.

I have no idea why Gretchen left him. When Ed Tickle had a stroke last January, Gretchen came back to Shelocta to help Abby take care of her father. She's been here ever since; according to our mom, things are strained in Gretchen's marriage at the moment, but it might not be over for good. I'm not convinced she knows what she's talking about. I can't imagine Gretchen sharing that kind of detail with any of us, least of all our mother. My dad is the only one she has much of a relationship with. She was always his favorite, even after everything that happened with Turtle.

I can tell Gretchen is trying to be as close to invisible as possible when I'm around. She spends a lot of time in her bedroom with the door closed. She goes to bed early and gets up late. But how can she not expect me to be fascinated by her? She is impossibly beautiful—even more so than our mother—and her looks are so startling, so unnerving, that I can't imagine ever feeling comfortable being in the same room with her. She must know what she has, right? That classic, all-American look that girls everywhere struggle for—blond hair, blue eyes, clear skin, impossible hip-to-waist proportions—comes so easily to Gretchen. Even though I haven't seen her use it, she must be aware of the power that comes with her kind of beauty, the Helen-of-Troy implications that will follow her throughout her life. Even Hannah already knows damn well that being pretty makes everything easier.

Gretchen doesn't acknowledge me as I stand in the doorway. She just stares at the cup.

"Gretchen?"

The cup goes flying as she flinches, then scrambles to regain her grasp. She tucks the cup into the folds of her bathrobe, as if she's trying to keep me from seeing it.

"The Mitchells are downstairs." I take a few tiny steps forward, inching my way into the room.

She barely reacts. "Okay," she says, staring at the wall behind me, unwilling to make eye contact. Neither one of us says anything for a moment.

"Are you going to say hi to them?" I ask.

No answer.

"I could, uh . . . I could tell them you're still in the shower. I could tell them you're busy."

She finally looks at me. "Why would you do that?"

Most of our conversations have been like this recently: tentative and agonizing. "Is Remy here, too?" she continues.

I shake my head.

"Have you talked to him lately?" I think I detect the slightest hint of accusation in her voice, but can't be certain. Gretchen has lived in Texas for the past ten years, and she's developed a heavy southern accent. Its effect is unnerving for two reasons: first, when I talk to her, I feel like I'm speaking to someone who is almost my sister, but not exactly; it's like she's Bizarro Gretchen. Second— and far more disturbing—I know her thick drawl is mostly an act. Her speech couldn't have changed so drastically in one decade. So why is she faking it?

Before I can escape, she stares at me with milky blue eyes that don't blink as she pats the space beside her on the floor. "Sit with me for a minute." Sensing my hesitation—those eyes have a way of unnerving me like nothing else—she says, "Please? Not for long, I promise." She has these occasional bursts of interest in me that come out of nowhere, small explosions of tenderness that she shrinks away from before they blossom into anything meaning-ful. When she tugs the towel from her hair, the smell of strawberry shampoo settles around us, rippling every time she turns her head. Her skin is translucent. She was never going to take the beauty queen route with her looks. She's a jeans and T-shirt kind of woman, always has been.

"Do you hate me, Samantha? You can tell me. I won't be mad."

How does a person respond to such a question? "I'm your sister."

She drags her fingers through the old shag carpet beneath us to create patterns in the worn-out fibers. They remind me of crop circles. I imagine our parents' bedroom as a tiny universe within our larger reality, whole civilizations of microscopic dust mites sur-rounding us.

"Gretchen. I love you."

"Mom hates me."

"That's not true." It might be true, though—at least a little bit. Especially of *our* mother, if only because her efforts to be kind and loving to her oldest child are so transparently forced. I'm sure she loves Gretchen plenty. Of course she does. All mothers love their children. But I know, too, there's a tiny splinter of hate in her soul for my sister. I don't see how there couldn't be. Maybe it's very small, so small that a person wouldn't notice it even if they took a hard look, but it's still there. It's not the worst thing in the world; a person can feel love and hate at the same time for the same individual. It's easier than you might expect.

When something terrible happens, everybody wants someone to blame. It's natural human behavior; years of therapy have taught me that much. In the case of Turtle's abduction, there was plenty of blame to go around. I've come to think of the events surrounding that night as a line of dominoes. And depending on how carefully you examine the situation and exactly where you choose to mark the beginning of the story, there's a case to be made that Gretchen was the first domino to tip. In a way, everything that happened started with Gretchen.

My sister holds the red Solo cup close to my face. "Do you see these?" she asks, pointing at a crooked row of indentations running along the rim. "This was Turtle's cup. It's the cup she was drinking from that night. Those are her bite marks, Sam."

If what she's saying is true, the cup is over ten years old. Where has she been keeping it? How does she even know it was Turtle's? Gretchen wasn't home that night; she was three doors down, at Abby's house. By the time anyone thought to wake her up, our sister was long gone.

I'm barely breathing as I run a finger over the marks, imagining my little sister chewing on the edge as we sat on the living room sofa that evening, bored, watching the grown-ups in our lives behave like teenagers, shining examples of the "do as I say, not as I do" style of parenting. It was too early for them to send us to bed, so they tried to ignore us as much as possible. The three of us—Turtle, Remy, and I—were drinking orange soda, which was a huge deal at the time; we were almost never allowed sugary drinks. I tilt the cup and see a mess of tiny fibers and minuscule shreds of lint and dust stuck to the inside. The white plastic has a dull, orange tint. It hasn't been rinsed, not once in ten years.

"Where did you get this?" Somehow the cup makes me feel different than I do when I'm looking at a photograph of my long-lost sister or holding a stuffed animal that belonged to her. Her mouth sipped from this very edge, probably leaving behind DNA. Her baby teeth made the marks in this plastic. It's more than something she once held; it's an artifact.

"I should put it back," Gretchen says, taking it from my hands. She puts it in our mother's top dresser drawer.

"Has it always been there? Ever since it happened?"

She nods. "I think so. Every time I've checked."

"How did you find it?"

Gretchen shrugs. "How does anyone find anything? I was going through Mom's stuff. You know, snooping around. You've never done that?"

"Not really, no."

My sister stands in the doorway, her blond hair spilling over her shoulders in thick, wet pieces. Her robe is knotted so loosely that it's coming apart, revealing a sliver of her naked body, which doesn't seem to bother her one bit. The sight causes me to tug my shirt more tightly closed and pull my knees up against my chest, as though I'm the one who's exposed.

Gretchen presses an index finger to her lips as she stares at me. From downstairs, we hear the screechy sounds of our mother laughing about something with Mrs. Mitchell, just like old times—almost.

"You and I, Samantha," my sister says, "are very different kinds of people."

She's right. I'm seventeen, and I've never even officially had a boyfriend. By the time she was my age, Gretchen had already gone through more than her share of boyfriends. The boys she liked were always older, always getting her into some kind of trouble. One of them—I don't remember his name—burned a hole in our new sofa when he dropped a cigarette. Another one, Mike, rode a motorcycle without a helmet. Ross Daniel, her junior year prom date, brought her home the morning after the dance so drunk that she couldn't get out of bed for the rest of the weekend.

I know about all these boys, and their relationships with my big sister, mostly because they've been assembled into a catalog of sorts in the bestselling nonfiction book *Forty-Eight Minutes of Doubt*. Early in chapter 4, author Davis Gordon devotes a few paragraphs to summarizing these teenage romances, and what they might say about Gretchen, as a lead-in to the book's real person of interest: Steven Handley.

Steven was the last guy Gretchen dated before she left for college. He was older, and he was much worse than any of the others. My parents couldn't stand him, which only made Gretchen like him more. The relationship lasted a few months. It ended badly when Steven was arrested for killing Turtle.

◆ ◆ ◆

**Partial List of Items Seized as Evidence
from 11 Cardinal Lane, Shelocta:**

2 Santa Claus costumes, OSFA (one size fits all),
including shirt, coat, pants, socks (4 total), gloves
(4 total), and suspenders

2 pairs OSFA adult boots, black

122 hair and fiber samples, among which two hair
samples were identified as potential matches to
Tabitha Myers

1 Garbage Pail Kids trading card with cartoon of
"Toxic Tabitha," a female child whose face and body
have been repeatedly assaulted with a nail gun

Forty-Eight Minutes of Doubt, p. 25

chapter three

New Year's Day, 1986

Remy's pants were all wet. When he opened his eyes, I could tell just from looking at him that he'd been awake the whole time, only pretending to sleep. The boy in him wanted to be tougher than any girl, but the fact that we were both children was all that mattered. He didn't want to leave his sleeping bag because he'd wet his pants as we lay there with our eyes shut, unable to sense anything beyond the breath of the stranger beside us. Now he was crying while I said it didn't matter, tugging him upstairs with me to get help.

"Santa Claus took Turtle away." I reached for Remy's hand, which was sticky and damp.

Our parents stared at us, uncomprehending.

"He took her," I repeated.

"Who took her?" As my dad stood up, Susan Mitchell noticed

her son's wet pajamas and beckoned him over. He tugged me along beside him, refusing to let go of my hand.

"Santa Claus." I knew it sounded absurd. I could feel the blood rushing through my head but not the floor under my feet, and before I knew it my knees were wobbling, followed by my legs, until my whole body trembled with panic and I fell crying into my mother's lap. "Why aren't you helping her? He took her!"

"Sweetie, calm down. Nobody else has been in the house. We've been here all night."

"Christmas is over, Samantha. Santa's back at the North Pole." Mike Mitchell, who was halfheartedly concealing a glass pipe in his cupped hand, tilted back his head and blew three perfect smoke rings. In *Forty-Eight Minutes of Doubt*, Davis Gordon would make frequent mention of all the precious seconds wasted as a result of Remy's and my parents' failure to act quickly. But it's easy for outsiders to look back on any tragedy and insist they would have handled things better. It's been suggested more than once that our parents were unforgivably negligent, but that's simply not true: it couldn't have been more than a full minute before they *did* act. Our fathers hadn't yet reached the bottom of the basement stairs when my dad hollered for someone to call the police.

We heard my father and Mike shouting for Turtle as they searched everywhere she might be hiding: the bathroom, the mudroom, the laundry room, the garage. When they didn't find her, they searched in less likely spaces: beneath the sofa, the cabinet below the bathroom sink, the washer and dryer. They shouted her name while they looked everywhere her small body could have managed to fit, and some places where it couldn't. Later, they would hate themselves for not going outside sooner, where they would have seen a single pair of adult footprints going from the house to the woods. She had only been gone a few minutes by then; they might have been able to find her simply by following the prints before they were covered in fresh snow.

I don't remember everything that happened after that, but there are bits and pieces of the hours that followed that I can recall in perfect detail, the sights and sounds chiseled permanently into my memory. My mother was so upset that she didn't even try to make it to the bathroom before vomiting a belly full of booze and pretzels onto our carpet. The first floor of our house—the kitchen and living room in particular—quickly became the kind of mess she would have stayed awake all night to clean up under normal circumstances: Empty beer bottles crowded into sloppy rows on the coffee table next to a pile of sticky playing cards and an ashtray, two cigars still burning within. Dirty dishes filled the sink, spilling onto the surrounding countertop. Though I didn't know what it was at the time, nobody bothered to hide the bag of marijuana on the bar. The TV was tuned to ABC's *New Year's Rockin' Eve* wrap-up show, hosted by a somehow-still-alert Dick Clark, his energy rippling over the airwaves even with the volume muted. When the heavy winds interfered with our satellite signal near the end of the show, the screen froze on his sign-off for the night, his mittened hand raised in a wave. It stayed like that for days. When someone finally thought to turn it off, Dick remained, his silhouette literally burned into the screen. The rest of the mess would remain, too, until Mrs. Mitchell decided to clean it up almost a week later; by then the smell of stale beer and vomit was impossible to get rid of. Eventually we replaced the carpet and slapped a new coat of paint on the walls. It was the best compromise my parents could come up with. My dad didn't want to change a thing about our house after that night; if he'd had his way, we might still be living in the same filth. On her worst days, my mom begged him to let her burn the whole place to the ground. I don't think any of us would have been surprised if she'd gone through with it.

I'm not sure why the police barely spoke with Remy and me until so much later. They at first seemed far more concerned with their search for Turtle than finding out exactly how she'd gone missing, which seems like a real no-brainer in hindsight. Maybe it was because we were so young. It was well after midnight, and we were two children struggling to manage our terror and exhaustion, along with all the unspoken fears that were displayed so clearly on our parents' faces as they waited, not knowing where Turtle was—if she was warm or cold, fast asleep or awake and panicking, alive or dead.

Each of us—especially as a child—wants to feel secure and protected. All my life I'd looked to my parents for reassurance that things were under control amid all the chaos and uncertainty of life. When I was afraid, they soothed me. When I was sick, they healed me. Because this was my reality, I felt certain at first that they would quickly find my sister and bring her home safely. It seemed impossible that they could fail. In the same way, I believed the police would arrest her abductor and throw him in jail, easy as that. It was the only outcome I could imagine: my parents would protect Turtle, and the police would protect everybody else by capturing the man who'd taken her. Good things happen to good people, and bad people get punished. We tell ourselves these things because we have to, and there's nothing more frightening than when this curtain of comfort is yanked away to reveal the truth: life often doesn't make sense; it isn't fair, and sometimes it is far more cruel than kind. We are never fully protected. To a child, these facts are incomprehensible. To an adult, they are reason to fear the worst—the fact that tragedy can swallow a person in one gulp without so much as a moment's warning.

Because nobody asked, it simply did not occur to me to mention whether I'd recognized the man inside the ill-fitting Santa suit. I'd seen enough of his features as he stood beneath the floodlight in our yard; they were mostly hidden by the white beard strapped to his face, but I'd still recognized him.

The previous summer, my parents had hired a landscaping company to build a retaining wall on the hillside in our backyard. The soil on the hill was too unstable for grass or plants to put down roots, and my mother couldn't stand the constant accumulation of pebbles from the steady erosion. Ed Tickle had promised to help my dad with the project months ago, but then he'd gotten too busy. He ran the local hardware store and did small construction jobs on the side; my dad knew Ed could have done a good job on the wall, but he didn't want to be pushy. He'd already built a playhouse for Remy and me at the edge of the Mitchells' backyard that summer. He'd done it for almost nothing, too, because he said it was good for the neighborhood.

Since Ed wasn't available, my mom hired a guy named Lenny

LaMana, because his bid was the only one my family could afford. His company was called Landscaping by Lenny. My father had seen him around town and thought he was a sleaze. "His name might as well be Lenny Leisure Suit," he'd complained. "I mean, come *on*—the guy wears a freaking pinkie ring!"

My mother is terrified of awkward conversations; as a result, she's polite to the point of absurdity. She once ate a hamburger at a restaurant because the waitress got her order wrong and my mother didn't want to embarrass her by correcting the mistake. My mother is a vegetarian.

"I already hired them," she said, referring to Landscaping by Lenny LaMana/Leisure Suit. We can't back out now; it will be too uncomfortable. Besides," she added, "we'd lose our deposit."

"You gave him a *deposit* already? You think we have a money tree growing out back that you can go shake when you need some extra cash? Christ, Sharon, I was gone for less than two hours this afternoon."

"He won't even be doing the work. He's a salesman. He'll send a crew of local guys, I'm sure. They'll probably be college kids."

"Oh, that's just great. I'm sure he hires only the best and brightest. Did you ask him if he does background checks on them? Do they get tested for drugs?"

My mom laughed at him. "Should they? Do *you*? Listen to yourself, Paul. You sound like your father."

In the end, my dad gave in, like he always does with my mom. There were four men on the crew Lenny sent to our house the following week. Steven Handley was the oldest at twenty-three. He'd graduated from the local high school when Gretchen was barely twelve years old, but she'd still heard about him. Shelocta was a small town.

Everybody had known and liked Steven back in his high school days. He acted in the musical every year and played drums in the concert band. He had dark brown hair, long eyelashes, red cheeks, and teeth that could have benefitted from braces but didn't need them to accomplish his ordinary but well-scrubbed look of a country boy who had always listened when his mother told him to brush his teeth and eat his vegetables. He got decent grades and played varsity football; his dad was the team's assistant coach. His parents owned their own business and worked hard. They were comfortable, but nowhere near rich. Under different circumstances, he might have grown up and become a successful insurance salesman who coached his kid's Little League team on weekends, and he might have been perfectly satisfied with life.

At Steven's senior prom, which was held at the local Marriott that year, he did a backflip into the wrong end of the hotel swimming pool and smacked his head against the cement floor, splitting his skull open underwater. He was bleeding buckets and was unconscious for more than six minutes before the ambulance showed up. He needed one blood transfusion, eighteen hours of surgery, more than a hundred staples in his head, and three months of physical therapy to repair hairline fractures in several vertebrae, but by fall it seemed to doctors like he'd made a miraculous recovery.

He hadn't. The people closest to Steven—his parents and his girlfriend, Amy, who was also headed to Penn State—could tell right away that something had gone wrong during his reassembly. It was as if he'd woken up a whole different person.

He and Amy left for college in late August as planned, but things went downhill from day one. Steven started getting high with his roommate almost immediately; Amy said he was heavily into LSD, which would have been a big deal to his friends and family. Steven and his roommate supposedly got so tripped out on Halloween night that when Amy tried to leave the room, they tied her to the bed and kept her restrained for hours. They even stuffed a sock in her mouth and put tape over it so she couldn't scream for help. She got away at dawn when Steven decided to set off all the fire alarms in the building and run screaming up and down the halls, pounding on everybody's door to warn them of the approaching apocalypse.

Steven might have been a different person five years after flunking out of school and moving back into his parents' house, but Gretchen hadn't known any previous version of him to use for comparison. My parents knew his name and story, mostly because Susan Mitchell was the high school band director. Steven's all-American looks still held up after everything he put his body through; the only major difference was the twelve-inch scar running from the top of his head to the base of his skull.

My mom and dad weren't the kind of parents who kept track of their kids' every movement. Maybe they didn't notice when my sister and Steven started flirting every day. Maybe they truly believed she was out until midnight or later most nights with Abby, at the movies or the mall. She lied to them all the time, and she usually got away with it. They didn't ask too many questions.

Steven and the rest of Lenny's crew worked in my yard the summer Remy and I turned seven. It was 1985. I remember going to the movies to see *Back to the Future* the weekend it was released, and hearing "We Are the World" every time someone turned on a radio. It was also the summer my family and I gathered in our living room to watch the press conference at which Vice President George H. W. Bush introduced America to Christa McAuliffe, the social studies teacher from New Hampshire who had been selected from among thousands of applicants to be on board the *Challenger* space shuttle when it launched the following year.

"What do you think, Sam? Would you ever want to be an astronaut and go up to space?" My mom was beside me on the couch, putting her hair in foam curlers while we watched TV.

I used to love looking at the stars, but I felt no desire to see them up close. "No. I'd be too afraid."

As she looked at me, she reached up to remove a bobby pin she'd been holding between her teeth. "Good girl," she said, patting my head. "Sometimes it's smart to be afraid."

chapter four

New Year's Day, 1986

From the moment I came unfrozen after Turtle was carried off into the cold night, I cried without stopping. Even when I was silent and otherwise seemed calm, the tears continued, and there didn't seem to be any point in trying to hold them back—not that I wanted to. None of it felt real. It was like we all had been actors in a pleasant but uneventful long-running play—*Childhood: Not a Musical*—but tonight we'd somehow wandered onto the wrong stage and picked up the wrong scripts. *Tonight, the part of Terrified Mother Who Cannot Stop Screaming will be played by Sharon Myers. This is a big change for Ms. Myers, whose previous role as Pretty Suburban Housewife did not require much screaming.*

While our fathers searched, Susan Mitchell walked down the street to retrieve Gretchen from Abby Tickle's house. My mother stayed by the front door and prayed the Rosary, which I'd never seen her do until that night. Remy and I sat at the kitchen table with a friendly cop—he told us to call him Officer Bert—who took notes on a small yellow legal pad as we talked.

"The man you saw tonight—can you tell me what he looked like?"

"He looked like Santa Claus, except he was skinny. I already told you." Beside me, Remy nodded in silent agreement. I thought he'd been asleep while it happened, but now he insisted he'd been faking.

"Okay, we know that. But other than his costume, did you see what he looked like?"

"Oh. Well, yeah." My voice was soft and hesitant. All I wanted was for my sister to come home. I didn't want to get anybody in trouble. You have to understand that my world was so small and safe back then; the idea that someone whom Turtle knew and trusted would hurt my sister seemed impossible. "He looked like Steven."

Officer Bert stopped taking notes and put down his pen. "Who's Steven?"

"Gretchen's boyfriend."

"And who's Gretchen?"

"My big sister."

"I see." A single strand of tinsel, probably from whatever party he'd been called away from, clung to the front of Officer Bert's sweater. "Did he only look like Steven, or was it actually him?"

"It was him."

Without taking his eyes off me, his right hand slid to the

walkie-talkie clipped to his belt. "What makes you sure it was Steven? Do you know his last name, sweetie?"

I shook my head.

"He doesn't have all his teeth." It was the first full sentence Remy had uttered since we'd come upstairs, and once he said it I knew there was no holding back anymore.

"His tooth is missing." I opened my mouth and pointed to an incisor.

"Hold on one second, sweetie." He left the room and found my mother, still praying at the front door. I couldn't hear their conversation, but it's not hard to guess how it went. Not thirty seconds after Officer Bert walked out, Remy's mom stepped in with Gretchen and Abby Tickle. They wore matching Billy Idol T-shirts instead of nightgowns. Abby was a little pixie of a thing, so her shirt reached almost past her bowed knees. She was still cute in a girlish way, whereas Gretchen was almost a foot taller and already looked like a woman. Except that she wasn't; she was seventeen, but I guess that fact was easy to forget.

My mom lunged toward Gretchen and pulled her into a hug. As they wept in each other's arms, my mother caressed my sister's face with strokes that grew increasingly aggressive until before I knew it they became outright slaps—one hard smack followed by another even harder one, at which point Remy's mom pushed her way between them, but not before my mom yanked out a fistful of Gretchen's hair.

"This is your fault. It's *your* fault." She pointed a trembling finger at my sister, who huddled between Remy's mom and Abby.

I screamed when I saw Gretchen's hair, which fell to the floor in lazy wisps, and my eyes stung from a fresh gush of tears. I wondered if a person could dry out and die from too much crying. When I tried to stop, the tears continued to flow, silent but steady. Other times I sobbed until I couldn't breathe. This lasted for days, even while I slept, and continued until there wasn't a drop left for me to lose. By then I was a husk of myself, dehydrated and exhausted. We all were. I had never been so thirsty in my life.

chapter five

Summer 1996

My parents are divided on the question of whether I should get a summer job. Dad says no; Mom says yes. She doesn't want me hanging around the house, doing nothing for three months. I don't have a driver's license, and even if I did, my mom needs her car to drive Hannah around most days. Mom wins, as usual, and I get the job of helping Susan Mitchell clean out her family's basement. Formerly occupied by Susan's now-deceased mother-in-law, the space is scheduled for some major renovations.

"Do you know what a 'man cave' is? My husband wants one." She sniffs the air in the dim, damp basement. Even though the layout is identical to ours, I can barely tell because of all the stuff crowding the room. "Mold," Susan announces, wrinkling her nose. "I'm sorry, Sam. It's a potpourri of mold and mildew down here.

We kept a dehumidifier running for Betsy. We never would have put her down here by herself, but she became very paranoid toward the end of her life. You remember her, Sam, don't you?"

"Of course I do. We called her Grandma Bitty."

Susan smiles. "I know. She was a wonderful woman. I couldn't have asked for a better mother-in-law. But once she developed dementia, she became a whole different person. She was mean. Have you been around anybody with dementia?" Susan doesn't wait for me to answer. "It was heartbreaking. Just heartbreaking. She was obsessed with the idea that someone was spying on her. She kept notebooks to document everything that happened. I'd leave her alone here to run to the grocery store, and by the time I got back she would have called the police to report an intruder. It didn't matter how many times they searched the house; at first she thought they weren't taking her seriously—which they weren't, to be honest, not after the first twenty times—and then she started thinking we were all in cahoots to drive her crazy. It was very sad, and it never gets better with someone that age; it only gets worse.

"She'd get up in the middle of the night and barricade her bedroom door shut because she was afraid someone would sneak in—the intruder, I guess—and hurt her. Then she'd wake up in the morning and wouldn't be able to open her door. I don't know how someone her age had the strength to move all that stuff to begin with. We tried taking her door off its hinges, and it only made her furious. The names she called me . . . Eventually we had to move her down here for her own safety, but she couldn't bear to be apart from all her . . . *stuff.* She was a pioneer when it came to hoarding. That's what it's called when someone keeps everything—did you know there's a name for it? It's an actual mental disease. I didn't know that, not until I saw a *Phil Donahue Show* episode about it, and then I thought, *Oh, my goodness, that's Bitty to a T.* For pretty much all her adult life, she had piles and piles of junk stashed in every corner of her house. You should have seen it. This is *nothing* compared to what it used to be like. Oh, it was absolutely insane. The first time Mike took me over to meet her—I was only seventeen—he was so embarrassed that he cried afterward." She pauses. "Maybe I shouldn't have told you that. Don't tell Mike you know about it, okay?" Susan plops a box of heavy-duty black garbage bags into my arms. "Anyway, you don't need to worry about pitching anything valuable, because I'm pretty sure it's all junk. Go ahead and throw everything away. Make it look like she was never even here."

It has been a full two weeks since my family's return, and I have yet to exchange a word with Remy. He's constantly coming and going with one friend or another from the same group of four or five teenage boys. If not for the different cars they drive, I don't think I would have realized they're four separate individuals. Through my window, they look like out-of-focus, shaggy-haired extras from the background of a Nirvana video. There are, however, small distinctions among them: Blue Minivan's hair is the longest, his heavy blond waves stopping just past his shoulders. His car has a JUST SAY NO bumper sticker on its back window. I can always hear Silver Pickup before I see him. He likes to blast his music—he's always playing something from the last Beastie Boys album—with his windows down. He always leans on the horn to let Remy know he's outside, instead of getting out and ringing the doorbell. Honda Civic and his brother (I think), who rides shotgun, are both easily forty pounds heavier than the rest of the group. Their bumper sticker is an anti-Nazi one, a swastika in a circle with a line drawn through it. It seems odd to have a sticker proclaiming something that most people would assume is a given in any decent human being. Why the need to announce it? You might as well have one that says I DISLIKE PAIN or KITTENS ARE CUTE.

Most nights after Remy has been out with friends all day, his girlfriend comes over and stays until after I'm asleep, although her car is always gone by the next morning. She drives a red Jeep, which was still parked on our street when I finally went to bed last night at around 1:30. It's almost noon when Susan and I hear Remy walking around in the kitchen above us.

Susan flashes the ceiling a frown. "Nice of you to get out of bed today," she murmurs. Her gaze is an apologetic wince. "I'm sorry for the way he's been treating you, Sam. I don't know what his problem is lately." She pauses. "Heather is such a clingy girl. I wish he'd spend some time apart from her."

I want to tell her that I don't care about Remy's life, or whether I ever talk to him again. It's not like I've been pining away for him all these years. It's true that we were close once, but ten years is a long time to be away from someone, especially when you're our age.

"Heather?" I can't help it. I do care. I care more than anything.

"Heather Bonterro. She's a year behind you in school."

"Oh."

"Her father is an undertaker. Her whole family lives at the funeral home. Can you imagine?"

"Not really."

Susan glances around the room. "Can I be honest with you, Sam?"

"Excuse me?"

She leans in a few inches and lowers her voice to an exaggerated hush. "I don't like her one bit."

I don't say anything.

"Well? Don't you want to know why?" She blurts it out before I have a chance to answer. "She's one of those needy girls. Clingy, like I said. And she smokes, I happen to know—that child must think I'm a *fool* sometimes—and I found a note she wrote him in his pants pocket while I was doing laundry—but I wasn't snooping, Sam, I respect Remy's privacy, I want you to know that—and this note, oh, my *lord*, I've never heard such filthy things. She's trouble. She's dirty, and she's trouble, and I don't like her face."

Susan finally stops speaking in order to breathe. She stares at me from behind her square, purple-framed glasses with the gleaming eyes of someone drunk on the relief of her confession.

At first, all I can think about is her claim—*I've never heard such filthy things*—and what a lie it is. I remember every word of the joke Remy's dad told on New Year's Eve, and the way Susan and my mom cackled with laughter. They seemed downright delighted by its filthiness.

"Oh, no. I hope I didn't make you uncomfortable." Any trace of relief in her expression is gone. "I shouldn't have said all that to you."

"No, it's okay."

"Maybe you could try to reconnect with him. Do you think he'd listen to you?"

"About Heather?"

"No, not just about Heather. Remy is different now. I know how boys get when they become teenagers, believe me, but he's . . . It's more than that. He doesn't tell me anything." Now Susan looks like she might start crying at any moment. "I just want to know he's okay."

I don't know what to say, so I say nothing. All the while, the joke keeps running through my mind: *This beautiful woman walks into her gynecologist's office . . .*

After a pause, Susan says, "Well, anyway, I'm sorry. I don't mean to put a bunch of pressure on you. But sometimes I feel like I don't know him anymore. I just want to hold on to him a little bit longer, Sam, before I have to let him grow up all the way." She looks past me, at the playhouse near the edge of the yard. It still looks great; Ed must have kept up on the maintenance. Now that he's paralyzed from a stroke, I wonder if anybody will bother with the task. "Remember all the time you two spent out there?"

How could I not remember? We spent entire days there, playing out whatever realities we could imagine, anything the space could accommodate. We did the standard childhood scenarios: school, house, hospital. After Turtle disappeared, we played detective and, eventually, courtroom, swapping the roles of lawyer, judge, and defendant without any understanding of how the scenes would have made our parents feel, not to mention any child psychologist who might happen to pass by.

Once Susan leaves me alone in the basement, it becomes clear Remy's grandma has left a mess that is more staggering for its utter uselessness than anything else. Aside from a bed and a dresser, the room is packed with back issues of *Muscle & Fitness* magazine that are stacked in floor-to-ceiling columns against the far wall. There are hundreds of them, the most recent of which is from August 1974. Piles of cardboard boxes hold disorganized collections of items that fall just a hair outside the category of garbage: tangled masses of plastic bead necklaces, most of which appear to be hand-strung by either monkeys or children; maybe a thousand keys that could open an endless number of theoretical locks; dozens of fist-sized wooden armadillos whose gaping mouths function as bottle openers; six convection ovens, their boxes postmarked from the Home Shopping Network; piles and piles of old photographs that were exposed to so much moisture they have fused into bricks of lost memories; an unused candle shaped like the Virgin Mary, its wick protruding from her folded hands; nine packages of Polaroid film, but no camera. Everything stinks of mildew and rot. The only source of natural light comes from a small window near the ceiling above the bed.

It's clear that my job here is just an excuse to keep me occupied, the same as when my mom used to pay me a dollar to organize our silverware drawer. The fact that I'm getting ten dollars an hour to sort through garbage annoys me more than it should. I could have gotten a real job somewhere in town, someplace where I'd have the chance to meet people and maybe even make some friends. At the very least, I could be working aboveground.

And it feels wrong to chuck all of Betsy's possessions into the trash, even if that's where they belong. How would she feel if she knew that her family wanted to get rid of every worthless item she treasured? It seems cruel of the Mitchells, even though I know they don't mean it that way. I'm more selective than I need to be as I decide what to keep or toss, and I can tell Susan is disappointed by my lack of progress at the end of the day, even though she's too polite to say anything. As she counts five ten-dollar bills into my hand, I see Remy watching us from the playhouse, gazing at me with steady eyes even when I stare right back.

chapter six

Summer 1985

Before she became a beauty, Gretchen was a fat girl. Our mother was horrified by my sister's weight but tried not to show it. She did her best to reassure my sister that lots of kids are chubby, but her daily reminders that everything was going to be fine someday only reinforced the idea that Gretchen wasn't fine to begin with. It didn't help that Abby was so petite ("Lilliputian," our mother called her), making Gretchen seem even bigger in comparison.

Even after Gretchen's awkward days were long behind her, our mom still talked about how much it had pained her to watch the two girls play together. "I'd see Abby flitting around like a little whisper of a child, so sweet and dainty; and then, hulking along behind her, would be Biiiiig Gretchen." She even did an impression of my sister, stomping across the floor with her arms held straight out like Frankenstein's monster and her faced fixed in a dumb stare. Our mother seemed to assume that, just because Gretchen was no longer oafish, the comparisons weren't hurtful, which was stupid of her. But she had no way of understanding how it felt to undergo the kind of drastic metamorphosis that her oldest daughter had experienced during puberty. Our mother did not know how to be anything but beautiful, and she believed that Gretchen must have shared her disdain for the younger, less attractive version of herself, as though the fatness was an unflattering outfit that she'd simply decided to strip off one morning.

My sister's first few years at school were spent trying to blend in well enough that none of her classmates had reason to single her out for ridicule. The strategy was less than successful, because kids don't need a reason to make fun of one another. Just as Abby put up with her fair share of teasing for being so tiny, Gretchen went through elementary school as one of the token fat kids. Some of the older boys on the school bus even made up a song about her, which they sang every morning as she walked to her seat as though it were as mandatory as the Pledge of Allegiance. It was only one line, repeated over and over for as long as it took for my sister to either bury her head between her knees or start crying: "Too many Twinkies . . . oink, oink!" (They were cruel, but not all that creative.)

During the summer between seventh and eighth grade, Gretchen's body decided that enough was enough. Over those few months, she morphed into a young bombshell with such alarming speed that our dad insisted she see a gland specialist, even though we couldn't afford it. It was as if she were molting, wriggling a little farther out of her old skin each day, not from effort so much as intuition: *This is what I am meant to become.* She didn't have to

put herself on a diet or exercise every day like other girls; she needed
only to surrender herself to the genetic lottery whose check had
finally cleared. Her unflattering lumps shifted themselves into
sleek, symmetrical curves. Her hair grew fast, as thick and long
as unspooling silk. Her legs stretched, her shoulders broadened,
her spine corrected itself from a slouch to an arch. Twenty extra
pounds seemed to dissolve as easily as snowflakes in hot water.
When school began the next fall, people whom she hadn't seen all
summer didn't recognize her. The Twinkie song was all but forgotten (until two years later, when poor Donny Levin started sixth
grade).

It didn't take long for Gretchen to understand that what had
once been impossible for her—physical beauty—was now effortless. She was thirteen but looked seventeen. She rarely wore
makeup, but it didn't matter. Her knowledge of these facts brought
power, and with great power comes great responsibility. Unfortunately, because she was still a thirteen-year-old girl, my sister had
the emotional maturity of a thirteen-year-old girl. She believed
she knew everything about life, when in fact she knew virtually
nothing. In short, she was the complete opposite of responsible.
And while our father understood that much, our mother wasn't
as quick to catch on. Because she'd been born beautiful, she'd
had plenty of time to grow into an understanding of what such a
role required from a person. Gretchen didn't have the first clue.

But she had plenty of opportunities to practice over the next
few years, and by the time Steven Handley strolled into our yard
to build a retaining wall one hot June morning in 1985, sixteen-
year-old Gretchen had been through a handful of boyfriends who

had barely managed to unclasp her bra without hyperventilating. They were nice enough—she stayed away from the ones who had teased her most mercilessly—but they were all disappointments in their own way: Ben the soccer player had acne all over his back (bacne); Michael the dentist's kid seemed to have no idea what to do with his tongue besides shove it in her ear; Scott the drummer desperately wanted a mustache but did not possess the necessary ability to grow facial hair, so he constantly looked like he'd forgotten to wipe his mouth after drinking chocolate milk; Greg the future flight attendant had issues he hadn't even begun to acknowledge; Adam mysteriously smelled like hush puppies all the time; and Hank always wore the same shirt as though he thought nobody would notice.

Put anybody under a microscope and their flaws will become unbearable. What Gretchen didn't realize was that none of those boys made her happy because they were all so *eager* to make her happy. Nothing is more unattractive than desperation, and the boys at her high school reeked of it—especially around Gretchen. By age sixteen, Gretchen was bored with them. She set her sights on Steven, thinking he would be a challenge.

She was right. At first he didn't pay much attention to her. It was part of his job description: Lenny gave all his employees explicit orders not to screw around with any of the clients' underage daughters.

"What's the matter with him?" Gretchen asked Abby Tickle, the two of them peeking into our yard from my sister's bedroom window, studying every move of the landscaping crew with an intensity befitting Official Retaining Wall Construction

Supervisors. "It's like he doesn't know I'm alive. Maybe his sex drive got damaged when he split his head open."

Abby was still tiny, but she wasn't a sweet little girl anymore. Lately she'd been cultivating a wild streak that sent occasional flickers of manic instability across her face. The words tasted good in her mouth as she spoke them, like a swig from the bottle of peach schnapps that Darla kept in the linen closet for emergencies. "There's nothing the matter with him," she said, her eyes shining with all the sordid possibilities. "It's because he's a *man*."

◆　◆　◆

Partial Transcript of Interview with Helen Handley, Conducted January 5, 1986, by Detective Jake Wyatt

Detective Wyatt: How old was Steven when he first started having problems with his anger?

Helen Handley: Steven doesn't have anger problems.

DET: I'm not sure how you can say that.

HH: I'm saying it because it's true.

DET: Tell me how he got his tooth knocked out. It happened in a fight, didn't it?

HH: There was no fight. It was a misunderstanding.

DET: Were you there? Did you see what happened between your son and Mr. LaMana?

HH: Steven wasn't angry. All he wanted was the money he'd earned. It was nothing.

DET: He wasn't angry that Mr. LaMana had fired him for screwing around with a client's teenage daughter?

HH: Please don't use that kind of language.

DET: What language? You mean "screwing"?

HH: (*unable to transcribe, inaudible*)

DET: That word offends you? What word would you prefer me to use instead?

HH: I don't know.

DET: How about "fucking"? The teenage girl your son was fucking.

HH: Stop it.

DET: They weren't holding hands, you know. Your son, your twenty-three-year-old adult son, was getting

it on with a high school student. That's called statutory
rape.

HH: (*inaudible*)

DET: Excuse me?

HH: I said that Myers girl is a trashy little slut.

(*twenty-six-second pause in conversation*)

DET: I'm sorry, which Myers girl are you talking
about? The one your son was fucking? Gretchen? Or
did you mean Tabitha, the one he murdered?

HH: Gretchen. Let me tell you something: I walked
into my living room one day, and that girl was naked
under a blanket with my son, doing things I didn't even
know about at her age. Steven didn't force her to do
anything. That's not the kind of boy I raised.

DET: Okay. Calm down. Tell me what kind of boy he
is, Helen.

HH: He's a good boy. He doesn't have a temper.

DET: But he must have been angry when his
supervisor fired him.

HH: He wasn't happy about it, but he wouldn't have
gotten violent toward anyone. When Stevie was a boy,
he found an injured squirrel in our yard and kept it in a
shoe box. He nursed it back to health. It would sit on
his shoulder sometimes while he watched television.
He loved that squirrel. Do you understand? He
wouldn't hurt a living creature. Not even a squirrel! He
cried for days when the poor thing died.

DET: But he did hurt someone, Helen. Maybe he

didn't mean it. If something happened to Tabitha by accident, now is the time to share that information. Later is no good for anyone, okay? We don't want to see your son throw away the rest of his life. We want to help him.

HH: You're a liar. You police all lie.

DET: I'm not lying to you, Helen. Steven was upset because he'd been fired. He went to see his boss, Craig, to beg for his job back. Craig says no. Steven gets angry. Maybe he shoves Craig, so Craig punches him and knocks his front tooth out. That's what happened, isn't it?

HH: I told you I wasn't there, but I know my son didn't attack Craig Maxwell. Craig is a friend of my husband's. Steven has known him for years, and he knew it wasn't Craig's fault. His hands were tied. Steven knew that. All he wanted was his money.

DET: So you're saying he wasn't angry with Mr. Maxwell.

HH: No, he wasn't angry with him.

DET: Because Steven knew Mr. Maxwell had no choice but to fire him?

HH: Yes.

DET: But he was still angry with *someone*, right? He was upset with Paul Myers.

HH: Yes.

DET: How upset?

HH: Stevie didn't hurt that little girl. He was home all night. He was asleep when someone took that child.

DET: See, that's confusing to me.

HH: What?

DET: That you say he was sleeping.

HH: Why? It was the middle of the night.

DET: Steven works for the township, doesn't he?

HH: Yes, sometimes. He tries to get as much work as he can find. He's a hard worker. Before he met that girl he never missed a day of work, not in years.

DET: What does Steven do for the township?

HH: He works for the maintenance department.

DET: Doing what?

HH: Mostly driving a snowplow.

DET: What shift does he work?

HH: The night shift.

DET: So he's used to being up late at night?

HH: Yes, I guess you could say that.

DET: Don't you think it's strange that he fell asleep so early that night? You said he was home before midnight. I thought everyone tries to stay up late on New Year's Eve.

HH: Yes, he was home around eleven thirty. He picked up the load from Armando's earlier in the day, so it had been sitting in his truck all afternoon. He tossed it in one of the laundry bins on his way into the house. He ate some shepherd's pie for dinner and went to his room, and that's where he stayed.

DET: And you're certain this was all before midnight, correct? Had you and your husband been drinking?

HH: I had a glass or two of white wine. I don't drink much.

DET: Did you see Steven drink any alcohol?

HH: I didn't notice him drinking, but he's a grown man. I don't make it my business to count how many drinks he has in a night.

DET: So you did see him drinking?

HH: It was New Year's. Everybody was drinking. But Stevie went to bed after dinner. He was in bed before the ball dropped.

DET: Why was he so tired, Helen?

HH: He's been under a lot of stress. He hasn't been on a good schedule lately.

DET: Why has he been under so much stress?

HH: You know why.

DET: I want to hear it from you.

HH: Because of Gretchen and her family. What they did to my son, those pe—(*stops abruptly, begins crying*). I want to see Stevie. I don't want to talk to you anymore.

Forty-Eight Minutes of Doubt, pp. 77–79

chapter seven

Summer 1996

I'm pushing Hannah on the wooden swing set across the street from our house, which has degraded into terrible shape since Remy's dad and Ed Tickle put it together more than ten years ago. (I vaguely remember Mike inheriting an unused circular saw from a friend who died before ever getting a chance to use it.) The two of them spent entire weekends drinking beer and practicing carpentry as though it were the only thing they'd ever dreamed of doing with their lives. The air in our cul-de-sac smelled like sawdust all season.

Now the air smells like exhaust as Abby Tickle's ancient yellow Volkswagen Beetle comes sputtering down the road. I don't recognize the woman in the passenger seat as Gretchen, not even after she gets out and starts walking toward us. Since I last saw her a few days ago, she's cut almost all her hair off, and now looks like

Mia Farrow in *Rosemary's Baby*. The difference in her appearance is startling. She looks like she's dropped ten pounds in as many days. I can make out the ridges of her collarbones beneath her skin.

"It's going to rain, you two. You should go home."

"Mom is mopping the floors. She told me to stay out of the house all afternoon."

"She's probably getting baked in there, not mopping the floors. That's really why she wanted you to leave." Enter Abby, resting her head against my sister's shoulder and flashing me a quick, insincere smile.

Gretchen elbows her, nodding toward our little sister. *Hannah*, she mouths to Abby.

Abby rolls her eyes. "She doesn't know what I'm saying."

Hannah hops off the swing and onto the sidewalk, her tap shoes clicking crisply against the pavement. "Watch me!" she says as she starts dancing for us. Her tap routine is a three-minute performance of "Animal Crackers in My Soup," during which she also sings.

There's a flicker of lightning so brief that I'm not sure I actually saw anything at all, followed a few seconds later by the low rumble of thunder. "It's going to rain," Gretchen repeats. She holds up her right arm and flexes her wrist back and forth. "I can always tell."

Behind them, another car turns onto our street. It's Remy and his girlfriend, Heather, in her little red car. Remy makes it a point to keep looking straight ahead when Heather slows down to get a better look at us.

Hannah keeps dancing, ignoring her surroundings, focusing instead on every clickety-clack of her feet. The show must go on.

There's a strange, sudden burst of activity. Maybe it only seems odd because I'm so distracted by Remy and Heather, who are sitting in her car across the street when a beat-up purple minivan turns onto Point Pleasant and parks at the far end of the street.

Gretchen notices the minivan just as a short, gray-haired old woman steps from the driver's side with a stack of paperwork held against her chest. Helen Handley, Steven's mother, has spent the last ten years insisting to anyone who will listen that her son was in for the night by 12:15 a.m. on New Year's Day, 1986. She's lying, and everybody knows it. At first she told police Steven walked in the door around 11:30, which they knew wasn't true. Even Steven admitted it. He claimed he got home a little after midnight, upset and exhausted over his fight with Gretchen, and fell asleep without even taking off his boots.

According to Remy; Gretchen; Abby; Helen Handley; her husband, Jack; and me, as well as five additional witnesses including *himself*, Steven was dressed up like Santa Claus from the time he got to Abby's house until he was booked into jail thirteen hours later. He'd put the costume on over his clothes before walking to Abby's house, he said, just to be stupid. He said he wanted to make Gretchen laugh.

As the owners of Precision Cleaning, what was then the area's biggest dry cleaning operation, Steven's parents were the go-to cleaners for Armando's Tuxedo and Costume, which was the area's sole supplier of Santa Claus costumes. Armando had three of them, and they'd all been rented out to local churches for the holiday.

On New Year's Eve, 1985, Steven made his usual Thursday afternoon visit to Armando's at around five to pick up any tuxes that had been returned with marinara stains or whatever else you could imagine after a weekend wedding. He'd done the same thing almost every Thursday for the past year and a half. (Armando's also boasted a wide selection of VHS rental tapes and a small arcade; most weeks, Steven would stick around to pick out a video or two for the weekend and play pinball until he ran out of quarters.)

By Thursday the thirty-first, all the Santa costumes had been returned to the overnight deposit box. When he showed up to get the dry cleaning order, Steven told Armando he didn't have time to stick around and play video games. He said he was about to start his shift driving his truck through the storm in the dark, plowing roads for the county. It didn't matter either way to Armando. He was far more concerned about Steven's mouth, and his missing tooth, and the fact that Steven was clearly upset about whatever had caused it to fall out.

Steven finished his shift at eleven and drove straight to my neighborhood. He parked his truck a block away under a broken streetlight, so my parents wouldn't see it on our street. He walked down an alley to Abby's house, where she and Gretchen were expecting him.

Of course, they noticed his mouth right away. Despite the distraction of his Santa suit and the white polyester beard covering part of Steven's face, it wasn't the kind of thing anybody would miss.

He lied about it at first. He said there had been a mechanical problem that morning at Precision Cleaning and he'd accidentally hit himself in the face with a socket wrench while he was making the repair.

The three of them hung out in Abby's basement until a few

minutes before midnight, when Steven finally admitted the truth: he'd been fired from his position with the county. His supervisor had learned about Steven's relationship with an underage girl. He'd called Steven into his office and explained, more or less, that he wasn't worth the trouble it might cause. Steven lost his temper. He took a swing at the supervisor, who swung back, and Steven felt his tooth getting knocked down his throat.

His story must have scared my sister a little bit, because she told him to leave after that. She said he was acting crazy, which only made him more upset. He started to fall apart once it was clear he'd taken things too far, and Gretchen wasn't ready for these kinds of stakes in a relationship. It was all because our father had been so hell-bent on keeping them apart lately; he'd been doing everything he could think of to keep Steven away from Gretchen. He was probably the one who called Steven's boss.

Our father was always closer to Gretchen than he was to me or Turtle, and sometimes even our mom was jealous of how much he obviously adored their oldest child. When push came to shove, Gretchen's loyalty was to our dad. She told Steven she didn't want anyone else getting hurt. She didn't exactly break up with him that night, but it was pretty close. It was enough to make him frantic.

Once Gretchen and Abby managed to get Steven out the door, he stood there in the cold, pounding on the glass with his fist while he begged my sister to kiss him when the ball dropped at midnight, even if it was for the last time. Abby turned out the basement lights and switched off the television. She and Gretchen went around the corner and sat on the stairs, in the dark, while they waited for him to go away. They heard the New Year's countdown on the upstairs television; Darla kept it turned on at a high volume pretty much twenty-four hours a day.

It was so black in the stairwell that all either of them saw were each other's eyes reflecting fractals of light no larger than specks of dust. They stayed close while they waited, resting against one another, and together at that moment they felt perfectly balanced: little Abby Tickle with all her darkness, reaching up to meet Gretchen's towering beam of light.

"She's going straight to your front door," Abby says to me as we watch Helen walk down our street.

"Sam," Gretchen commands, "go over there and stop her."

"What? Why do I have to do it?"

There's more lightning. Hannah's dancing has taken her nearly all the way to Abby's house.

"Go stop her. Hurry up!"

"What am I supposed to say?"

"I don't care! Just go!"

But I can't move, not until Gretchen grabs my arm and shoves me into the street. At the same time, Abby says, "Her shoes!" and takes off running toward Hannah. She scoops up my little sister and tugs off her tap shoes, throwing them into the grass. It takes me a minute to realize why she does it.

The old woman standing on our porch is much shorter than I remember. Obviously, I've grown, but she's also shriveled; I guess you could say the years have not been kind to Helen. She smells strongly of chemicals. She tries to smile, but there is fear behind her milky gray eyes.

"Is that you, Samantha?" She brings a shaky hand to her mouth. "Oh. You've gotten so pretty."

The last thing I expected was a compliment, and it catches me so off guard that for a second I forget who she is and why I'm supposed to hate her; instead she becomes a stranger, somebody's grandma. Her skin is crinkled into a map of fine, deep lines, the bags beneath her eyes full and dark. It's hot outside, but she wears beige polyester slacks and a long-sleeved cotton shirt. I imagine sending her flying off the porch with a flick of my finger.

From behind the front door, my mother's voice is full of barely controlled rage. "Samantha, come inside."

Helen gives me a desperate look. "I only want to speak to your mother for a minute—"

My mother opens the door but doesn't step outside. "Get in here, Sam!"

I shake my head at Helen. "You have to leave right now."

"Please. I know she doesn't want to see me." She holds up her clasped hands, shaking them under my nose, the chemical smell wafting around me. "I am begging you."

My mother rushes outside in her bare feet, slamming the door behind her and ignoring me altogether as she grabs Helen by the shoulders, forcing her to take clumsy steps backward to avoid falling over.

"Get the *fuck* off my property. Get the fuck out of here now. I'm calling the police."

Helen puts her hands up in surrender, her stack of papers scattering onto the street. "I'm sorry, Sharon. I'm leaving now. I didn't mean to upset you. I'm sorry."

"You didn't mean to *upset* me?" My mother shrieks, her voice pure hatred. I wish I could say I've never seen her so upset, but this transformation—calm one moment, furious the next—has happened many times throughout the years. It is as if she is constantly balancing on a tightrope, a hair's breadth away from crumbling. You'd think it would get better as more time passes, but it doesn't, at least not by much. Every day, for her, is the worst day. Until Hannah was born, that's what she would say. She always apologized afterward. "It's not your fault, Samantha." But we all know it sort of is. "It's not your fault, Gretchen." But she undeniably played a big role. "It's not anybody's fault except Steven's." But her pain—and my father's—cannot stay so sharply focused on him. The blame oozes onto everything and everyone connected to that night; it is impossible to keep it neatly contained; it is too slippery, and there is far too much of it. And just when you think you've managed to get it under control, you find more seeping from cracks that you didn't even realize existed.

Helen rushes to her car without attempting to collect the papers she's left to scatter up and down the street. She fumbles through her purse as she looks for her keys, glancing over her shoulder every few seconds to make sure my mom isn't about to pounce.

It feels like we're on stage, the whole world watching the drama of our sad lives playing out on our dead-end street. Mrs. Souza peeks out her front door to gawk at the scene, but she would never do anything besides stare at us with her big, droopy eyes and open mouth; I don't think I've heard her say one word in my entire life. The whole time she's looking at us, she keeps a withered hand on the neck of the German shepherd sitting calmly at her side.

Susan comes running out the door and wraps her arms around my mother from behind, wrangling her back into our house as the rain starts. In our living room, my mom sobs into Susan's chest while Gretchen and Abby—Hannah still in her arms—hurry into the kitchen.

"Shh, shh," Susan says, stroking my mom's hair as if she were a child. "She's gone, honey. It's okay now."

"It's not okay. It's never going to be okay. Never, never, never, never."

"Shh. I've got you. Take a deep breath." Susan meets my gaze and mouths *Call your father,* but I don't know where to find his work number.

"It's never going to be okay."

"Shh. I know. I know. I know it won't."

Through the living room window, I can see Remy walking around in the downpour, trying to pick up the papers Helen left behind, though most of them have started to dissolve into pulp that will easily wash away with the rain. Hannah's tap shoes dangle from his free hand. When he sees me staring at him, he waves the drippy papers and gives me a slight shrug, as if to say it's no problem for him to clean up the mess, even though it's not his.

•   •   •

I felt for his family more than anything, you know. Jack and I go way back, all the way to Little League. This didn't used to be the kind of town where people had crazy secrets and kids couldn't play outside without having to worry about getting pestered by perverts. It was a nightmare for that whole family from the time Stevie had his accident in the swimming pool. It was like the doctor left a couple of wires unattached when he was putting Stevie's head back together, but most of the time it didn't seem like a major malfunction. He got headaches all the time and forgot little things he'd known all his life; Helen was always reminding him what their phone number was. Other times, though, something would misfire and he'd screw up big. Their neighbors who lived at the end of the street had a bunch of kids of all different ages. I guess they left their house unlocked a lot of the time because the kids came and went at all hours. One day the wife comes home with her twins and a trunk full of groceries—in the middle of the day while the other kids are all at school and her husband's at work—and she sends them right upstairs for a nap and then finishes bringing in her groceries and putting them away, and when she goes up to check on the kids she finds Stevie asleep in her bed. He was fast asleep under the covers, as if it were the most normal thing in the world.

After the thing with the Myers girl, people would hardly look at them. It wasn't more than two or three months before the business went under. Helen would sit there all day by the register without seeing a single customer. Jack told me they were eating supper one Sunday when a condom that someone had filled up like a balloon with shit came flying at the window and exploded all over the place. They didn't deserve all the hate people shoveled onto them—as people, you know? They weren't bad people. It broke my heart to see things end that way for them. Back in high school, we thought Jack would walk on the moon someday, and Helen would be pretty forever. You know what I mean? It seemed that if something so awful could happen to Jack and Helen, then probably we were all fucked.

So if you're asking do I think it happened the way they say, what do you expect me to tell you? Yes, I think he killed that little girl. Otherwise he's just the unluckiest bastard who ever lived. But nobody can figure out what he could have done with her after. She's not in his house, I know, because we tore that place apart from top to bottom. I hated to do it, but it's my job, and here's how decent Jack and Helen are: they let us into the house and didn't say a word the whole time, because they knew we didn't have a choice in the matter, and afterward I shook Jack's hand and said I was sorry but what else could I do, and he said it's okay, Tom, I know, but Stevie didn't hurt her.

Even so, I don't know that he should have been tried for murder. Not without a body. I'm not saying I think she's alive, but shouldn't the court have to prove it? You get a miracle every now and then—remember that girl in Canada who'd been missing for twenty years? Didn't they find her a mile from home, locked up in someone's wine cellar? All I'm saying is, it happens.

I'm still friends with Jack and Helen. I'm a Christian, and I'm not going to abandon them in their hour of need. I don't blame them for not believing Stevie could have done anything to that little girl. Would you want to believe it about *your* child? He's their only kid; that's what parents are supposed to do. People want to look at Stevie and think, *Oh, they all must be monsters, the whole damn family.* They're not. They just got a bad egg.

Forty-Eight Minutes of Doubt, pp. 66–67

chapter eight

January 1986

The way our lives unraveled over the next year made for a captivating story for those whose curiosity outweighed their grief, from our neighbors to the local news audience, and eventually the rest of the country. Prior to that day, our town had little experience with major crimes; aside from some garden-variety domestic violence and a handful of drug users who sometimes required legal attention, the worst thing that had happened was the 1979 suicide of Marvin Gill, a sixteen-year-old boy who'd hung himself from a beam in his attic one night after a Boy Scout meeting. (Whenever they drove past the Gill residence after Marvin's death, my parents would wonder out loud how his parents could possibly stand to keep living in the same house.)

Our town had twelve police officers, none of whom had any experience with kidnappings. Ego was never an issue in the investigation; state police were called in immediately and given full control. They divided Shelocta into a grid and organized the citizens to conduct shoulder-to-shoulder searches of every square inch. Teams worked in shifts to scour the town for sixteen hours each day. Everybody wanted to help: anonymous casseroles showed up on our doorstep with such regularity that most of them ended up in the trash. A tip line received dozens of calls each day, none of which yielded any valuable information. Housewives distributed thermoses of coffee and hot chocolate to the searchers, who persisted in spite of single-digit temperatures and a growing tremble of doubt that Turtle would be found alive, if at all. Throughout all of this, Steven was in a jail cell less than six blocks from my house.

Two weeks into the new year, an overnight storm dropped fourteen inches of fresh snow on Shelocta in less than eight hours. Police called off their official search. If Turtle was anywhere outdoors, she wasn't alive.

I slept with my parents most nights for years afterward, either between them in their bed or on the floor beside it. Long after they'd both swallowed their last sedatives of the day and gone to sleep, I stayed awake with my eyes closed and kept track of their breathing, constantly reassuring myself that there was nobody in the room but the three of us. My brain replayed the same nightmare every time I slept deeply enough for dreams: Remy and I were building a snowman in the woods behind our houses when I looked down to see Turtle's face staring up at me, her mouth wide open and frozen in a permanent scream beneath a sheet of ice.

In Davis Gordon's book, he uses the word "colored" to describe how my life, in particular, was changed. He talks a lot about the coloring of my worldview, my sense of security and vulnerability. All I can ever picture is a large, shadowy villain hovering above me, wielding a handful of crayons. It's funny how much we rely on euphemisms to soften the blow of an ugly truth. When my parents spoke about things like "bringing Turtle home," what they meant was bringing her *body* home, but nobody would dare say it that way. Even today, we still do it. There's an expression in journalism: "If it bleeds, it leads." It didn't take long for my parents to realize that we were entertainment for plenty of people, a status that made the most horrific details of Turtle's case the most sought after. Steven's parents had it worse in the press, but there were still plenty of stories that stung. "Parents of Missing Toddler Were Intoxicated, High on Night of Disappearance." "Tabitha Myers: Could She Have Been Saved?"

Davis seemed different from the other reporters. More than anything, he claimed he wanted to help us find closure. That word gets thrown around a lot in situations like ours, and usually people don't understand how impossible it can seem in the thick of all the pain. As if what happened that night is a book we've all been reading together, and one day we'll come to the last page and finally be able to put it down forever. But that would mean our lives follow a predictable narrative that is required to make sense somehow in the end, which is so clearly not the case.

Davis meant more to my dad than he did to anyone else in our family. My father had always been the kind of person who preferred calm to chaos. After Steven went to prison and my family moved away, it seemed as though even the smallest ripple in his thoughts could set off days of emotional agony. He talked about the past with Davis, and how the smallest decision could change a person's whole future for better or worse without any rhyme or reason. But if you can't figure out the moment when something starts to happen, how can you determine when it ends?

My mother had no patience for my father's meandering thoughts. She followed a different path. It led her through fields of marijuana to mountains of Valium and Xanax, where a river of codeine flowed into a lake of Everclear. By then she was chewing whole pills into dust—sometimes three or four at a time—between her teeth instead of swallowing them with water.

Davis was willing to listen to my father's miserable philosophizing all day, if he thought it would help. He seemed to truly care about us. When he told us all he wanted was to help us find some peace, we believed him. Why shouldn't we have done so? He'd devoted his career to solving other people's mysteries. His first book had followed his own modern-day investigation into his aunt Carolyn's 1966 murder, which he eventually solved. "I made a promise to my mother before she died," he told us, "that I would find the person who killed her sister, and that's what I did." And he showed us a picture of his aunt. She was a pretty girl, barely eighteen years old when her naked body floated to the surface of Keystone Lake on a summer morning during the Age of Aquarius, ruining one unlucky fisherman's day.

My family was living in Virginia by the time Davis took an interest in us. He traveled back and forth between there and Shelocta throughout the spring and summer of 1988. He interviewed everyone who knew anything about the case and followed up on every tip the original investigators had dismissed as irrelevant, scrutinizing them for any hint that might lead to my sister's body. My mother kept a picture of his aunt Carolyn on our fridge, and sometimes I'd catch her staring at the dead woman whose face had become hope personified for us, as though she were a benevolent force from beyond guiding us toward the closure we'd heard so much about but never experienced.

Davis spent hour after hour at our home, where he looked through photo albums with my mother and listened as she described every detail of my sister's interrupted life. His fingers touched the blanket that had swaddled Turtle as a newborn at the hospital; they felt the blunt ends of the lock of hair my mother had saved from Turtle's first haircut. My father kept in frequent touch with Davis long after he finished his research and returned to his home in New York to start writing the book. His wife sent us a Christmas card that year, and Davis watched Super Bowl XXIV at our house. He even bought me a pogo stick for my tenth birthday.

But it turned out he'd spent plenty of time talking to Steven and his parents, too. We knew that, of course, but we had no idea that he'd reached out to them with a promise similar to the one he made us. Maybe he liked them more. Maybe Helen Handley makes a better lasagna than my mom. Maybe she and her husband guaranteed Davis a lifetime of free dry cleaning. Or maybe he's just an asshole. From the moment his book hit the shelves six years ago, Davis has spent every penny of the profits on a new defense team for Steven.

In *Forty-Eight Minutes of Doubt*, Davis uses words like "mercy" and "compassion" and "forgiveness" when he discusses the broader issues of crime and punishment and the many failures of the American justice system. My father read the book before anyone else in our family. He stopped talking for a few weeks after he got to the end. I don't mean that he was quieter than normal—I mean he stopped talking altogether. He began staying home from work for days on end to smoke weed in our basement and sort through boxes of his old baseball cards. He lost job after job for not showing up, failing a random drug test, or giving everyone he encountered the creeps by refusing to make eye contact with a single one of his coworkers for months.

My mother didn't read the book at all. She changed our phone number and donated my pogo stick to Goodwill, but she left the picture of Davis's aunt Carolyn on our fridge. It stayed up for almost a year, finally disappearing a few weeks before Hannah was born.

The book was an instant bestseller. Because of it, there are plenty of people who have some level of doubt about what happened to Turtle that night. Theories range from the unlikely to the impossible to the insane. People—especially those who aren't fully informed—came up with some impressively creative scenarios. An unlikely one: the idea that Steven didn't act alone, and that Turtle is still alive out there somewhere. I can't tell you how many times I've imagined it: one day the phone rings, and the voice on the line informs us that my sister has been living for a decade in another state, happy and well cared for by some individual (or individuals) who only wanted a daughter to love. Now that her true identity has been realized, she is swiftly returned to her rightful home and family. Ten years of misery evaporate in a moment as she falls into our arms, looking exactly the way we've pictured her all these years. That night, we all sit around the kitchen table and eat hot dogs and coleslaw, Turtle's favorite meal. Our family lives happily ever after. Roll credits.

Impossible: despite having a motive and opportunity—and despite the fact that both Remy and I clearly identified him as the man we'd seen carrying Turtle away—Steven Handley was wrongly convicted of a crime he did not commit.

Insane: the idea that one of my or Remy's parents might have been involved, or even me and Remy ourselves.

The truth is not nearly so exciting or complicated. No matter what happened to Turtle that night, it's delusional to hope that she might still be alive. Even finding her grave—if she has a proper one somewhere—seems like too much to wish for most days. There have been countless tips and theories that have provided my parents with grains of hope over the years, but none of them have blossomed into anything but disappointment, each letdown another tiny death for us to grieve.

The biggest comfort at this point is also the most gruesome: though none of us ever says it out loud, we all understand that our only real wish is for Turtle to be long dead. Let her spend eternity oblivious to the ugliness that seeped into every empty space she left behind.

◆   ◆   ◆

Letter from Steven Handley to Gretchen Myers

Dear Gretchen,

I hope you like the flowers. I'm not sorry about what happened today. I don't know why your father is destroying my life. His cruelty makes me sick, when all I've done is love you and treat you like the princess you are. He sits in his house like a king playing a twisted game with his subjects. I am not obsessed, I am IN LOVE. How would he act if someone yanked away the person he loved most in the world for no good reason? He's messing with the wrong man. Nothing changes; we'll just have to be careful. I'll be in the school parking lot on Friday morning. Same spot, same time (unless it snows and I have to pick up a shift.)

I love you!

—Me

Reprinted with author's permission.
Forty-Eight Minutes of Doubt, p. 81

chapter nine

Summer 1996

We were pariahs in Shelocta as much as we were celebrities. How many people can say that their fifteen minutes of fame was also the single worst thing that's ever happened to them? At first everybody wanted to help, but once they all realized Turtle was never coming home, nobody knew how to treat us. Most people tried to avoid my family as much as possible.

Even Abby, who had barely spent a day apart from Gretchen in years, pulled away for a long time. Her dad and Darla showed up to volunteer for the search parties that assembled at the end of our street every day for almost two weeks. They tried to help in other ways, too, even though they weren't always successful. Ed Tickle got into a fistfight one day with a reporter who'd followed Gretchen all the way home from school, asking her if she ever thought about killing herself over what had happened to her sister. Darla brought over her makeup kit one day and spent hours giving me a makeover while my mother stayed in her bedroom. Darla liked to have the television on while she worked; she said having soap operas in the background kept her mind engaged. During a quiet scene in *The Days of Our Lives*, we could hear my mother sobbing all the way upstairs. Darla turned up the volume and kept right on dabbing my lids with eye shadow as if nothing had happened, but I remember thinking it was taking her an awfully long time to finish my makeup. When she was done, she braided my hair and painted my toenails before starting to work on her own manicure.

"You don't have to stay here all day with me," I told her. "I'll be okay."

"I don't mind if you don't mind." Darla always seemed so glamorous to me, but her heavy makeup and shellacked hairdo weren't nearly as impressive up close. "When I was a little girl, about your age, my mom left me home alone all the time."

"Really? That's so cool."

"Yeah, well, it ain't legal."

"Did your mom get in trouble?"

Darla's lips trembled into the briefest of half smiles. "She was always in some kind of trouble."

But Abby stayed almost completely out of sight until after we moved away; I don't even think she came over to say good-bye the day we moved out. She and Gretchen didn't reconnect until a few years later. I don't know exactly why it happened that way, but my best guess is that Abby figured my parents hated her for being Steven and Gretchen's go-between, which they did.

I wonder if Abby realizes how hard it was for Gretchen to lose her best friend and her sister at the same time, or if there was a reason for the rift that I don't know anything about. Either way, nothing seems to have changed about their relationship. They are inseparable once again, spending most of their time at Abby's house. Ed Tickle needs almost constant care since his stroke last winter. Gretchen told us she doesn't think he'll live much longer. She's been here with Abby, on and off, since February. Darla and Ed split up years ago; without Gretchen's help, Abby would be looking after her father alone.

I'm surprised to realize how jealous I am of their friendship. I don't know why it bothers me so much. Maybe it's because the Remy I've remembered for so long does not exist anymore; instead he's been replaced by an aloof stranger, way more interested in his friends and girlfriend than he is in me. I've never had a friendship like Gretchen and Abby's.

I barely see Gretchen. When she is around, she always seems to be either coming or going in a hurry. Our only consistent interaction happens most mornings as she's getting ready for work. She takes the longest showers of anyone I've ever met, hogging the bathroom and leaving me with no hot water, wet towels thrown on the floor for someone else to worry about. She is always running late. As I brush my teeth one morning, she strolls in without knocking and sits down on the toilet. She doesn't acknowledge me as she props her foot against the edge of the garbage can and begins to clip her toenails while simultaneously peeing.

"Do you mind?" I spit into the sink. "I'd appreciate some privacy."

"You're seriously foaming at the mouth, Sam." *Clip. Clip.* "Guess what I just saw outside. Remy was sneaking that chick out his basement door. She *clearly* spent the night. I watched him walk her outside, and I felt like I should be paying them for the show they were putting on. No joke. They were like a couple of octopuses." She pauses. "Is it 'octopuses' or 'octopi'? Anyway, you know what I mean." *Clip, clip, clip.*

I rinse my mouth and slide the garbage can out of her reach with my foot. "Get out."

She blinks innocently at me. "What's wrong?"

"Get out."

"Sam, calm down." She grasps my arm. "You're way prettier than her. She's built like a ten-year-old boy. You could steal him in a second if you wanted to."

"Why do you need to use my bathroom every morning, Gretchen? Why don't you just stay with Abby all the time instead of making everything harder for us here?"

She's silent for a moment, drawing her hand away from me and crossing her arms. "This is my family, too. I have as much right to be here as you do." Her wedding band sparkles on her finger. It seems strange that she's still wearing it when she hasn't so much as mentioned her husband since she arrived.

"You're still wearing your ring."

She glances down at it, wiggling her finger. "Yeah. So what?"

"I thought you were getting a divorce."

"It's not that simple, Sam."

"You seemed happy together."

"Well, things aren't always what they seem."

"So you're giving up."

"We're working on things."

"Isn't it hard to work on things when you're up here and your husband is all the way down in Texas?"

She flings a hairbrush into the sink. "You're such a brat. You think you know everything, don't you? *I am here. To help. My friend.* Her father is dying. I didn't want her to go through it alone. I know—I'm such a bitch, right?"

"Don't you ever worry that she's taking advantage of you, Gretchen?" I ask, echoing the suspicion our mother has been muttering to herself for weeks. "She could hire a nurse, couldn't she? It's not like she couldn't pay for it. Mom says Ed has veteran's benefits."

Gretchen's irritation softens into sadness. She looks at me with an unsettling expression of aching, sincere regret. She feels *sorry* for me, I realize, because I don't know what such an intimate friendship feels like.

"Abby isn't taking advantage of me. Trust me, Sam—you think you know all about her, but you don't have a clue. Nobody knows her like I do. She's going to surprise everybody someday." She pauses. "You just wait."

chapter ten

Summer 1996

I'm still working on the Mitchells' basement at the beginning of July. Susan is at some kind of teachers' conference today, so I'm supposed to let myself into her house and get started on my own. So far, my days in the basement have been unrelentingly dull reminders that I have no friends or social life here, but after my fight with Gretchen this morning, I was looking forward to being alone. So of course, when I walk into the kitchen, Remy is standing over the counter with his back to me, nodding along with whatever's playing on his headphones as he butters a piece of toast, oblivious to my presence. He starts to sing and dance along with a Bob Marley song, the one about three little birds.

I've been watching him for less than a minute and have barely moved an inch since walking through the door, but somehow Remy can tell he's not alone. He spins around and we make eye contact.

His face freezes in mortification. His arm bumps the counter, sending his toast flying from his plate onto the floor. All he's wearing is a pair of Smurfs boxer shorts. He tries to cover himself with his arms for a second before realizing that it doesn't help much, so he switches tactics by running out of the kitchen and down the hallway. He forgets to grab his Discman from the kitchen counter, and it falls to the floor and breaks into three pieces when his headphones snap away, but that doesn't slow his exit. We haven't exchanged a single word yet.

When he finally comes back—fully dressed—I hand him the Discman. "The hinge on the lid is broken. Sorry." *Bob Marley's Greatest Hits* rests safely on the index finger of my other hand.

"Damn it, Samantha, I won that playing skee-ball last week at Cedar Point. I had to spend, like, seventy bucks on tokens."

"You could have bought one for less than that."

"That's not the *point*." He stares at his now-ruined toast, which landed butter side down on the linoleum.

"I thought you knew I'd be coming over. I've been here every morning for a week."

"I'm not monitoring your every move. I don't even know what time it is." He's trying to brush the dirt from the floor off his toast. I think I see a pubic hair among the debris.

"Please don't eat that." I reach for it.

"Five second rule." He pulls his hand back.

"Remy, it's been sitting there for at least three minutes. Throw it away. There are ways to get more toast."

He sits at the kitchen table and tries to fix the Discman, without success, while I make him a new slice.

"Did you find anything interesting downstairs yet? My grandma kept everything she ever saw or touched, pretty much. My dad says it's because she lived through the Great Depression. We used to take her to the buffet at the Howard Johnson's on Sunday mornings. You know, the one down by the old Family Dollar? She'd stash bacon in her bra to eat later that day. One time we caught her stealing the little salt and pepper shakers. It was humiliating."

"When did she die?"

"Back in March. She just didn't wake up one morning."

"I'm sorry."

He shrugs, chewing nonchalantly. "Don't be. She was so old that it wasn't even sad, not really. I mean, she was out of her mind, so it was more of a relief than anything. I know I'm not supposed to say that, but it's true. I'm the one who found her. Did you know that?"

"How would I know that?"

"I don't know. It seemed like a big deal to me at the time. I told lots of people." He pauses. "Her eyes were open. I wish they would have been closed."

"I thought you said she died in her sleep."

"She must have opened them, maybe right before it happened. Her light was out. It would have been dark in her room." Another pause. "It would have been better if they'd been closed. You remember her, don't you?"

I nod. "A little bit."

"But she was normal back then. She was crazy toward the end."

"Yeah, your mom told me about that."

"You don't know how bad it got. She was paranoid. She used

to set up all these weird little booby traps to see if someone was going through her things. Like, she'd put little pieces of tape on the edges of doors or drawers or whatever, so she'd know if someone other than her had opened them. She did it all over the house, and sometimes she'd forget about them for days. Her memory went in and out like that. One minute we'd be watching *Wheel of Fortune* together and everything would seem fine, and the next she'd be begging me to drive her to a violin lesson."

"Your grandma played the violin?"

"Uh, *no*. That's what I'm trying to explain. She had dementia on top of being paranoid—or maybe she was paranoid because of the dementia, I don't know, I'm not a doctor or anything—so even when she could think clearly, she was still insane. Like with all those pieces of tape; she'd forget about them, and we'd all go about our business living here, and when she finally remembered what she'd done, all the tape would be broken or out of place. It was awful."

He takes a bite of toast, staring at me while he chews. It's so quiet in his kitchen that I can hear his jaw muscles moving as he works the food around in his mouth. He swallows, takes a swig of milk directly from the open half-gallon jug beside his plate, and repeats the chew-and-stare process all over again. He can tell I'm uncomfortable, but he seems to be enjoying the power of his silent gaze too much to let it go. When I can't stand it for another second, I blurt out the first thought in my mind: "You have a big hickey on your neck."

More silence. His expression only changes a smidgen. If he's embarrassed, it doesn't show. "I know that."

"Kind of trashy, don't you think?"

"Who cares?"

"People care."

Remy squints at me as if he's trying to make up his mind about something. When he starts talking again, everything about him seems suddenly detached, as though he's flipped a "disengage" switch in his brain. "Okay, Sam. I'll try to conduct myself in a way that's less embarrassing for you from now on."

"That isn't what I meant."

"You don't know anything about me. Not now."

"I know I don't. I didn't mean—I wasn't—I should go downstairs." I try to rush past him, but he grabs my arm with buttery fingers.

"You don't look anything like I thought you would." He says it like an accusation.

"Neither do you."

Outside, someone gives a car horn three long honks.

"That's Luke." Remy lets go of my arm, and I feel an invisible wall moving back into place between us before he's even left the kitchen. "I have to get dressed. I'll see you later, Samantha." He doesn't even turn around to say good-bye.

"I bet his girlfriend hates your guts." Abby rarely comes into our house unless my parents aren't here, which means it's not hard to avoid her most of the time. Tonight I'm not so lucky. My dad is out, probably drinking beer with Mike at the American Legion. My mom is at an all-day gymnastics camp with Hannah. I don't have anywhere else to go, so I'm stuck with my sister and her trusty sidekick, who are snuggled together on the opposite end of the living room couch, a blanket spread across their laps. Abby's head rests on Gretchen's shoulder. We're eating pizza and watching *Dirty Dancing*. I'd pass on movie night with them under any other circumstances, but I'm starving, and what kind of girl turns her back on *Dirty Dancing*? (No kind of girl. Everybody loves *Dirty Dancing*. Everybody.)

"That doesn't make any sense. Remy and I aren't even friends."

"Who said it had to make sense?" Gretchen doesn't take her eyes off the television screen.

"That is why you fail, Samantha." Abby is still as petite as always, especially compared to Gretchen, but she's nowhere near as pretty as she was a decade ago. Her whole person, from her face and body to the way she moves and breathes, has the look and vibe of a woman who knows that whatever potential she might have possessed in her youth has long since faded away. It wasn't that noticeable at first, but it became obvious once I'd spent some time with her. Her face is a shade too thin, her eyeliner a touch too heavy; her fingernails are uneven, their polish chipped; her dark hair is littered with strands of gray. There's a weariness emanating from within her that never goes away, not even when she's cuddled up beside her best friend in the world.

I guess that's what happens when you sacrifice your whole life to take care of someone else, which is what she's doing for her father. He might live for another thirty years with Abby caring for his broken body, his working mind trapped inside without any possibility for either of them to escape until his heart stops beating. I want

to loathe her, but it feels too cruel, even though she gives me a reason to every time she opens her mouth.

"She doesn't need a good reason to hate you," she continues.
She's still talking about Heather, Remy's girlfriend. "She hates you
because you're a pretty girl who lives next door to her boyfriend."

"But I've barely even spoken to Remy."

"You will," Gretchen says. "You were best friends."

"That was ten years ago."

"Ten years isn't that long."

"Maybe Samantha doesn't like boys," Abby suggests, flicking
her tongue at me from between her fingers. Mid-gesture, her gaze
lands on my necklace. I'm wearing a silver locket that I found in
Remy's basement in a shoe box filled to the brim with old jewelry,
most of it too tarnished or tangled to bother with.

"Where did you get that?" Her eyes narrow in accusation.

"From Remy's basement. It was his grandma's."

"Oh, yeah? It's pretty."

"Thank you."

"Whose picture did you put inside?"

I put my hand over the locket. "Nobody's."

Gretchen laughs. "That sounds about right."

"Shut up. I *do* like boys, you know."

"You could have fooled me."

"I'm busy with other things."

Abby snorts through her perky little nose. "Well, that's a lie."

"God, Samantha, you're no fun at all!" My sister lights the joint
she's been rolling for the last ten minutes and gets it burning nice

and steady before passing it to Abby. Abby offers it to me, even though she knows I don't want any. Once I've refused, she starts blowing smoke rings in my direction and singing under her breath: "*Don't smoke, don't drink, goody-goody-two-shoes.*" She pauses before adding, "I'm talking about you, Sam."

"Oh? I didn't realize."

"Wait a minute, you two—stop bitching at each other. Tell me this, Samantha: have you ever been on a date? Like, a real one?"

"Why are you so interested in my love life all of a sudden?"

Gretchen shrugs. "Because you're my sister, I guess."

For a moment, the world around me is all background noise and static, and I can only think of Noah. My parents called him my boyfriend, but that's not what he was. One night together at a Holiday Inn does not a boyfriend make, but it's not like it mattered; my parents made sure they put an end to any relationship we might have had before it ever got started. But if Gretchen knows about Noah, she isn't letting on.

Beside my sister, Abby digs through her purse until she produces an oversized bag of candy corn, which she begins to eat by the handful. The sight disgusts me. "I wasn't aware anybody ate that stuff on purpose."

"I have to agree with Sam on this one," Gretchen says. "Candy corn is the worst. That shit will rot your teeth faster than anything." She works part-time as a dental assistant three mornings a week. Even if she and her husband *are* trying to "work things out," I don't think she's planning on going back to Texas anytime soon. Otherwise, why bother to get a job here?

Abby smiles. Her teeth are already stained orange and black.

"I brush twice a day," she says. Tiny flecks of spit go flying from her lips onto the blanket. Gretchen wipes them away.

"That isn't enough. You have to floss every time you brush, too, or you might as well not bother at all."

"Shut up. You don't know what you're talking about."

"Yes, I do! You know what I hear at my job at least once a week? I mean at *least*. Take a guess."

"I don't know. Tell me, oh wise and lovely dental assistant." They're both giggling like maniacs. Neither of them seems at all concerned that the entire first floor of the house reeks of pot. It's no surprise that Abby's not worried, but Gretchen should know that our parents would likely frown on the scene if they happened to walk in with Hannah. She hasn't even bothered to open a window or turn on the ceiling fan. If I had smoked some of the joint, would I be as relaxed as she and Abby seem right now? I can't imagine how it feels. I've never smoked marijuana, although I've smelled it plenty of times. I've never even been drunk.

"I hear, 'Is that a popcorn kernel? I don't even remember the last time I ate popcorn.'"

Abby laughs with her whole body. She butts her head against Gretchen's shoulder and kicks her bare feet with glee. "That happened to me! I swear to God, it happened to me the last time I had my teeth cleaned!"

"Popcorn," Gretchen repeats. "It's always stuck between molars or below the gum line. People are always so surprised. 'How did that get there?!'"

"Stop!" Abby throws a handful of candy corn into the air like confetti. "It's too funny! I can't take it! I can't breathe!"

"You're making a huge mess," I say, picking pieces of candy corn from my hair. "It's getting all over the floor, Abby. Who's supposed to clean this up?"

"You are!" she screeches, throwing another handful. I look at Gretchen for help, but she couldn't care less. She taps the ash from the joint onto the floor and tilts her head back while she sucks in another lungful of smoke, which she's still holding when Silver Pickup turns onto our street a minute later. The song "Get It Together" is blasting from the truck's open windows. The vehicle barely comes to a full stop long enough to let Remy jump out before the driver makes a U-turn in the cul-de-sac and speeds away.

"Excuse me." I stand up and start walking toward the kitchen as casually as possible. "The smoke is bothering me."

"Bring me a beer, Sam," Abby shouts, but my hand is already on the back door. I need to get out of this house. I need air, and a place where I can be alone. From the edge of our yard, I can still hear Abby's laughter carrying on the breeze.

I don't have my driver's license. Even if I did and could leave the house by myself, it's not like I have any friends in this town. There's nowhere for me to go. For a millisecond, I think of calling Noah, but that's a terrible idea. As a kid, I always hid in the playhouse whenever I needed time to myself. Why can't I do the same thing now?

The playhouse door isn't locked. Inside on the floor are a pillow, a short stack of books with an ashtray resting on top, and the *Star Wars* sleeping bag that Remy has had since we were toddlers. There's a half-empty gallon jug of red wine and a deck of playing cards. A small hummingbird feeder hangs from a loop of silver wire in the window.

It's a warm night; the sleeping bag is enough to keep me comfortable for now. Remy's bedroom light shines through his open window at the back of the house. I watch him pacing the room in slow circles while he talks on the phone, pausing once in a while to look at himself in the mirror or flip through the channels on his TV. His conversation lasts about five minutes. After he hangs up, he strips down to his boxer shorts and walks out of the room, probably heading to the shower.

It gives me a strange thrill to be in here, watching him, without his knowledge. I know I shouldn't be doing it, but it's not like I'm hurting anyone. Besides, it's really Remy's fault for not closing his blinds. I settle deeper into the sleeping bag. I gather a handful of fabric in each fist and feel the rough, worn-out cloth in my hands, convinced that I've earned the right to trespass, that a part of Remy still belongs to me—will always belong to me—whether he likes it or not.

◆　◆　◆

"I want to die." He was as calm as a stranger asking for the time. "Sometimes I think it already happened. Maybe we're all dead, and this is hell. It's possible, isn't it?"

By then I considered Paul a friend. He wasn't the kind of person to exaggerate things. I'd spent hour after hour with him and his family, and I felt a sense of kinship as a fellow husband and father. We sat across from each other in a corner booth at Denny's. He ordered coffee and didn't touch it. He was only forty-four but looked at least sixty. The restaurant was three short blocks from the Hilton he'd checked into a week earlier with the intention of ending his life. He told me in detail how he'd tied a rope around his neck and stood on a chair for over two hours while he tried to work up the courage to kick it away. In the end, he couldn't do it.

I did the only thing I could: I listed all the reasons I could think of for him to keep living. I reminded him of the people he'd be leaving behind. What would happen to Sharon, Samantha, and Gretchen? What would they do without him?

"That's the thing. That's what makes it a hell. All I want to do is die, but I can't. People always say the worst thing would be to lose everything. They say that, don't they? If you lose everything, you have nothing left to live for. But they've got it all wrong. The worst thing is to lose *almost* everything, because then you have to keep going for whoever's left down there with you in the steaming bog of shit that life becomes. You have to keep treading through the shit together just to keep everyone's head above the surface. Forget any chance of escape. Forget it. We'll never get out, none of us. We're in it together until we die. One big happy family. And my daughter, my baby girl, is out there alone, and I can't do a goddamn thing to help her. What if she's alive? I know it's impossible. I know that. And I'm glad about that, for her sake, because at least she's not alone, wondering when someone will finally save her. The point is that I didn't help her. You want to know the first thing I think about every morning? Before I even open my eyes? I wonder whether she called out for me or Sharon. Was it cold? Was it dark? She must have been so scared. Did she die while calling out for us? That's how I start my days. And I deserve that. Don't shake your head, because you know it's true. This is my life and my hell, and this is where I have to stay, because if Sharon or Sam or Gretchen calls my name and I'm not there . . . I don't know. I can't think about it. It kills me every morning. I hear her screaming for me every morning."

Forty-Eight Minutes of Doubt, p. 77

chapter eleven

Summer 1996

It's so nice to have found a place of my own in the playhouse, even temporarily, that I try to forget the fact that it doesn't belong to me and I don't have permission to be here. Several nights have passed since the first time I spied on Remy from the playhouse, and each evening I've found myself returning after dark to this little room, with all its remnants of the long-lost comforts of my childhood.

Tonight I've brought along a cardboard box filled with Grandma Bitty's old photos from the basement. Except for the silver locket, the box is all I've kept so far. The only light I have to see the pictures with comes from a strand of multicolored Christmas lights strung around the playhouse ceiling, but it's enough. Go look sometime at pictures of yourself as a cute, happy little kid, when life was easy and everyone wore ridiculous clothing. It's a blast. I hover over a bunch of photos spread out across the floor, sifting silently through stack after stack, my eyes straining to stay focused in the dim light.

For a second, I think I hear a light tapping on the door. I pause, holding my breath to listen. Nothing.

"So there's this beautiful woman who goes to see her doctor one day for a checkup," Remy says, sticking his face through the open window.

"What are you doing out here?" I scramble to hide the photos, shoving them back into the box and underneath the sleeping bag, but it's too late.

"What am *I* doing out here? That's funny, Sam. This is my yard. What are *you* doing out here?" His gaze flicks around the tiny room. "You'd better not be drinking my wine."

"Don't worry."

Remy lifts his right hand to show me the six-pack of Rolling Rock he's brought. "It feels like more of a beer night, anyway." He sits cross-legged on the floor beside me, cracks open a can, and takes a few gulps. "So, as I was saying, this hot woman goes to the doctor. When he comes into the room, he's stunned by how beautiful his patient is. The doctor considers himself a professional and a gentleman, but sometimes a person can't help himself. He tries to do the exam as usual, but eventually he starts rubbing her thighs."

"I've already heard this one."

"I know." He offers me one of the beers. "But it's a good one."

"Maybe if you're twelve years old." It's the same joke we overheard Remy's dad tell that New Year's Eve.

"Oh, I think it's universally funny. When she tells the doctor she's there to be tested for herpes, but they've already had sex? What's not funny about that?"

"Right. Because the best jokes are the ones you have to explain."

"No, the best jokes are about naked women."

I close my eyes for a few seconds, hoping that he'll be gone when I open them. It doesn't work. "Why are you out here?"

"Don't you want this?" He means the beer.

"No." I could cry. Now that he knows I've been coming here, it's ruined. "Why are you here, Remy? What do you want?"

"I told you, it's my yard. I can come out here whenever I want. You, on the other hand, cannot."

"Why do you get to decide that? This place isn't yours, either, not technically. You didn't build it."

"But it's on my property."

"It's *barely* on your property. Ed built it for all of us. He only used your yard because the tree was the right size."

"Ed's not in charge of much around here, Sam. Not lately."

"Your parents wouldn't care, either."

He shrugs. "Maybe, maybe not. But I care." He glances down at all the pictures. "Were those my grandma's? Did you steal them?"

"I didn't *steal* them. Your mom told me to throw them away, but I kept them instead."

"So you stole them."

"No! I told you, I only—"

"Relax, Sam. I'm kidding."

"Oh."

He picks up a stack of photos and brings them closer to his face as he looks through them. "Are you sure my mom meant for you to throw away all of these? Some of them look like ones she'd want to keep."

"I think so."

"Wow, these are crazy. I forgot they existed." His eyes flash with nostalgia as he takes in each picture, and for a moment I think I see the Remy I remember.

Looking at the photos makes me self-conscious about the fact that Remy and I used to spend so much time together. There are only a handful of shots of him that don't include me. "Did we do *anything* without each other?" He flips through a few shots of us naked in the tub together, our lower bodies obscured by a thick layer of bubbles. The date scribbled on the back reads 8/25/79; we weren't even two years old. In another—this one from October '85—we're standing shoulder to shoulder on the sidewalk in Halloween costumes. Remy's a cowboy; I'm an Indian princess. Gretchen is in the background, posing like an aspiring model in her witch costume. Her black skirt is too short for a sixteen-year-old, and her legs seem unsteady as she balances on five-inch stilettos. Turtle stands on the periphery of the scene, her form blurred as she twirls gleefully in a pink ballerina costume. It is Halloween night, exactly two months before she disappeared, and the fact that her features are fuzzy gives me a sick, dizzy feeling. It's as if she was already starting to fade.

"Why did you come back?" Remy flicks the photo aside and fixes his gaze on me. "I'm not talking about Gretchen; I know why she's here. Why did the rest of your family come back?"

"My dad lost his job. We had no choice."

"No jobs in Virginia, eh?"

"It's temporary."

"Everything's temporary, Sam."

"That's so philosophical of you."

"I'm a pretty deep guy." He looks pleased with himself, which makes me want to scream.

"Listen, Remy, I know it's weird to be here, okay? I get it. But what were we supposed to do?"

"I don't know. Weren't you upset that you had to leave all your friends with only one year of high school to go? Wasn't there anyone you could have stayed with until graduation? It's not like your parents would be across the country. It's only a four-hour drive."

"There was someone." I pause. "But it didn't work out. It wouldn't have worked out, so I didn't stay with him."

"I see. With *him*. How interesting."

"Stop it."

"What was his name?"

"Rudolf Schmidt." Obviously, I'm lying.

"That's funny. So here you are, anyway."

"So here I am. Here we are, Remy."

"What are you like now, Samantha? Because here's how I remember you: you were loud and funny, and you could fart on command. We used to play this game with my plastic army men and your humidifier; do you remember the one I mean?"

"Yes!" I almost shriek. Remy leans away from me, as if to create more room for my enthusiasm, and I feel embarrassed that I've let myself show so much excitement over a children's game. "Sorry."

"Don't be sorry. That was the best game! We used to make such incredible special effects with the steam from the humidifier." The air in the playhouse is hot, and the cool breeze from the open window has the pinch of a bee sting when it hits my face.

"You have the same ears." He reaches out, brushing my earlobe with his fingertip. "So what are you like now? You didn't answer me."

"I'm not sure what you mean."

"Well, here's what I'm like." He pauses and pulls his hand away from my ear. "Sorry. I'm not trying to grope you or anything."

"It's only my ear. I don't feel groped."

"Yeah, well . . . the thing is, my girlfriend maybe wouldn't quite, like, be *excited* to know that we were in here alone at night and I touched your ear, okay?"

"Oh, okay. I won't bring it up right away the first time I meet her, then, because that's what I was planning to do."

"I see. You're clever." He taps his nose and points at me like you would in a game of Charades.

"I don't know about clever. I'm smart. I get good grades."

"I almost didn't pass my junior year," he says. "My parents are concerned that I'm wasting my potential."

"My parents don't worry about me," I tell him. "I'm good. Boring and good. I've never even drunk a beer."

Remy makes the same perplexed frown that I've seen on Gretchen's face so many times before. I'm a disappointment to both of them, but Remy doesn't want to accept it so easily. "Oh, yeah? That's about to change." He reaches for the six-pack.

"I don't—"

"Shush. It's my playhouse; I make the rules." He stares at me, dead serious. "It's international playhouse law, Samantha. A smart girl like you should know that."

Remy opens a beer and brings it closer and closer to my lips until I reach out and take it. He wipes his forehead with the back of his hand and watches me as I drink. I take a few little sips. It's not bad. I mean, I've tasted alcohol before—a sip here and there from one of my dad's cans of Coors when I was younger, just to see what it was like—but I've never been drunk. There are circles of sweat beneath the arms of Remy's T-shirt, and he smells the way you'd imagine a teenage boy would smell at the end of a hot summer day. It's the strangest feeling to go from then to now with ten years of static in between; I remember him as a boy who was nothing but my best friend, but now it's impossible not to notice that his body is all grown up.

"So you're the smart one and the good one," he repeats. "It's, like, your role in your family."

"Yeah." I force down a few more mouthfuls of beer.

"Do you want it to be?"

"I guess so." The truth is, I've never given the matter much thought before now. "It's easy for me. I've never had any problems in school. I don't cause trouble. It makes my parents happier."

He looks disappointed. "No trouble at all?"

I pretend to try to remember. "I stole a Kit Kat from a gas station once."

"Really?"

"No."

"Oh, God. If that's the worst thing you were willing to *make up* . . ."

"I told you, I'm very well behaved."

"Obviously. It's disgusting. So if you're the good one," he continues, "what does that make Gretchen?"

"Do you have to ask?" I shuffle through a stack of photos taken in Remy's living room during one of Darla's in-home Mary Kay Cosmetics parties.

"Fair enough. What's with her haircut? Isn't it supposed to be a sign of, like, huge emotional distress when a person chops all their hair off out of nowhere? And she's, what—divorced? About to get divorced?"

"I don't know, Remy."

"Does she seem normal to you?"

"I don't know! Maybe. I have no idea what normal is for Gretchen." I hold up my hand and start ticking off everything I can say for sure about her on my fingertips: "She showed up at our house at the end of May, alone, and I don't know what's going on with her husband, Michelangelo, or if she's ever going back to him. She's a dental hygienist over in Penn Village. My mother hates her. Gretchen's probably permanently, irredeemably fucked up forever and ever, no matter what, because of what happened to Turtle. And she's rocking the short hair."

"Okay, I get it. What about Hannah?"

I wince at the sound of her name. "You know what she is."

"She's the replacement." He stretches out each syllable as he pronounces it, taking his time to let the implications settle in the air around us.

"My mom would have died."

"What do you mean?"

"I mean she was almost dead already, even though she was still walking and talking and breathing. Before Hannah was born. You don't know what it was like before then, and it got worse when Davis's book came out. She was so sad, Remy."

"And now she's happy? The pageant stuff with Hannah is creepy, Sam."

"It's not creepy. Lots of kids do it. Hannah has been taking dance lessons since she started walking, so it makes sense for her."

Remy shrugs. "My mom thinks it's gross."

"She does?"

"Yes. She and your mom aren't going to be close again, you know. She doesn't even like my dad hanging out with your dad all the time." He's staring me right in the eyes. I don't remember him being this mean.

"I don't believe you. Our moms are best friends."

"They *were* best friends, Sam. Things are different. Your family moved away ten years ago. You think my parents want to think about this stuff all over again? It's not like we can just pretend nothing happened and start up a bowling league. We haven't exactly been dying to get the old gang back together."

Maybe he finally realizes how upset I'm getting. He breaks away from my glare, looking at the floor and slumping like someone who's blurted out something they immediately regret, but I bet he's more relieved to have said it than anything.

"Thanks, Remy. Why don't you leave me alone, then?"

He laughs. "Because you're in my playhouse! Listen, Sam, what happened was hard for us, too. I know it was worse for you guys," he adds quickly. "I know it was way, way worse for you, worse than we could ever imagine. I'm not saying anything different. But it's not like we weren't there that night."

"I know."

"And it's not like your mom even has time to hang out with my mom. She's always busy with Hannah. And you said she's happy, so everything is okay. Right?"

"I didn't say she was happy."

"You didn't?"

"No. I didn't answer you yet. But I will now. She's not happy, Remy. She'll *never* be happy. But at least now she doesn't sleep for twenty hours a day. Now she doesn't have to use prescription eye-drops because her eyes are so dried out from crying—crying every day for so many years that it's starting to permanently affect her vision."

"Does Hannah know about Turtle?"

"She's only four, Remy."

"Does she know, Sam?"

I pretend to be absorbed in a photo of Remy's mom and Grandma Bitty together. Maybe I'm enjoying these pictures so much because we don't have many old ones on display in my house. Before Hannah was born, my mom kept pictures of Turtle all over the place. Now they're in a box in our garage somewhere. I can understand why she did it. When they were around the house, I went out of my way in order to not see Turtle's face, until the day my mom finally packed them all away.

"Look here," I tell him. "See the locket your grandma's wearing? It's this one, isn't it?" I hold up my necklace for him to see.

He glances at it, disinterested, and then squints at the picture. "Yeah, I guess so."

"Do you think your mom will mind if I keep it? I haven't asked her yet."

"She won't mind. My grandma probably got the necklace at a yard sale. She loved buying junk."

"It's not junk. It looks like real silver."

"You can keep it. My mom will neither notice nor care."

"Are you sure?" I hold it up by the long chain and watch the locket twinkle as it twists in the breeze.

"Of course I'm sure. My grandma used to drive her crazy. She never wants to see most of the garbage down there again."

"It's going to take me forever to finish."

"So? Do you have anything better to do with your time?" He smirks.

"Thanks," I say flatly.

"I'm sorry. But I don't get it: Why did you really come back?" he presses. "It would have been so much easier for you to stay in Virginia for one more year. Finish high school, go to college if you want . . . When I get out of here, I'm never coming back. Not for anything."

"I already told you, I couldn't stay in Virginia. It wouldn't have worked out."

"Because of that boy? What's his name?"

"Noah. But he's not the reason."

"Then who is?"

"Kate O'Neill."

This time, Remy is the one who winces. How could anyone not?

"Yeah. *That* Kate O'Neill."

◆ ◆ ◆

From the earliest stages of the trial, Steven made little effort to give the jurors a good impression of himself. He showed almost no emotion and kept his head down most of the time, avoiding eye contact, sketching on a legal pad. He'd shown talent for and interest in art since childhood, and had gotten quite good at portraiture over the years. Throughout the nine-day trial, he filled almost an entire sheet of paper with detailed drawings of Gretchen's face. Sheriff Jeff Bates remembers seeing the pictures for the first time: "It was little stuff that you barely noticed until you took a close look. For instance, in one of them her earrings aren't hearts as they seem but two-headed snakes eating through her earlobes. Or her eyebrows are crawling with centipedes. Her necklace is a noose of knotted rope; that kind of thing. My first thought from the moment I saw them was how much they reminded me of those Garbage Pail Kids. It was before I knew about the Garbage Pail card they found in his room, the Tabitha one. When I saw it in court later on, I just about threw up. I mean, maybe it's a coincidence, but *wow*, kid. You sure know how to dig your own grave."

Forty-Eight Minutes of Doubt, p. 111

chapter twelve

January 1996
Virginia

Little Kate O'Neill was supposed to be in school the day a pair of teenagers found her body in the woods more than a hundred miles from where she'd gone missing. It happened like this: Kate was at church with her family on December 24 for the Christmas pageant. She'd been cast as one of the three wise men. She was sitting near the stage with the rest of her Sunday school class, waiting for services to end so the pageant could begin.

She kept nudging her mother—who was also the Sunday school teacher—and complaining that she was too cold in her short-sleeved costume. Her mom told her to deal with it, but Kate continued to bug her, until her mom finally passed her the keys to the family minivan and sent her outside to get a sweater from the back-seat. It was nineteen steps from the church doors to the parking lot and the O'Neills' Dodge Caravan. She never got the sweater.

Kate's mother didn't even notice that her daughter hadn't returned until the pageant had already begun and she realized there were only two wise men lined up in the wings.

Before their only child's body was discovered, Kate's parents went on television to beg for her life. They talked about the Christmas presents waiting for her at home, still wrapped and sitting under the tree. They said she was a sweet little girl who loved horses and ice-skating. She had a hamster named Midge. She was excited for the church carnival coming up in a few months because it fell on her birthday that year, so it was almost as if she were getting her own personal birthday festival. She wanted funnel cake instead of a regular birthday cake, they said; it was her favorite treat, and she only got the chance to eat it a few times each year.

It might seem odd to some people, but it can help to share those kinds of little details about a missing person. In theory, it's harder to hurt someone if you know them and recognize their humanity, if even only a little bit. Sometimes it works. Not this time.

After confirmation came that the body the teenagers discovered was Kate's, the press managed to leak two especially horrid details: her long red hair was gone, shaved all the way down to the scalp; and, much, much worse, her autopsy revealed her stomach to be full of undigested funnel cake.

chapter thirteen

Summer 1996

Police don't have any clue who killed Kate O'Neill, but at least
they found her body. At least her family could lay her to rest
with some semblance of dignity, which is probably more than
Turtle will ever have.

But our graves don't last forever. Did you know that? After we
die, our bones only belong to us for another hundred years; after
that, the ground and everything within is available to the highest
bidder. In today's case, that bidder is a man named Francis Cane,
owner and CEO of Cane Industries. He builds malls, and he believes
the town of Erie, Pennsylvania, is long overdue for his services.

The plot of land that Mr. Cane has in mind for his mall is mostly
forest. The only structure still standing on the acreage is an abandoned Episcopal church. The land surrounding the church is all
cemetery, but it hasn't been an active burial ground since the early

1900s; it's not as if anybody will have to deal with the thought of their dear aunt Margaret getting dug up after only a few months or years in the ground. Besides, nobody in their right mind would want that; it's a recipe for a horror movie, or at least for an unpleasant experience for a few unfortunate bulldozer operators.

Still, the local historical society was not pleased with Mr. Cane's plan to disturb the eternal slumber of so many souls. They filed a lawsuit against Cane Industries, only to learn that it is, in fact, perfectly legal to dig up a cemetery once its inhabitants have been dead for at least one hundred years. That's all we get, people: one hundred years, and then our remains can be exhumed in order to provide the living with easier access to a Spencer's Gifts.

Even though what Cane Industries plans to do is perfectly legal, the public consensus is that it is, at the least, in poor taste—or so the plaintiffs claimed. The parties agreed to a compromise: instead of digging everything (and everyone) up, Tasmanian Devil–style, Mr. Cane and his people agreed to be a little more meticulous about the whole process and carefully excavate each grave and then transplant it to a separate parcel of land twenty miles south, essentially creating a new cemetery from all the old-as-dirt corpses. To sweeten the deal, Mr. Cane sponsored the new cemetery all by himself. As a result, the people of Erie get their mall (with a food court and a movie theater!), and their ancestors will continue to rest in peace—save for a few brief moments' transit via air-conditioned tractor-trailers to their new eternal resting spots—for at least the next hundred years. Everybody wins.

Everybody, that is, but a man named Chester William Stark. Mr. Stark (known aliases include Charlie Steems, Bill Steems, and

Charlie Starker; he clearly lacks creativity) has been in prison for the past twelve years, serving a life sentence for the kidnapping, rape, and murder of a sixteen-year-old girl who disappeared while she was walking home from tennis practice on a sunny spring day back in 1978. Her name was Jenna Moses. She wanted to become a veterinarian, but now that will never happen, because Chester/Charlie/Bill decided it was more important for him to kill her a week before her seventeenth birthday, two weeks before she would have attended her junior prom, ten years before she might have become somebody's wife and (eventually) mother and grandmother. Chester Stark decided to say "Fuck it" to those possibilities because he has trouble controlling his impulses. So there you have it.

Anyway, for years there was suspicion that this same gentleman was responsible for the disappearance of twelve-year-old Bethany Taylor, who vanished in June 1980. She was at the drive-in with her family to see *The Empire Strikes Back* when Bethany went by herself, in the dark, to use one of the Porta-Potties at the edge of the parking lot. She never came back. Several witnesses remembered seeing her talking to a man who seemed to match Chester's description, but it was hard to be sure without enough light. Her body was never recovered. She'd run away from home once before. Because of this, police were slow to take her disappearance seriously—even though in the previous instance she'd only run to her friend's house a few blocks away from home, and she was gone for only a few hours before she felt guilty enough to call her parents to let them know she was okay. Regardless, the incident was on her record, and Chester was undoubtedly long gone once the search for Bethany really heated up by the end of the weekend. And this is where the careful relocation of the Erie Episcopal cemetery becomes relevant: as the workers dig new holes for all the displaced coffins, one of them notices a suspicious-looking assortment of bones among the contents of a loaded backhoe shovel. Because he's a good guy, the backhoe operator halts operations and insists that his foreman call the local police. Upon closer inspection, it is determined that the bones in question are indeed those of a human, most likely an adolescent female. A search through the national database of missing persons for teenage girls from the past twenty years whose remains were never recovered reveals over seven hundred potential candidates. That seems like a lot, doesn't it? Police think so, too, so they narrow their search parameters: they focus on unsolved crimes within a two-hundred-fifty-mile radius of the discovery, which brings the number of possibilities down to sixty-seven, which still seems like an awfully shitty too-high number to me.

Meanwhile, Chester Stark claims to have developed a close, personal relationship with Jesus Christ since his incarceration. This relationship, he claims, has prompted him to do an enormous amount of soul searching. He realizes that Jesus, who we all know was firmly in the "don't rape and murder anyone" camp, wouldn't want Bethany's parents to go another day without knowing for certain what happened to their pretty daughter, a gifted ballerina who practiced her dancing for an hour and a half every morning before school, even when she didn't feel like it (you might say she had exceptional impulse control for such a young person). When Chester's attorney alerted him to the discovery at the cemetery,

Chester decided to save everyone some time and further narrowed the search parameters. It was Bethany's body, he admitted. If Chester hadn't murdered her, she would have turned twenty-eight last month.

At the local support group for families of murdered children— another unfortunate thing that exists—the recent discovery of Bethany Taylor's remains is very big news. Her mother is here tonight, along with Bethany's brother, Noah, who is nineteen. Bethany's dad died a few years ago; unfortunately for him, Chester Stark's relationship with Christ didn't develop soon enough for Bethany's dad to learn where his little girl's body had been dumped.

My parents and I (Hannah is at home with Gretchen, who only attended one meeting, years ago; she stayed in the bathroom almost the whole time, and has shown zero interest in returning) are among the twenty or so members of this ultra-exclusive club, which meets in a church basement in Pittsburgh once a month. People come from miles around to attend, and it's a fairly tight-knit group regardless of the distance anybody travels; it's not like these kinds of organizations are set up on every street corner. After we moved, we still showed up a few times a year, although our attendance made a sharp decline after Hannah was born. Sometimes we shared the drive with the Taylors, who live twenty minutes from our old house in Virginia. This is the first meeting we've been to in nine months, and in that time, the group has gained a handful of additional members. I don't recognize any of the new people (although they all have the same look: faces either blank with unnatural, forced and/or medicated calm, or frozen with grief if they haven't yet given in to the allure of prescription sedatives), but they sure as hell recognize my family, and my parents in particular. Out of all the dead children who are mourned at these meetings, Turtle had the highest profile, the most media coverage. For a few months in the winter of 1986, she was America's angel. They were holding candlelight vigils all the way over in California.

Sheila Keller is the unofficial leader of our chapter, which she founded more than a decade ago. Her son William was sixteen when a mugger shot him in the face. He'd been out walking his dog. He didn't even have a wallet with him; he traded his life for less than two dollars in pocket change. The Kellers are African American, and William's murder got far less attention than it should have because he wasn't a pretty little white girl. Sheila jokingly refers to my family as the RWPs: the Rich White People. We aren't rich by anybody's standards—completely the opposite, actually—but I can see why we've earned the distinction in Sheila's mind. When my sister was kidnapped, it was front-page national news for weeks, from the night it happened until Steven's sentencing months later. When William died, he got two sentences on page sixteen of the local paper. That's it. Meanwhile, his murder is still unsolved. It's the kind of injustice so heinous that you would almost have to ignore it unless you were face-to-face with his mother; the prejudice of the system is the kind of thing most people can't stand to acknowledge, because they aren't willing to accept what that says about the world we all live in.

Sheila runs a small bakery in the city; she brings trays of homemade cookies and pastries to every meeting. Tonight everyone is nibbling small squares of lemon torte off Styrofoam plates. We sit in a circle of metal folding chairs. Sheila opens the meeting with the Serenity Prayer. In this group, nobody's faith is lukewarm: people either cling to God or reject the possibility entirely. As we sit with our heads bowed, my mom and I stay silent while my father and some of the other members recite the prayer with Sheila.

Unlike at other meetings I've been to, Sheila doesn't have to ask for volunteers to get the conversation started tonight. Everybody stares at the Taylors, anxious to hear how it feels to experience some supposed closure. We're like a bunch of virgins hanging on every word while a friend describes how it feels to have sex. There might as well be a spotlight shining on their faces. Bethany's mom, Darlene, is almost giddy with happiness. It might seem bizarre to anyone who hasn't lived through something similar, but we all have at least some idea of how she feels. I'm sure I'm not the only person in the room who is trying to suppress some jealousy over the sense of closure she must be holding, and it's clear she's holding it as close to herself as she can, basking in the relief she thought would never come. Yet here it is, and she shares it with us, she says, to give us hope that anything can happen.

"I'm sure you all remember when we went on *The Judy Stone Show* a few years ago," Darlene says, and most people respond by trying not to roll their eyes. Judy Stone is a talk-show host whose most frequent guests include women who are unsure which of the men in their lives have fathered their children, as well as pretty much anybody who is willing to go on national television and take a lie detector test that could potentially reveal any number of unpleasant truths to the viewing public.

Every Friday, Judy hosts a psychic who calls herself Mary Marie Boon, an overweight, wrinkled woman in her sixties who claims to be able to communicate with the dead as easily as you or I might pick up a phone and order pizza. She has written over a dozen books detailing her many supposed encounters with the "other side"; apparently, dead people have nothing better to do but stand around and wait for a chance to shoot the breeze with her. She talks often and in great detail about her experience as one of Cleopatra's ladies-in-waiting in a former life. She is bright and charismatic; she is also a grotesque fraud. When Darlene appeared on the show and begged Ms. Boon to contact Bethany, Mary Marie told her she couldn't do that, because Bethany wasn't dead. "She's okay, honey. There was a reason she left you that night; there was something going on in her life that you didn't know about. But she's out there, I promise, and she is most definitely alive. When she's ready to let you into her life again, she will come to you."

"Nobody could understand why I was so upset," Darlene says. "Well—you all understood, I think. But my friends thought I'd finally lost my mind, because I couldn't even get out of bed after the show, not for weeks. I knew Mary was wrong. I guess I knew she was lying to me, trying to make me feel better or give me some hope, but she did just the opposite." Darlene looks around the room, trying to make eye contact with every single person, desperate for confirmation that we understand. "After so long, you just want to know that your child isn't hurting. It can never be over for us, but it can be over for her. That was all I wanted, but instead I found myself imagining my little girl out there, wondering why I hadn't found her yet."

"I like what you just said, Dar." My mom and Darlene have always gotten along well; they're both around the same age, both beautiful. "But I think it can be over for survivors, too. Maybe not completely, but at least a little bit. You know, we have only a few more months to go before Steven's time runs out." What she means is that she and my dad are hoping he'll tell people what he did with Turtle. It wouldn't be that unusual, since he's trying to avoid the death sentence hanging over his head.

Noah has been quiet throughout the meeting. He hasn't made eye contact with me once tonight, and I'm surprised he's here at all. When she found out we were moving, Darlene offered to let me stay with her and Noah for my last year of high school. At first my parents said yes, even though they knew by then that something was going on between the two of us. My father had walked in on us kissing in my bedroom one afternoon. Noah's hand was up my shirt. It would have been easier if my dad had yelled at me or punched Noah in the face before dragging him from the room, or done *something*. But he didn't do anything like that; all he did was stare at me for a second with a look of complete heartbreak before walking away. He even quietly pulled the door shut on his way out.

Maybe my parents weren't concerned about letting me live with Darlene because they knew Noah was in college already; he only came home on the weekends, so how much would we really have even seen each other? Or maybe they knew I wasn't the kind of girl to lose her mind over a boy, and they trusted Darlene to watch out for me.

That all changed a few weeks after my father walked in on us. If I'd been smart about things, I would have known to stay away from Noah after the incident, at least for a little while. But I guess

I wasn't thinking straight, because instead I did the opposite. That's how we ended up spending the night together at a Holiday Inn, although it wasn't for the reasons everyone assumed. When I realized what a mistake I was making the next day—although I guess I'd already made it by then—Noah took me home, but the damage was done. Our parents were waiting for us when Noah pulled into his driveway. That was in April. We haven't seen each other since, until now.

Noah sits up straight in his chair and laughs too loudly, saying, "Some asshole on death row is gonna say whatever he can to stay away from that needle. I bet he'd tell you he kidnapped the Lindbergh baby if it meant the death penalty got taken off the table. It's basic evolution; we're all wired to do whatever we can to stay alive. That doesn't change when somebody goes to prison."

Nobody reacts in any noticeable way; we all look at Darlene, who seems mortified by her son's outburst, for guidance. "Noah has some strong feelings about the, um, darker side of human nature." She pauses. "I don't think he's getting enough sleep, either. You know . . . *college.*"

It was supposed to be funny. Nobody laughs.

Noah has never acted this way in front of the group before. And the last I knew, he was doing fine at school. "I'm getting plenty of rest." He stares across the circle at me and my parents. He doesn't look so hot, actually. The whites of his eyes are glassy and bloodshot. His clothing has the dingy, wrinkled look of an outfit that's been slept in. His intensity is just a hair past a comfortable level.

There's the slightest tremor to his hands. He grips his knees, struggling to hold them steady. "What if the guy who took your daughter never tells you anything, and then he dies? What does that accomplish? Once he's gone, you'll never know what happened to Turtle." He pauses. "That's if Steven is even guilty. Lots of people think he might not be."

My mother's body stiffens. "Excuse me?"

"Noah. I thought we talked about this." Darlene tries to put a hand on his shoulder, but he flinches away from her. When the legs of his chair scrape against the floor, I swear I can almost taste the metal in my mouth.

"It shouldn't make you happy when he dies. And it won't. You don't know it yet, but it won't make things any better."

My mother looks as lovely as can be as she takes another stab at maintaining diplomacy. Her voice is flat and only a little shaky. "I understand why you might say that," she manages, "but if that's what you believe, Noah, then you have been grossly misinformed. Steven was convicted by a jury, and that's all I'm going to say about the matter. And who are you to say how we'll feel when he dies? The day they kill him will be a good day for our family. He doesn't deserve the life he's been living for the past decade. He gets a warm bed, three meals a day, plenty of rest. No. No. He doesn't deserve that. He gave up the right to be treated with even a hint of compassion or mercy when he decided to *kill my child*."

It's the word "child" that sends her controlled response veering all the way off course into rage. "This isn't your intro to philosophy class, Noah. It's very simple, you see? I have a problem. My problem is that my daughter is dead, and the man who murdered her is still alive. I want that problem to be resolved, Noah. Do you understand?"

I expect him to back down, but he is unfazed. "I understand that's how you're hoping to feel, Sharon, but I think you're going to be disappointed. Steven will die, and it won't change anything. It won't bring your daughter back. He'll just be dead."

"I know it won't bring her back. I know that." My mom's voice is shrill and singsong. It's the voice of someone else altogether, some nightmare facsimile of my mother, her vocal cords warped and dripping with hot tar, the surrounding muscles bruised.

"You *think* you know. You *think* you'll have a sense of closure anyway, because at least he's dead. I just wouldn't bet the farm that it's going to work out like that. What if it doesn't make any difference? What if it makes you feel worse, because now somebody else's kid is gone? He has a mother just like everyone else, you know, and her heart will be as broken as yours is. Is that going to make you happy? Breaking his mother's heart? Taking her baby away? Everybody was somebody's baby once, Sharon. Even him."

My mother opens her mouth to respond, closes it, then opens it again, but says nothing. Noah appears almost breathless, his face flushed. Beside him, Darlene stares at a plate of half-eaten lemon torte in her lap. The pastry seems out of place here, like red balloons at a funeral.

"Maybe we should give this topic some breathing room," Sheila says, nudging her way into the conversation.

But my father has had enough. "You cocky little shit." He says the words quietly. Beside him, my mom is crying without making any sound, which she's really good at.

Noah isn't this tough. I know it. He knows it. Everybody in the room knows it. He pauses for a beat too long to keep the momentum of his aggression going.

"You stupid *boy*," my dad says. "You stupid goddamn infant. How old were you when Bethany died?"

Noah doesn't blink as he responds. "Why does that matter?"

"You don't remember a thing, do you?"

"I remember plenty."

"But what do you remember, specifically? Can you tell me one story about her? Do you remember the sound of her voice?"

"Yes. We have lots of old home movies of her. I've seen them all, plenty of times."

"That doesn't count. I'm talking about the way she was in real life. For example, do you remember what she smelled like? Here's a memory for you: Turtle, my daughter, smelled like peppermint. I don't even know why."

I do. Ed Tickle was an Altoids addict. Anytime Turtle saw him, she'd beg him for a handful of mints. She'd eat one or two and stash the rest of them in her pocket. "I'm savoring them," she'd tell us. That was the actual word she'd use: "savoring." Our mom used to keep a list of all the big words Turtle used. She was such a clever kid. She would hoard the mints in little hiding places around the house to make sure they lasted until the next time she saw Ed. That's why she always smelled like peppermint.

My dad rubs his eyes with balled-up fists as his breath stutters and catches in his throat, eventually erupting into sobs. He looks weak, like a frightened coward, when he cries. I'll never get used to it. It's another one of those unwritten universal rules: a father doesn't let his kids see him cry. Fathers are supposed to be able to keep their shit together, even when things aren't looking good. It's in their job description, sort of how flight attendants are trained to stay calm even in the worst turbulence. They know the passengers are watching them for reassurance that everything will be okay.

I guess the rule applies no matter whose father is doing the crying. Noah can't stand it, either. He slumps in his seat and stares at the floor in a posture of surrender. He rubs a threadbare spot on his jeans as the circle waits for him to summon a response. It doesn't come. Even though I'm not looking at her, I can discern the wavelengths of my mother's gaze, her uneven breath rippling across the circle. She's still crying without sound. Now that it's started, she won't be able to stop it for hours.

Noah's chair scrapes against the floor again. "I need air."

"Noah, stay here." Darlene reaches for one of his belt loops but misses by inches.

"I need air," he repeats. Before he leaves the room, he tosses her the car keys. "Don't worry, Mom. I'll come back."

The moment the heavy metal doors close behind Noah, Sheila suggests a five-minute break. She spends most of it in a corner of the room with her hands on Darlene's shoulders. Even though I can't hear them, I can tell from their body language that Darlene is apologizing for Noah, and Sheila is telling her not to worry about it. I'm sure she's giving her some version of the whole "boys will be boys" line of reasoning, with a twist for the unique circumstances:

something like, "boys who lost a loved one to a senseless and violent death at a young age will be boys who have some issues."

Sheila wants to move on with the meeting. The break is over; Noah is still outside; Darlene has managed a quick trip to the ladies' room to reapply her lipstick.

"Can I ask you something, Paul?" Mary Shaw's ex-husband killed their son before turning his gun on her and then himself. She was the only survivor. Because of her injuries, her mouth barely moves when she speaks, even though there is otherwise no physical damage to her face. Her brain didn't make a full recovery; somehow it wiped out the filter between her thoughts and her mouth. She'll mention how fat someone has gotten right in front of them, with zero awareness of how insensitive she's being. It's not her fault. At many of these meetings, she flatly states her wish to have not survived the gunshot. She talks about it with the same level of emotion as someone expressing a preference for chocolate ice cream instead of vanilla. "How *do* you think you'll feel? I'm talking about before he dies, when you get to look at him."

It comes off sounding like pure curiosity, as if she were asking "Does this dress come in any other sizes?" instead of "How will you feel when your daughter's killer meets his maker?"

He answers right away, and it seems as though he's given the question plenty of thought before this moment. "Like my body is a cyst full of pus that's finally bursting open."

Mary's eyes and mouth do not move. Her voice seems to come from the air. "That sounds wonderful."

"Sam?" Sheila ventures. "Let's give your dad a break. Do you want to talk about your feelings?" She catches me with a mouthful of lemon torte, and it occurs to me how morbid it would seem to an outsider: all these people sitting around eating cake while discussing dead children and the pros and cons of state-sanctioned murder. But that's why everyone is in this room tonight: we're the only ones who can understand how it feels. When you've lived with this kind of thing for as long as most of us have, you get used to talking about it. It never gets better or easier, but it does get different. It has to—otherwise most of the people here would be long dead. After a while, the simple act of living would get to be too much.

I don't think anybody has ever asked me how I'll feel once Steven is dead, at least not directly. I try not to think about it. Even though it has been helpful to listen, I've never felt like I wanted to talk about these things as much as most of the people in the group. "I'm okay for now, thanks."

Mary Shaw leans across the bodies that separate us and speaks loud enough for the janitor mopping the hall outside to hear her: "Samantha, your breasts have gotten huge." It's off to the bathroom for me.

And there's Noah on the stairs outside the bathroom, playing Tetris on his Nintendo Game Boy with unnecessary intensity, his thumbs moving as though the future of humanity depends on his score. He doesn't look up from the screen. "Making a run for it, are we?"

"And where would I go, exactly? Somewhere with you?"

He smiles, still playing the game. "That didn't go so well the last time, Sam."

"So? Did you expect it to?"

"I didn't expect to be your chauffeur. At least, that wasn't *all* I expected to be for you."

"You weren't my chauffeur."

He rolls his eyes. "Whatever you say, Sam."

"This isn't cute, Noah. Would you wipe that stupid smile off your face?"

He beams at me. "Your breasts *have* gotten awfully large. One thing about Mary, she calls 'em like she sees 'em."

"Thanks. You're a real gentleman."

"And they say chivalry is dead." He sets the Game Boy aside and promptly loses. The tinny, computer-generated sound of breaking glass builds and then fades away before the screen goes blank and resets.

The fading afternoon sunlight streams through the stained glass window in front of Noah, projecting a mosaic of color onto the beige wall behind him. Each time a car goes by outside, it blocks enough light that all the colors shift and fade momentarily, as if we're inside a kaleidoscope.

"Why are you acting like this?"

"Don't play dumb, Sam."

"I'm not playing. You're being an asshole."

"I'm not trying to be an asshole."

"Well, you're making it seem pretty effortless."

"You think I'm an asshole because I don't believe we should go around killing people because we think it *might* make us *feel* better?"

"You made my parents cry. You made my dad cry, Noah."

"I know. I'm sorry."

"Your mom is in there crying, too, now. Are you happy?"

He smirks at me. "That doesn't strengthen your argument, Sam. I've seen my mother cry over expired yogurt. She's not, like, a pillar of emotional fortitude, in case you hadn't noticed."

"Can you blame her?"

"No. I don't blame her. But Sam—be honest with me for a minute, okay? Don't you get a little bit sick of all this? And don't pretend you don't know what I mean, because I know you've been through the same things I have, more or less. My mother has spent my whole life holding a perpetual wake. You know that. You've seen the shrine in our house. It got to the point where even my dad couldn't take it."

"Your father died of cancer, Noah."

He laughs. "Right. It was some kind of cancer, I guess. They said it was his pancreas, but you know what I think? He just sort of rotted away. By the end, he couldn't wait to get the hell away from her. She's so fucking *sad* all the time, and it's not because she doesn't have a choice, Sam: it's because she doesn't want to be happy. It's easier for her to be miserable, and she doesn't care what it does to the rest of us. My dad didn't even get out of bed for a whole month before he died, but in the last few days he had all this energy; he was so excited, like a kid on Christmas Eve. He practically leaped into the grave."

"Stop going home, then. You have a dorm room. Stay at college."

"I'm home for the summer." He gives me a loaded stare. "You know that."

"You could still move out. You're nineteen. Get your own apartment."

He shakes his head. "I can't do that. My mom doesn't have anybody else, Sam."

"She has the group."

"Screw the group. I hate coming to these things."

"Then why did you bother? You drove three hours to get here today, and for what? So you could show up and put all of us in our place? So you could enlighten us about how we're grieving all wrong?"

"That's not why I'm here."

"Then why did you come? For the lemon torte?"

"No, Samantha. I came to see you." He reaches out to snatch my hand, and I don't have a chance to pull it away in time. "Meet me somewhere. We need to talk."

"Now? Where are we supposed to go?"

"Not now. Soon, though." Noah yanks me a little bit closer. He smells like rotten chicken broth. It's the smell of someone who hasn't showered or changed his clothes in days. His pupils are so dilated that, aside from a slim thread of color around their edges, I can barely make out his green irises. "My mom is going to visit my aunt Laurie in Florida at the end of the month. I'm driving her to the airport. I'll have her car for a whole week."

"I still don't have my license. You'll have to drive all the way to Shelocta. It's a long drive."

Squeezing my hand more tightly now, trying without success to stop his own fingers from trembling, Noah says, "I know that, Sam."

"What's the matter with you? Did something happen?" The Noah I remember is nothing like the panicked kid staring up at me. He was polite and soft-spoken. He was an honor roll student and a varsity baseball player. His biggest screw-up in nineteen years had been . . . well, I guess it was me.

"I'll tell you. Promise you'll meet me, Sam, and then I'll tell you everything."

"Noah . . ."

"Promise me." Even his eyelashes are dirty, littered with tiny crusts of sleep.

"Fine. I promise."

chapter fourteen

January 1987

I tried to hide the day we moved away. My parents were busy loading our things into the U-Haul. Along with Remy's parents, several other neighbors volunteered to help without being asked: Ed Tickle showed up with a dolly and some extra boxes; Darla cleaned out our fridge and mopped our floors, which were covered in muddy footprints by the end of the day; Mrs. Souza, in a rare gesture of humanity, brought over a pan of homemade manicotti. It was January, and the weather was bone-cold. Remy and I hid in the playhouse. We huddled beneath a blanket in our winter coats, holding on to each other's mittened hands and keeping quiet when we heard our parents calling our names. I don't know what we expected to accomplish; it wasn't as if we actually believed our plan would work.

It was Abby who found us. I don't remember where Gretchen

was that day, but she must have been around. Abby was in her yard, smoking a cigarette, when she noticed my face as I peered at her through the playhouse window. She wasn't wearing a coat when she came in and crawled underneath the blanket to sit between us on the floor. She must have been freezing.

"You have to go with them, Sam. Your mom and dad are waiting." She could have told my parents where I was hiding instead of dealing with it herself. I don't know why she bothered trying to comfort us. It was the first time she'd ever been even remotely kind to me, and I didn't know how to react.

"Why can't I stay here and live with Remy?" He squeezed my hand more tightly beneath the blanket when I asked the question.

"Because you have to do what your parents say. I know it sucks, but that's how it goes."

"But I want to stay."

"I know you do, kiddo, but it's not up to you." She reached over to wipe my tears, and I flinched as though I expected her to hit me. She didn't try to touch me again after that.

We heard my father shouting my name from the back porch, and I knew he or my mom would find us any minute; we didn't exactly have the best hiding place. When I think about it now, it's obvious they knew where to find us the whole time.

"It will be easier if you don't fight it," Abby said. "Trust me."

But we wouldn't listen; her words just made me cling more tightly to Remy. When she finally gave up and left, it was only another minute or two before my dad came knocking at the playhouse door.

It took both of our fathers to pry us apart as we screamed and kicked and held on to each other as tightly as we could with fingers numb from the cold. Once they managed to separate us, my dad threw me over his shoulder and carried me to the U-Haul. Remy watched from his living room window as we drove away, crying and waving until we turned out of sight. It was no proper good-bye for two kids who'd known each other all their lives. My arms were scratched and bleeding from where Remy had tried to keep hold of me.

We weren't yet out of town when I had an idea. "What if Turtle comes back and we aren't home? How will she find us?"

Remember, I was seven. I knew Steven was in prison for my sister's murder, but she'd been alive the last time I saw her.

Beside me in the tiny backseat, Gretchen grabbed my wrist and squeezed so hard that I had a bruise the next morning. "Shut up, Samantha. Turtle's never coming back. She's dead."

"Don't say that!"

"Why not? It's true. She's dead. She's gone forever. Right, Mom? Tell Samantha it's true. Tell her."

Our mother didn't answer. Our dad turned up the radio to drown out the sound of our voices. Gretchen stopped talking and stared out the window, and I fell asleep shortly after we pulled onto the highway. As I dozed off, I thought I heard her speaking softly to herself, although it might have been a dream. But I could have sworn I heard her whisper, repeating the same sentence over and over again: *This can't be how it ends. This can't be how it ends. This can't be how it ends.*

◆ ◆ ◆

In the past five years, Paul and Sharon Myers have allowed themselves to hope for closure no fewer than eight times. Every instance is different: once it was the discovery of Turtle's shoe alongside a highway; another time it was bone fragments that ended up belonging to another missing woman waiting for another family to claim her remains and the heartache that came with them. Several times, an especially promising tip shriveled into nothingness upon closer inspection, and there have been two very convincing false confessions. Each of these events bears one thing in common: unlike the diminishing returns that tend to occur with multiple instances of good news, the Myers' grief over each new disappointment has not yet begun to sting any less. And perhaps "sting" is too mild a word for what they endure.

"Imagine you've been cut open and had your insides pulled out," Paul tells me. "You'd think that eventually there would be nothing left, but that isn't how it works. Somehow it keeps filling up, over and over again. You think it won't hurt as bad the next time around, but somehow it manages to get worse. I never knew this capacity for misery could exist within one person, and it's fucking endless. Will it stop after I'm finally dead? Where will it go? I'll tell you what I think—what I know: there's no getting rid of it. It's self-generating. Once I'm buried, it will just find somewhere else to grow. Those scientists who are trying to invent a perpetual motion machine—would they settle for discovering perpetual pain? They ought to cut me open and have a look inside."

Forty-Eight Minutes of Doubt, p. 136

chapter fifteen

Summary 1996

The first time my parents' lawyer called to tell us that my sister's body might have been found was eight weeks after she disappeared. It was March 1, 1986. By then, every day bled into the next like an endless waking nightmare for my family, especially for my mom. I remember prescription pill bottles taking up a whole shelf in the bathroom closet. My mother may not have been able to pull herself together enough to do laundry or cook dinner, but she always managed to go to the pharmacy or the liquor store.

By early March, Steven was in jail on charges of aggravated kidnapping and second-degree murder, which struck some people as odd, since there was no hard proof that my sister was dead. My parents hadn't given me any inkling of that as a possibility, not yet. They were still holding out hope that Steven had stashed Turtle away somewhere—maybe at a friend's house—and that she was alive and unharmed. Because I was seven years old and had never known anyone who died, death was still more a vague idea than an inevitability; it was something that happened to old people, something—so I'd been told—that I wouldn't have to worry about for a very long time.

Back then I still believed in God. Every morning when I got up, and every night before I went to sleep, I prayed for him to send my sister home. I tried to be as clear as possible about my request: *Please let Turtle come home.* I don't remember ever asking for my parents to stop being sad or for Gretchen to stop acting crazy; I knew getting Turtle back would solve all of my family's other problems.

Imagine Point Pleasant way back in 1986, when the neighborhood was still new enough that even our row of cheap, cookie-cutter town houses had some sheen to it. When Channel 4 News anchorwoman Stacy Middleman stood in our driveway to film a segment on Turtle's kidnapping, she described us as living in "a quiet family neighborhood in a small community." She spoke to my parents a few times, her film crew lugging its gear into our living room and taking all afternoon to set up, while Stacy and my mom sat at our kitchen table and looked through the carefully assembled photo albums that documented my sister's brief, interrupted life. Imagine me peeking around the corner to get a glimpse of the celebrity who was drinking tea with my mother. (Until Turtle's kidnapping, my mom had been a dedicated coffee junkie, but now her stomach was too weak to handle anything stronger than green tea.) I wanted to ask for Stacy's autograph, but I was too shy.

We got used to seeing news vans parked outside our house. I

guess they felt it made a better story if they filmed their segments at the scene of the crime. They all seemed like nice people who didn't want to interfere too much with my family's attempt to keep our pain and worry from bubbling over, which used to happen at the slightest provocation or reminder of Turtle's absence: back then, just seeing a kid with blond hair was enough to make my mother lose it. All the reporters and behind-the-scenes tech guys did their best to be kind and respectful, but at the end of the day they wanted a good story more than anything else.

When the police found Turtle's red shoe on the side of Route 22, somehow the press found out before my family. We came home from the mall to find Stacy Middleman reporting live from our sidewalk, holding up a shoe similar to the one that had belonged to my sister; I guess it made a good visual aide. It had been almost a week since the last swarm of reporters had shown up at the house, so we knew right away something big must have happened to prompt their arrival. Gretchen had opted out of our trip to the mall that day; she was alone in the house when the Channel 4 News van pulled up, and she saw the shoe in Stacy's dainty, well-manicured hand. After closing the curtains and turning off most of the lights, Gretchen took a few of our mom's Xanax pills and spent the afternoon drawing shallow lines across the skin on her Achilles tendons with a steak knife. The wounds weren't deep enough to do any lasting damage, but you can still make out the scars if you look closely enough.

But back to the shoe: it was a real blow to our family, but it could have been worse. Lots of little girls owned the same kind of shoes, which our mom had bought from Kmart. Plenty of those same little girls had to have worn the same size. There was a chance—a small one, but still a chance—that it wasn't her shoe at all. If they'd found, say, Boris, the stuffed bear she'd been clutching when Steven carried her away, it would have been worse, I think, because there would have been no doubt that it had belonged to Turtle. Because Mrs. Souza had used purple thread to reattach his ear, he was unique. There was only one Boris.

The discovery of the red shoe was the first of many false alarms regarding the recovery of my sister's body. (Even now it makes me shudder to use those words, but they're better than the alternative of calling them her "remains.") The police initially thought it was a big deal because of the location of the ditch along a secondary road two miles away from the home Steven Handley shared with his parents. The road was surrounded by woods. At first, the theory was that Steven had tossed the shoe out his car window before or after dumping Turtle somewhere nearby—or maybe it had fallen off without him noticing—and then he'd quickly returned home.

Police and volunteers searched within a two-mile radius surrounding the drainage ditch for fifteen days. They used four cadaver dogs. They scanned from above in a helicopter. They found nothing.

Things like this have happened again and again over the years: someone finds some bones in the woods that look as if they could belong to a human child, authorities are called in to investigate, forensic tests are conducted, and my family waits for weeks, only to learn that the bones belong to an animal and not somebody's daughter. A tipster in upstate New York calls the police because his downstairs neighbor has a quiet little girl who looks like she could be an older version of Turtle, and our hopes soar at the possibility that every fact we know about her disappearance is somehow wrong. We ignore the ridiculousness of our new theory, in which Steven had an accomplice—someone for whom he was willing to go to prison—who'd whisked my sister away in the night in order to raise her in a middle-class suburb eight hours' drive away. It's not impossible. Miracles happen. Never give up hope, people used to tell us; hope will sustain you. Hope only sustains for so long before it corrodes into fantasy. Without evidence, hope becomes delusion. After enough time, people stop grieving *with* you and start grieving *for* you. It's a lonely feeling.

Last year, on Christmas morning, my family got up to find that a sealed white envelope had been slid through our mail slot overnight. Thinking it was a card from a neighbor—there was no stamp, which meant that someone had hand-delivered it—my mother opened it right away.

It was a photograph of Turtle from when she was three years old, asleep in bed. Nobody knows who took the picture. Nobody knows where it came from. When we called the police, they told us it was probably someone's idea of a sick joke.

Things like this happen more often than you'd think, they said. The world is full of people who like to watch their friends and neighbors suffer. And we're still supposed to hold on to our hope—even knowing something like that.

chapter sixteen

Summer 1996

Hannah and I are sharing cotton candy on the Ferris wheel at the local Fireman's Carnival when I spot Remy and Heather below us. It's a sunny Saturday afternoon, almost dusk. Lines are already forming at most of the rides. The cloudless sky is a mellow blend of reds and yellows near the horizon. Remy and his girlfriend are watching some friends shoot baskets, trying to win stuffed animals. He's standing behind her, his hands in the front pockets of her white denim shorts. She reaches up to drag her fingers through his hair, and he leans over to bite her neck, which makes her giggle. I feel a wave of nausea as our chair lurches forward.

"I see Remy," Hannah says.

"Me, too." It will be a nightmare trying to avoid them. The carnival isn't big enough.

We're playing Skee-Ball when they come strolling out from behind a hot dog booth, their arms around each other's waists. Before I have a chance to distract her, Hannah notices Remy and calls out his name.

If it wasn't for my little sister's enthusiasm, I'm certain the three of us would have been able to stay away from one another and still manage to have fun. Remy and I have been spending time alone together, mostly late at night, but he's also been around more often in the afternoons and evenings lately. I know he hasn't been with Heather as much as usual. I haven't asked him why.

He has a startled look in his eyes, glancing back and forth from me to Hannah, trying to figure out how he should react.

"I'm Sam. It's nice to meet you." I give Heather an awkward wave with my fistful of game tickets. "You're Heather, right?"

She's pretty and petite, even in wedge sandals that add a few inches to her height. Her tank top is cropped to show off her flat stomach and pierced belly button.

"Yeah . . . ," she says. She gives Remy a death stare. "How does she know my name, baby?"

I look at him, too. "What?"

He looks at my sister. "Hey, Hannah. I like your overalls."

"Thanks." My mother makes sure Hannah is always well dressed, even in play clothes. Before we left for the fair tonight, she put my sister's hair in two braids with yellow ribbons tied to the ends. Her lips are stained dark red from the cotton candy we ate on the Ferris wheel.

There's noise and activity all around us, but silence settles over us like a methane cloud while Heather and I wait for Remy to answer her question.

"So you and Remy have talked since your family moved back? I didn't know that," Heather says to me. She gives Hannah a fake smile that is all teeth and gums.

"She lives next door, baby, so it's not like we weren't going to bump into each other." Remy tries to put his arm around Heather's shoulders, but she steps out of his reach.

"Why did you lie to me?"

He's staring at the ground. I can't tell whether he's afraid to look at her or embarrassed to look at me, or both.

Heather's attention shifts back to Hannah. "Is this your sister?" she asks me. Her mouth drops before I can answer. "Oh, wow." She puts a hand to her mouth in genuine surprise. "She looks so much like Tabitha." Her eyes are wide. For a second I don't understand how she would even know what Turtle looked like, but then I remember that my sister is something of a local celebrity. You'd have a hard time finding someone around here who would be able to take one look at her photo—the school picture from kindergarten was the one they always showed in the papers and on the news—without knowing exactly who it was. Everybody remembers what happened to Turtle.

Everybody but Hannah. "Who's Tabitha?"

"Your sister," Heather says. She's either very stupid or very mean.

Hannah shakes her head. "My sisters are Sam and Gretchen."

"Heather and I have to go now." Remy smiles at Hannah while

he backs away, dragging Heather along behind him. She starts yelling at him as soon as she thinks they're out of earshot, and I see her smacking his face and shoulders as the two of them disappear around the corner.

"Who's Tabitha?" Hannah repeats. Aside from the question, she seems unfazed by what just occurred.

"Don't worry about it. You don't know her."

"But that girl said she was my sister. She said I looked just like my sister Tabitha."

"She was confused."

"Oh." Hannah seems to accept the answer. "Can we stay a little longer?"

I can't see Remy or Heather anywhere now. If they're still fighting, they'll probably go somewhere where they can be alone. "Sure. We can stay as long as you want."

By the time we start walking toward the exit, I haven't seen Remy in over an hour. Once it got dark and we could pass through the crowds without being so visible, I actually managed to enjoy myself.

We didn't need a car to get here tonight. My house is less than a mile away, and most of the distance can be covered by cutting through alleys and fields. As we walk through the parking lot, I see Remy's car parked in a spot up ahead. I look at the windshield once I'm close enough to see all the way inside. Remy is alone in the driver's seat. His eyes are closed.

"Is that Remy?"

"Yes. We should leave him alone, though. Come on." I tug at Hannah's hand. She plants her feet in the packed dirt beneath us, shaking her head. "I'm too cold to keep walking. Ask him to give us a ride."

"Hannah, it's a short walk. Please don't argue with me."

She frowns, shakes her head, and skips away to knock on his window. He wakes up—if he was really sleeping in the first place—and rolls down the window to speak to her for a few seconds. I can't hear anything they're saying until Hannah turns to me and shouts, "Come on, Sam!" She waves me over with a self-satisfied grin.

As we're buckling up, I realize that Hannah, who is in the back, doesn't have a booster seat.

"She'll be fine." Remy has already shifted into reverse.

"My mom will slaughter me."

"What's 'slaughter' mean?" Hannah isn't smart, not in the same way that Turtle was. Turtle would have been able to figure out the word's meaning from the context.

"Never mind, Hannah."

"She needs a booster seat," I repeat, even though I know it's useless. We'll be home in thirty seconds.

"Why?" Hannah demands. "Why do I need one? I'm not a baby anymore."

"Because you're too short to ride around without one. It's dangerous."

"Ugh," she moans. "Everything is more fun when it's a little bit dangerous."

*   *   *

My parents still aren't home from their movie when Remy pulls onto our street. All the lights in our house are out; Gretchen isn't home, either. I don't see Abby's car anywhere on the street, which means the two of them are out together, doing who knows what until who knows when. And I don't have a key.

"You'll wait at my house. Stay as long as you need to." Remy has been mostly quiet on the short drive. He didn't mention Heather, and I didn't ask.

"You don't have to do that. We'll figure something out."

He doesn't answer me. He just rolls his eyes and walks into his house, leaving the door open for us to follow.

Susan and Michael are out for the night, too. Remy drinks a glass of water while I flip through TV channels until I find *The Muppets Take Manhattan* for Hannah. We dim the lights in the living room, and I spread a blanket over my sister's tiny body.

"Will you watch the movie with me?" Hannah asks when she sees that I'm following Remy toward the stairs.

"Sure. In a few minutes, okay?"

Hannah sighs. "You won't come back. You're trying to trick me."

"I am not."

"You think I'll fall asleep right away. You're tricking me."

"Aren't you tired?"

She sits up to shake her head at me. "I'm wide awake. You better come back."

"I will."

On the stairs, Remy murmurs, "You're going to watch the movie with her?"

I press a finger to my lips and hold up five fingers. She'll be asleep in no time.

"Okay, then. Let's chill out." Remy walks backward on his tip-toes, reaching behind his back to open his bedroom door. "Finally," he says, kicking off his shoes once he's inside. "What a night."

I freeze in his doorway. "You mean in there?"

"Yes." He laughs. "What's the matter? Are you a vampire? Do I have to formally invite you into my room?"

"No." But my feet are still planted in the hallway.

"Sam, get in here and shut the door."

"You aren't going to believe this." I'm too embarrassed to look at him.

"What is it?" In my peripheral vision, I see him tugging his T-shirt over his head.

"I've never been in a boy's bedroom. I haven't—it's not that— I'm not technically allowed."

"That's not true." He throws his T-shirt at my face. I duck, but it still lands on my shoulder: damp with Remy's sweat, smelling like summer and smoke and cotton candy. I can't throw it back to him fast enough.

"It is true."

"No, it isn't. You've been in here plenty of times before, when we were kids."

"That was different."

"Sam. You can't be serious. What are you afraid of? Is it this?"

He gestures to his bare chest. "Are you worried you won't be able to control yourself around me?"

"No!"

"I'm not going to attack you or anything."

"I'm not afraid of that."

"Then what's the problem?" He steps toward me and takes me gently by the arm, as though I'm an old woman he's helping across the street. We both stare down at my feet against his dull hardwood floor. "See?" he breathes. "Now you're in my bedroom. Nothing to it."

An entire wall of his room is covered in a collage of rock and punk band posters. Clothing—including underwear and socks—is scattered across the floor. Beside his bed, a turtle no larger than a silver dollar paddles around the shallow water inside a small aquarium. His desk is piled with CDs. The whole room reeks of aftershave. His unmade bed still has the same flannel *Star Wars* sheets from when we were young.

"I assume you don't want me to tell Heather I was up here," I say.

"Heather. Right." He picks up a framed photo of the two of them and stares at it. "I'm sorry about that."

"What exactly are you sorry for, Remy?"

"I know how it seems, but I didn't lie to her about you."

"It kind of sounds like you did."

"Look, it's not important what I did or didn't say to Heather. We've been having problems for months." He takes a deep breath, closing his eyes before slowly breathing in and out a few more times, as if he's trying to calm himself.

"Is Hannah okay?" His eyes are still shut.

"Yes. I told her it was nothing. She seemed to forget about it."

He looks at me. "Good. Then don't worry."

"But what happened with Heather?"

"The end happened, that's what. We got into a big fight, and she got so pissed off that she told me she fooled around with Noel Gilligan at a track meet last spring. I could never respect a girl who let *that* loser put his tongue in her mouth." He pauses. "Besides, she was dating me at the time."

Remy drops the picture—frame and all—into his trash can. The glass shatters dramatically, and he smiles. He grabs a box of Girl Scout cookies from his windowsill and tosses me an entire sleeve of Thin Mints, which I barely manage to catch.

"They're your favorite, right?" he asks.

I nod. "How do you—"

"I remember. That's how I know."

"Oh."

"Heather wouldn't eat them. She only likes the shortbread ones."

"Trefoils? Gross."

"I know. What a monster, right?" He sits down beside me on his bed, reaching into my lap for a few cookies. I'm not sure whether he notices my body tense up when he leans across me to reach into the aquarium and scoop the turtle into his hand. We sit side by side, our backs against the wall of posters, heads tilted together, watching as the turtle looks around the room, probably terrified. "I found this little guy in the parking lot outside Shop 'n Save. He was on his back in a puddle. No idea how he got there."

I don't say anything. From downstairs, I can hear Kermit singing "Right Where I Belong."

"Is it okay that I'm sitting here?" Remy watches the turtle pacing in circles on his palm.

"What do you mean? Beside me?"

"Yeah."

"Oh." I don't know what to say. The turtle reaches the edge of Remy's hand and peeks over the side before quickly shrinking into its shell. "He's scared," I say.

"I know." Remy leans over to return the turtle to the aquarium. When he leans back again, he shifts his weight a little closer to me. It's obvious what he's doing; I know it, and he knows that I know. I don't know how I'll react when he tries to kiss me. I'm not even sure I want him to try.

"Sam? What are you thinking about right now?"

I blurt out the truth before I have time to think it through. "I wish we hadn't come back to this town."

It's not the answer he expected to hear. From the look on his face, I know I've completely killed the mood. "Well . . . so do I, sometimes," he says. He sounds baffled by the sudden turn our conversation has taken.

"You mentioned that before. Thanks, Remy."

"Aw, Sam . . . come on, you know that isn't what I mean. It's just that before you got here, I had a pet turtle in my room, and now every time I look at him it's like I'm aware of the deeper symbolism because of your sister. I feel like my life has turned into a goddamn short story where everything has to *mean* something."

"Welcome to every day of my life for the past ten years."

"I know. I shouldn't complain, because I know it's so much worse for you. But you're the only one who knows how this feels," he continues. He turns around and brings his face close to mine. "If I'd never met you, none of this would have happened. But it did, and now you're the only one I can talk to about any of this."

I kiss him more to shut him up than anything else. He's surprised at first, but then his arms snake around me and he shifts his weight onto my body until I'm lying beneath him in bed, and it feels like the most natural thing in the world to let him keep going. Kissing Remy is nothing like kissing Noah. With Noah, I was at ease *until* we started kissing.

"Hey! No smooching!" Hannah stands in the doorway, her small arms crossed against her chest, a look of absolute disapproval on her face. She stomps a bare foot against the wooden hardwood floor and it thumps weakly, with neither the weight nor the authority she's going for.

"We weren't smooching." I wipe my mouth with the back of my hand. My lips and part of my face are numb and raw from the constant pressure of Remy's short whiskers, combined with the heat and moisture that our contact has generated.

"Yes, you were." She raises her right eyebrow in a practiced gesture. "I saw you with my own eyes, Sam. Those weren't family kisses. They were *wedding* kisses." Then, without skipping a beat, our make-out session instantly forgotten: "You said you would watch the movie with me."

"I know. I was going to come down in a minute."

"I want to sleep with you tonight," she says.

"You will. I'll be there soon."

"But I'm afraid to be alone."

Even though we are so much farther apart in age, Hannah and I are closer than Turtle and I ever were. I've always blamed Remy for this. If he hadn't been around to monopolize my time, Turtle would have been my natural playmate and closest friend. It's been a struggle not to punish myself for ditching her so often, either because she was too slow or too small to keep up with the differences in our development. When you're that young, three years is a big age difference.

Hannah crawls into bed between Remy and me, oblivious to the possibility that she's intruding. I remember feeling the same way when I was her age and would sneak into our parents' room at night after a bad dream: it didn't occur to me until years later that they were anything but thrilled by my arrival.

Remy produces his television remote from somewhere beneath the sheets. "You want to keep watching the Muppets, Hannah?"

She burrows closer to me, warm and soft as a little squirrel. "I'm afraid of the animal."

"You mean 'Animal.' That's his name."

"I don't care what his name is. He's ugly. We can watch it, okay? But you both have to snuggle with me in case I get afraid again."

On the screen, the Muppets are assembled onstage in a Hollywood theater. Remy reaches across Hannah's body to hold my hand. "I said *no smooching*," my sister mutters.

By the time the credits start to roll maybe fifteen minutes later, she is fast asleep between us, her tiny hands clenched into fists beneath her chin. Remy's eyes are closed, too. When I try to wriggle my fingers free from his grasp—my hand is starting to fall asleep—he only holds on more tightly, our arms forming a kind of gate across my sister's chest. The irony of the scene is not lost on me, and I lie there feeling like the two of us are traitors for keeping her so safe tonight. If I were Turtle, I think I would hate Hannah for the simple fact of her existence, and I would hate me for loving her so much, for locking the front door, for letting Hannah crawl into bed between us. There are so many reasons for Turtle to hate us, and I wouldn't blame her for a second. As I'm falling asleep, I pretend that we are in the basement again. The credits on the television screen could be the credits from any movie. It's not Hannah sleeping between us but Turtle. Our arms across her body have created a barrier in time, allowing everything in the room to age except for her. Remy and I have grown older, but Turtle is perpetually four years old. Our will is so strong that nothing, not even time, can touch her. And with my eyes closed and the music from the television in the background, I can almost believe it's true. Maybe that night hasn't happened yet; maybe what I saw was just a vision of a single possibility among thousands. Maybe if we stay like this, we can keep her safe forever.

. . .

Partial Transcript of Interview with Steven Handley, Conducted March 16, 1988, by Davis Gordon

Steven Handley: They didn't care about the other suspects. Ask that detective—ask him about Space Barbie.

Davis Gordon: Space Barbie?

SH: You don't know about that?

DG: No.

SH: Turtle wanted this Barbie doll. She went crazy one day at the store about it. I wasn't there, so I don't know exactly what happened; Gretchen told me later. But you can imagine, right? Turtle wanted the doll, her mom said no, and she threw a fit. But a couple of days later, when Gretchen was babysitting, I *was* there. We'd had these rolling blackouts—remember them? They started up in New York, I think, and then moved down the coast, and we didn't have power for two days. Remember?

DG: I do. It was around Halloween.

SH: Yeah, it was a few days after Halloween. Gretchen let the kids binge on their candy so they would leave us alone. It wasn't that she didn't care about them stuffing their faces. It was Halloween, you know? But their mom was so uptight about food. On Halloween night, she let her kids pick out two pieces of candy— only two—to eat, and then she hid their bags in her closet. Gretchen didn't think it was a big deal to get it down for them—would you? Anyway, Turtle threw up. Skittles—oh, man, I remember the Skittles. It was all over her shirt, so she went upstairs to change—Sam went with her—and she found a Space Barbie sitting on her bed. Brand new, still in the box. Well, she'd taken it out already before we saw it, but the box was still there on her bed. I wouldn't have guessed it was a Barbie if I hadn't seen the packaging; the doll looked like David Bowie. You know, like Ziggy Stardust? She had this short, spiky hair and crazy makeup, and she was wearing a jumpsuit. Gretchen told me they never could figure out who'd bought it for Turtle. It sure as hell wasn't me.

Forty-Eight Minutes of Doubt, pp. 165–67

chapter seventeen

Summary 1996

We're watching *Saturday Night Live* when one of those old anti-drug commercials comes on: a father confronts his teenage son with drugs he found in the kid's room. "Who taught you how to do this stuff?" he demands, his mustache twitching with emotion. "You, Dad," the boy replies. He looks at his father with this sad, weary expression, and you're supposed to be able to tell that he's already numb from life's disappointments, probably because his parents are potheads. "I learned it by watching you."

There's a tornado warning for the whole county until tomorrow morning. The weather has been breezy and humid all evening. The rain will be here any second, I know. In the last five minutes, the wind outside has built into a frenzy, gusting with enough strength to set off a car alarm a few streets over.

"It's true, you know." Remy holds a joint between his lips. He nods at the TV screen. "Parents who use drugs have children who use drugs."

The smell of marijuana makes me ill if I'm around it for too long, so I lie flat on the floor with my head beside the open window and breathe in as much fresh, cool night air as I can. The floor creaks beneath the weight of our bodies. When I close my eyes, I can feel the whole playhouse rock in the wind.

"This seems like a bad idea."

"What does?"

"Being out here in a storm. We could get struck by lightning." The TV is plugged into a long, thick extension cord that goes out the window and across the yard, all the way to the power outlet beside Remy's back door.

"Nah." But he unplugs the television anyway, and we're suddenly alone together in the dark. Any light from the moon or stars is blotted out by the clouds.

I don't say a word while Remy smokes. When the joint gets too short for him to hold without burning his fingers, he puts it out with a dab of spit and balances it on top of the TV. It's dark enough in the playhouse that I can barely make out his face as he lowers his body onto mine.

"What if the floor collapses?" This place wasn't built to support the weight of two horny teenagers in bad weather.

"It won't." He kisses my forehead, then my nose, and finally my mouth. I can feel the pressure building within his body as soon as we connect. There's an urgency to his movements. With electricity rippling from his palms, he inches his fingers up my T-shirt, slowly but surely trying to tug it over my head.

"Remy, wait a minute." I wriggle out from under him.

He sits up. "Did I do something wrong?"

The air is so thick with moisture that it's a little hard for me to breathe. "No. Maybe I should go home, though."

"Oh." He reconnects the television. The screen is nothing but static. "So . . . was that not okay?" he asks.

"No! I mean, yes, it was completely okay." My gaze falls to his lap. He's obviously not ready to stop.

"But you want to leave," he says flatly. "So obviously it's not . . . what you wanted. I mean, I'm not."

"That isn't true." I pause. "There's just so much between the two of us. There's so much background running through my head."

He looks dazed. I notice his glassy eyes and sweaty forehead. "You know what I do sometimes, Sam?"

"What?"

"I drive to Steven's house."

"Steven Handley?"

"Yeah."

"You mean his parents' house?"

"Yes."

"Why would you do that?" The whites of his eyes are bloodshot from the pot. Sometimes I feel like I'm the only person I know who isn't constantly seeking the next opportunity to muffle their thoughts.

"His mom still lives there. Did you know that? The business is gone, though, so there's just an empty storefront. She's all alone."

"I know." Steven's dad died a few years ago. Helen had to take a job with one of her competitors in order to support herself.

"I can't stop thinking about her sometimes. I feel sorry for her."

"Remy, what's the matter with you? Has she ever seen you there?" I don't know if I feel sick because of the smoke or because of what he's telling me.

"I don't think so. Calm down, Sam. I've never knocked on the door or anything like that."

"So what do you do? You spy on her?"

"I wouldn't consider it spying."

"What do you do there, Remy?"

"I . . . do things. A few times last year, I shoveled her driveway after it snowed. It was the middle of the night, Sam. She didn't see me."

I'm shaking. "Remy, you have to stop that. You can never go back there again. It's a terrible idea."

"She doesn't know it's me."

"That doesn't matter! What if she figures it out? Why would you do something like this?" I'm so furious that I'm starting to cry.

"I already told you, I feel sorry for her."

"Stop it. There's nothing you can do for her."

"That's not true."

"Yes it is, Remy. She doesn't want your help. She hates you."

He nods to himself. "I know. It's one of the things we have in common. We both hate me."

"Shut up."

"It's true." He stares at the static dancing on the television. I can recognize the sounds of Aerosmith performing "Janie's Got a Gun" on *Saturday Night Live*.

"Sometimes I think I ought to kill her, if I'm ever actually going to help her. She'd be happy if I did it. Don't you think so? She'd be glad it was all over. That's all anybody really wants, isn't it? More than anything, we want it all to be over." He sighs. He falls onto his back and stares up at me. He doesn't seem to register my anger; his mind seems galaxies away. He reaches for my hand, weaving his sweaty fingers between mine and squeezing them tight, as though he's already forgotten that I was getting ready to leave a moment ago. "Imagine that, Sam. Imagine how good that would feel."

◆ ◆ ◆

"I wish I'd never met him." Those are Gretchen's first words to me in the common room at her college dormitory, where she's reluctantly agreed to meet. She hands me a stack of unopened letters. They are all from Steven. He wrote to her twice a week for months after his arrest. "He was a lunatic. He thought we were in love. I never loved him. It was just a stupid crush. I liked the attention more than anything." Yet she's hung on to the letters for years, going so far as to bring them with her to college.

But does she think Steven is guilty? When I ask the question, she doesn't hesitate with her response. "We all saw him in his stupid Santa Claus suit that night. Sam and Remy saw him in the basement. Who else could have done it?"

I start to tell her about the numerous studies that have been done on the accuracy of memory. Eyewitness testimony is notoriously unreliable, especially when it comes from children. And what about motive? Why would Steven want to harm Gretchen's sister?

"To get back at my dad? Who knows? Why don't you ask him yourself?" I can tell she's already tired of my questions, but I'm not ready to leave just yet. I ask her if she thinks Steven deserves to die for his crime, and Gretchen goes quiet.

"What do you think he deserves?" she asks.

I tell her I'm not sure.

"Neither am I." She hesitates. "I shouldn't have said that. I didn't mean it."

Forty-Eight Minutes of Doubt, p. 191

chapter eighteen

1985

In a former life, my parents used to go out almost every weekend with Mike and Susan and leave Turtle and me—along with Remy—in my older sister's care. Abby usually came over to keep her company, but she left what minimal childcare was required to my sister. Gretchen had never been much of a babysitter before she met Steven; our evenings with her mostly consisted of us occupying ourselves upstairs while she and Abby watched TV in our basement. Occasionally my sister would holler up the stairs to make sure the three of us hadn't accidentally killed ourselves. My parents knew Gretchen was no Mary Poppins: they usually left money for pizza so she wouldn't have to cook, and my mom always got us changed into our pajamas before she and my dad left, in order to make sure my sister's workload was as near to weightless as possible. And things usually went okay; we never found ourselves in any real danger because of Gretchen's negligence. The worst thing she ever did was to let us watch any movie we wanted on cable. Off the top of my head, I remember seeing *Children of the Corn*, *Creepshow*, and *The Thing* all before my sixth birthday.

But it was different once Gretchen started seeing Steven. Because here's the thing: even though she never paid much attention to me and seemed almost unaware of Turtle's existence, we worshipped her. How could we not? She was so beautiful and so smart (at least she seemed that way to us), so wise to the ways of the grown-up world. She cursed in front of our parents all the time, and when they told her to watch her mouth, she only laughed. She was never mean to us; on the contrary, she let us do pretty much whatever we wanted as long as we left her alone. She didn't even get mad when we would spill a two-liter bottle of diet soda on the kitchen floor or get nail polish all over the coffee table. My point is this: all three of us loved and looked up to Gretchen. We didn't want to get her in trouble. So when she did things around us that we knew she probably wasn't supposed to be doing, we kept our mouths shut. In return, she always told our parents that we'd been perfect angels throughout the evening.

At first, Abby and Steven would both come over to hang out in the basement with Gretchen. As the weeks went by, we saw less and less of Abby. Gretchen said it was because Abby didn't want to get in the way. I thought maybe she didn't like Steven. But Remy, Turtle, and I liked him very much. Even now, I remember how cool he'd seemed at first. While Abby and my sister had always pretty much kept to themselves in the basement, Steven actually appeared to enjoy being around kids.

"I have little cousins," he told Gretchen. "They're a lot of fun. Kids are great; you can be as much of a jackass as you want, and they think it's funny."

My sister was annoyed by his enthusiasm about us. "I rented us a movie to watch downstairs."

"Later," he said, "after they're in bed."

It was Steven who taught me how to play War with a deck of cards. He stood in our kitchen and concocted bile-colored beverages that he called "zombies," which were just a mixture of whatever sugar-based drinks were on hand: Pepsi, orange juice, ginger ale. They were disgusting, but we drank them all the same. It was an elementary-school version of the kind of experimental mixing of adult beverages that I'd seen my dad and Mike Mitchell do so many times before. We tilted our heads back and held our noses as we gulped down our drinks with the enthusiasm of frat boys. We laughed so hard that, on more than one occasion, liquid shot from Remy's nose.

Steven taught us how to play Bloody Mary in the first-floor bathroom. He showed us how to cover the staircase with pillows and blankets to turn it into a slide, which we barreled down head-first. He brought us handfuls of the miniature peppermint patties that his mom kept beside the register at her dry-cleaning store. When Steven was around, even Gretchen seemed to enjoy our company, at least more than she usually did. Maybe she just didn't want Steven to think she was a shitty big sister. She'd tousle my hair or give Turtle a spontaneous hug for no reason. She called us sweet, made-up names like "Cuppycake." Because of this overall improvement in the quality of our Saturday nights, Turtle, Remy, and I began to look forward to them with an enthusiasm that pleased our parents even as it aroused their suspicions. More than once, my mom pseudocasually asked me, "What's so great about Gretchen all of a sudden? I thought she and Abby didn't play with you very much." (Abby was allowed to come over while my parents weren't home, because she was a teenage girl. As an adult male, it went without saying that Steven's presence would have been frowned upon.)

Over the years—especially in the weeks and months after Turtle's kidnapping—I have been given countless opportunities to sit down with a number of Caring Adults to discuss Steven's behavior when he came to our house on all those Saturday nights. A social worker once gave me a stack of blank sheets of paper and a box of crayons and asked me to draw the games we'd played with him or "anything else that might have happened." I made poor sketches of myself, Remy, Turtle, and Steven (Gretchen hadn't cared to participate) playing Bloody Mary; the social worker asked me if we played any other "bathroom games." My first therapist (there were several), Miss Russo, gave me a naked Raggedy Ann doll and told me to point to anywhere I might have been touched. I shrugged and handed the naked doll back to Miss Russo, explaining that I didn't remember Steven touching me anywhere, not even on the arm. A hypnotist did his best to relax me with his dull monotone before asking me what animal I thought Steven most resembled. I compared Steven to a grasshopper because of his long, skinny arms and legs. Even though all the Caring Adults claimed to be relieved by what I shared with them, I could tell a part of them was always just a little disappointed. I wasn't giving them the answers they were looking for, not exactly. They didn't want to hear that Steven had been friendly and funny, more so than Gretchen or Abby ever were. As much as they were glad Remy and I had been spared any abuse, they wanted confirmation that Steven was a monster. They wanted what had happened to Turtle to make some sense. In a world where all is right, nice men don't kidnap four-year-old girls in the middle of the night. They certainly don't murder them. They don't hang their heads and sob in court, pleading their innocence. But they also don't sleep with seventeen-year-old girls. So there's that.

My sister must have known that it was only a matter of time before our parents caught on to her lies about Steven, which were stacking up into a pretty impressive piece of fiction. In the end, it was Mike Mitchell who made the crucial discovery when he swung by our house in the middle of the evening to pick up the wallet he'd left on our kitchen counter earlier that day. He didn't knock or ring the doorbell, he just let himself in through the front door and strolled into the living room, where the five of us were watching *Gremlins*. Gretchen and Steven were cuddling under a blanket on the sectional sofa while Remy, Turtle, and I sat on the floor eating popcorn. Mike didn't get angry or act surprised; he just said hello to all of us, introduced himself to Steven, retrieved his wallet, and left as quickly as he'd arrived. I thought there was a chance he wouldn't even mention anything to my parents. But the next morning at breakfast, when I saw Gretchen glaring puffy-eyed at our mother over a bowl of Rice Krispies, I knew we'd been busted.

All these things happened in relatively quick succession during the last six weeks of the summer of 1985. Had Gretchen's relationship with Steven ended that Saturday night in August like it was supposed to, my memories connected to that summer would be quite different from what they are now. The older guy who'd dated my sister for a few weeks would be a distant memory, barely a footnote in an otherwise ordinary childhood. There were so many other, more significant events that took place during that decade: IBM introduced the first desktop; MTV premiered at 12:01 a.m. on August 1, 1981; the Senate confirmed Sandra Day O'Connor as the first female Supreme Court justice; the CDC announced its discovery of a new strain of deadly pneumonia, thought at first to affect only gay men. "Small-town teenage girl sneaks around with older guy" was hardly newsworthy, even to our neighbors. And it might have stayed that way; the relationship likely would have faded into nonexistence even in our memories. Years later, Gretchen, Turtle, and I might have reminisced while out to lunch somewhere about the guy who used to come over when our parents went out. "What was his name?" Turtle might have asked, unable to recall any details from that time in her life. Gretchen might sigh, her gaze rolling toward the ceiling in thought. "Sean? No, that's not right. But I'm sure it was something that started with an *S*." Then maybe she'd shrug, losing interest in the matter. "I don't remember. It isn't important." And we'd go back to doing whatever it was we'd been doing: getting our nails done, the three of us seated in a row at a busy salon; chatting softly in a movie theater during the previews; lying on a beach. We'd be all grown up. Turtle, with her long, silky hair and big eyes, freckles across her nose and cheeks as though someone had pitched a fistful of brown confetti at her face, would have been the most beautiful of the three of us. I think about these things sometimes, and what I feel is not quite sadness as much as abstract curiosity, a distant yearning that never quite gets too painful to tolerate, but never goes away completely.

♦ ♦ ♦

"Suddenly everyone's a detective. Give me a break. We investigated plenty. The other suspects? Eliminated every last one of 'em. Look, it was pretty simple: you have a suspect, two eyewitnesses, and a dozen other people who can corroborate. What reason do any of those kids have to lie? And what about the threats he made to her father? There were half a dozen *more* witnesses in the ice cream aisle at the supermarket when it happened. It was the morning before the crime! Paul Myers was grocery shopping when he ran into Steven. Sharon had found something in Gretchen's room a few days earlier— Polaroids. They weren't the kind of pictures any dad wanted his daughter posing for. He knew she and Steven were still sneaking around behind everyone's backs, so they had a few words. Things got heated. You know what Steven said to him? He yelled it, actually—like I said, there were half a dozen people who heard him. 'I'm going to destroy you.' That's what Steven said to Paul. 'I'm going to ruin your life.' He *promised*. If I had any doubts . . . Well, I don't have them. Steven Handley murdered that little girl the same night. I'd bet my career on it."

Forty-Eight Minutes of Doubt, p. 201

chapter nineteen

Summer 1996

It takes me almost eight weeks to finish clearing out the Mitchells' basement. Now that I've gotten rid of all the clutter, Susan is moving forward full speed with her renovation plans. The next step is to put a fresh coat of paint on everything. At least I'm not working alone now; Remy is helping.

While we're pushing all the remaining furniture away from the walls, I find a few more boxes of old photos underneath his grandmother's bed. Remy doesn't seem bothered when I sit down to look through them while he's doing all the painting prep. He tries to be nice to me in little ways like that—ways that are more like how a boyfriend might act, instead of a boy who's only a friend. I've never been treated this way before, not by Noah or anyone else. It's better than I could have expected.

Remy whistles at me. "You know you've been staring at the same picture for about a year, Sam?"

"What?"

"Yeah. You've been spaced out. Let me see that." He tugs the photo from my grasp to have a look. It's from our fifth birthday party. We're seated at the round picnic table in my backyard. My mom stands nearby, holding Turtle on her hip. Young Remy's chubby cheeks are smeared with cake and icing. Beside him, I look like I'm about to fall asleep in my party hat.

"Your mom sure is rocking those shoulder pads."

I don't laugh. I don't say a word.

"Come on. That was funny."

"Who's this man in the picture?"

Our dads are standing next to an open cooler filled with ice and cans of beer. Remy's dad, with his white shorts and pink collared shirt, looks like he just stepped away from the set of *Miami Vice*. There is a lit cigar in his mouth, its smoke winding into the sky in thick, blurry loops. Behind him and off to the side, a strange man is lurking at the edge of Remy's yard, watching the festivities. He doesn't seem like a guest at the party; more like an uninvited outsider. His clothing is ragged, yet almost formal looking: he wears a white collared shirt and black pants, which are odd choices for what was obviously a warm day.

"Are you talking about this guy?" Remy presses his thumb against the man's face as if he's trying to squash his head.

"Yes." His outfit looks like it came from the Salvation Army; his shirt is too big for his body, the sleeves too long, but his pants are a few inches too short. He has a full head of curly black hair. His face is pale and so slender that his cheeks have visible hollows even from so far away; it's less a face than it is skin stretched over a skull.

"I don't know," Remy says. "Just some guy, I guess."

"But what is he doing there?"

"I don't know, Sam," he says impatiently. "Maybe he knows Mr. and Mrs. Souza."

I frown at him. "Mr. and Mrs. Souza don't have any friends."

"You're probably right," he admits. "But I'm sure it's nothing. He's just a guy in the woods. There used to be dirt paths running all over the place back there. He looks confused, don't you think? Maybe he was lost."

"But we saw him somewhere else once. Don't you remember?"

"Should I?" He holds the photo closer to his face. He looks at it for only a second before flinging it back at me as though it's a Frisbee. "I don't know. Maybe. I've smoked a lot of weed since then, Sam. My memory's not so sharp."

"We saw him by the railroad tracks, Remy—the tracks that run along the river uptown. You have to remember it. It was Gretchen's fourteenth birthday. She and her friends went horseback riding, and we begged to go along to see the horses, but we were too little to ride. A couple of the girls who worked at the stables took us on a walk, and he was there."

Remy shrugs. "Sorry. I don't remember any of that."

I remember the girls' obvious resentment at having to babysit the two of us.

"We were on the tracks inside the tunnel. The stable girls were way back. They weren't paying any attention to us. Remember? We went into the tunnel and he was there, walking and singing a song. He gave us marbles. He seemed nice at first, and then he started singing that creepy song."

"He started *singing*?" Remy laughs at me. "Are you messing with me right now?"

Susan interrupts us, calling down from the top of the stairs: "Are you hungry, Sam? I made tuna salad." She pauses. "Is Remy down there with you?"

"Yeah, Mom, I'm here."

"Okay . . . You kids having fun?"

"So much fun, Mom. So much. More than you could ever imagine."

"You have to be a smartass, don't you? Listen, I have to run over to the school for a little while. Can you switch the laundry around for me?"

"Sure."

"You have to run the sheets on hot water. Don't forget."

"I won't."

"And keep the door cracked. You don't want to inhale all those paint fumes."

Remy sighs. "We will, Mom."

"There's Pepsi in the fridge. Sam, do you drink Pepsi?"

"I'm not thirsty right now. Thanks, though!" I can picture her standing in the doorway up there, her purse hanging from her shoulder, probably worried that if she comes down she'll see us half-naked or something. Remy and I listen in silence, tracking her foot-steps as they travel out of the kitchen and down the hall, until she leaves the house. We hear the garage door open and close, followed by the chiming of the grandfather clock in the foyer, announcing that it's noon. I realize I haven't eaten a thing all day, but I'm not the least bit hungry.

"Okay—what were you telling me, now? He sang to us?"

I nod.

"Let's hear it, then," he says, grinning, and I know he doesn't believe me. "Maybe it'll trigger a memory."

I try to remember the melody. When I close my eyes, I can remember seeing the words forming between his lips and glimpsing his tongue, which looked like it was growing a layer of white mold; I remember the way the skin at the corners of his eyes crinkled like old lace.

Oh, say, do you know
That a long time ago,
There were two little children,
Whose names I don't know.
They were stolen away
On a bright summer's day,
And left in the woods
In a place far away.

Then I see it: the briefest flicker of recognition in Remy's eyes. "Was he wearing a hat?" he asks.

"Yes! You're right—a cowboy hat!"

He frowns. "Yeah, maybe I do remember him. Why does it matter?"

And when it was night
So sad was their plight
The stars were not out
And the moon gave no light
They sobbed and they sighed
And they bitterly cried.

He pressed a marble into the palm of my hand, then gave one to Remy, but I never saw it. He kept his voice quiet as he sang, probably so the girls from the stable wouldn't hear him. They were behind us, maybe thirty feet away. I wasn't scared. It was the middle of the afternoon on a bright, warm day, and we were within shouting distance of dozens of houses.

And when they were dead
The robins so red
Took mulberry branches
And over them spread
And all the day long
They sang their poor song
Poor Babes in the Woods!
Poor Babes in the Woods.

I thanked him for the marble. "You're welcome, my dear," he said, and then he knelt down in front of us and held out his hand for us to shake. "If you keep that with you, wherever you go, I'll always know exactly where to find you."

I pulled my hand back. He smiled at me, his teeth so straight and white they might have been dentures. He jerked forward a few inches, snapping them at me, as though he were going to bite. I screamed, which got the attention of the teenage girls from the stable. Remy and I ran out of the tunnel, and I immediately felt safer in the bright sunlight. When I looked back at the man, he waved at us before he began strolling away slowly, hands clasped behind his back. A long, dark braid poked out from beneath his cowboy hat and snaked halfway down his back. The marble felt so hot in my palm that I dropped it onto the tracks. I could have sworn it was a swirl of blue, green, and white, like a tiny planet Earth, when he first tucked it into my palm. Now it was all black. It shined so fiercely in the sun, opaque as a piece of coal.

I remember. And I don't know why yet, but I know it matters.

chapter twenty

Summer 1996

Abby Tickle is raiding our refrigerator as if she hasn't eaten in days, which she used to do all the time when she and Gretchen were kids. It annoyed my mom back then, and I'm sure it would annoy her today. She's held a grudge against Abby's sort-of stepmother, Darla, that goes all the way back to when Gretchen and Abby were in the second grade together. Our mom volunteered to be their homeroom mother, but the title went to Darla instead. "She's not Abby's mother, she's her father's girlfriend. It's homeroom *mother*, not homeroom *girlfriend*."

There were other reasons why our mom didn't like Abby, long before Steven came into the picture. Abby refused to babysit me whenever Gretchen wasn't available. There was one time in particular that our mom never got over: she was cleaning our house and wanted me, Turtle, and Remy out of her way, so she marched

us down the street to the Tickle residence to see if Abby would keep
an eye on us for the afternoon. Abby said no, even though she wasn't
busy. She wouldn't even let us past her front door. My mom took
us home, and I ended up tripping over the vacuum cord and giving myself a bloody nose, staining our carpet.

As Gretchen got older, my mom was annoyed that my sister
preferred the Tickle household to her own. She resented Darla, who
was young and sexy and had a way with teenage girls that my
mother simply did not possess. Our dad thought it was funny. He
told my mom she was just jealous of Darla.

"Why on earth would I be jealous of that woman?"

"Sharon, calm down. She's a nice woman. She's a free spirit."

"A free spirit? Is that what people are calling it nowadays?" Darla
wore tight miniskirts and low-cut shirts and carried a bottle of
hairspray in her purse, which she would pull out and reapply
whenever the mood struck, even if she was in the middle of the
grocery store.

Abby is improvising a BLT sandwich in our kitchen, which is
to say that she's got the B but none of the L or T. She squirts a blob of
mayonnaise onto a heel of bread, spreading it around with her finger before smashing the whole thing together. She isn't using a plate,
and when she picks up the sandwich, she brushes the bacon crumbs
that are left behind on the counter onto the floor.

The TV in the living room is turned up loud enough that we
can hear the rerun of *Beverly Hills, 90210* all the way over in
the kitchen. The show was Gretchen's choice, and I haven't been

paying a bit of attention when a single thread of dialogue breaks away from the rest of the story and seems to be shouted instead of spoken, as though the words are deliberately finding their way to my ears.

"Steve Sanders? He would never hurt anybody."

"I'm telling you that Steve Sanders raped me, Brenda."

"You're lying."

"It's true. Steve Sanders raped me."

It's those tiny, inescapable things that can drive you crazy: hearing his name out loud, even when it's referencing someone else; every blond-haired little girl you see from a distance or up close; the sound of snow crunching beneath your feet. Look hard enough, and it's possible to see her in everything.

Does Abby even realize why she says what she says next? "Will you go to his execution, Sam?"

"Shut up, Abby," Gretchen says through gritted teeth, nodding at Hannah, who is coloring at the kitchen table.

Abby replies with a loud whisper that everyone can hear. "She doesn't know what we're talking about."

Cue Hannah, raising her head in interest: "What's an execution?"

Gretchen pinches her best friend hard on the arm. Abby yelps and drops her sandwich to free up both hands to smack my sister's face. They've always fought like a pair of feral cats, claws and all. Before I know it, Hannah and I are watching, open-mouthed, as they swipe at each other. Hannah is entertained. To her it's all slapstick; they're not swearing or yelling—they aren't speaking at all, actually, and the near silence makes it that much more mesmerizing. But she can't pick up on all the ripples from a thousand tiny sparks of friction that have been building up over the years, crackling in the air all around us. Gretchen slaps and claws, while Abby seems partial to hair pulling. The whole thing lasts for maybe only twenty seconds. When they stop, it seems more like they've been pried apart by an unseen force that drains their will to fight in an instant than that there's been a resolution. They both take a minute to catch their breath before shifting back into conversation as though nothing has happened. I close my eyes and see fireworks bursting against a black sky. I can almost smell the ashes as the last embers fade.

chapter twenty-one

January 1986

Remy and I waited only a minute or two, if that long, before we rushed upstairs to tell our parents that Turtle was gone. The rest of the night was an agonizing blur of time for everyone in our house, but Susan Mitchell managed to remember the crucial fact that, when Remy and I appeared in the living room, Eddie Money was on television performing "Take Me Home Tonight" live from the Times Square New Year's Eve celebration. The song lasted from 1:49 to 1:54 a.m. Police put the kidnapping sometime between 1:45 and 1:48 a.m. At the time, they told my parents that it was a great start on the investigation, and that whoever had taken my sister couldn't have gotten far. They told us that most of the time when a kid disappears in the middle of the night, nobody realizes what has happened until the next morning. I remember one of the detectives using the phrase "ahead of the eight ball," with a big smile on his face. Nothing to worry about, he said. We'll have her home by morning.

Of course, the same detective didn't bother to ask me or Remy if we'd seen the man who took Turtle. He left to search for her, and it wasn't until much later that his coworker sat us down in the kitchen with hot chocolate and finally asked the right questions. You hear all the time about police incompetence and botched investigations, and it's no joke: police detectives are only human. It was the middle of the night on New Year's Eve. Later on, we'd learn that three of the four officers who'd initially been dispatched to our house were drunk as skunks. They did a good job hiding it—missing children in subfreezing temperatures tend to sober people up pretty quickly—but they eventually lost their jobs, which I guess was the city's way of apologizing for such a monumental screwup. A few years ago, one of them died after falling asleep in his car while it was parked, engine running, in his garage. His ex-wife wrote us a letter afterward, telling us that he'd never forgiven himself for being drunk that night, and that we shouldn't feel bad about his suicide, because at least he had some peace now. She said it had ruined their marriage. My parents tore the letter up before they threw it away. As far as I know, they never responded to the woman.

By the time Remy and I named Steven as the man inside the Santa suit, it had been hours since he'd walked out of our basement with Turtle in his arms. That's a lot longer than forty-eight minutes. But Steven insisted he'd gone straight home after Gretchen and Abby kicked him out, and there were plenty of witnesses to back him up.

Steven's father, Jack, had spent his evening at the Moose Lodge with a few other men from the volunteer fireman's association. When the club closed down for the night around 12:30, they moved the party to Jack's house and started a game of cards. All five of the men were lifelong residents of the area. People who knew them considered them decent men, not the kind of folks who'd be willing to lie to protect a killer, even if he was the son of a close friend.

At 1:28 that morning, they got a call about a structure fire in the woods on the northern end of town. As one of them put it to police, "We knew the drill. You don't screw around getting pretty when something's burning. We were on our way out the door before Jack hung up the phone."

When they left the house around 1:30, Steven's bedroom door was open. Jack Handley and his friends all saw him asleep on top of his comforter, still dressed in the Santa suit. They arrived at the scene of the fire, an abandoned motor home at the end of a dirt road in the woods, about ten minutes later. The place was already half-eaten by flames. There was no saving the building. Jack and his friends stuck around for less than twenty minutes before they headed back to their card game. When they got back to Jack's house a little before three in the morning, Steven's bedroom door was closed.

Oddly enough, they were all able to verify the time based on what they'd seen on the television when they walked into the living room. Like my own family, and probably like most of the families in our town, the TV had been tuned to channel 4 all night, where Dick Clark was ringing in the New Year in Times Square.

When questioned separately, all five men remembered the same thing:

"Neil Diamond was singing 'Sweet Caroline' on the stage in Times Square."

"It was Neil Diamond, and he was doing that song—the one that goes 'bam-bam-bam.' You know the one I mean? I don't listen to music much."

"It was 'Sweet Caroline' by Neil Diamond. My wife's name is Caroline, so I'm pretty familiar with that one. She always makes me turn it up and sing along when it comes on the car radio."

"'Sweet Caroline.' I don't know who sings it—that Jewish guy. He looked ridiculous."

"Neil Diamond, 'Sweet Caroline.' Of course I'm sure. I don't live under a rock."

And they were right: Neil Diamond was the next-to-last performer on *Dick Clark's New Year's Rockin' Eve* of 1986; Stevie Wonder followed him to close the show, which ended at three in the morning. All five men were awake for the whole thing. If they were telling the truth, it meant that Steven had woken up—or he'd been pretending to be asleep—driven four miles to our house to steal Turtle, and made it back home and into bed in under an hour.

What could he have done with Turtle in such a small window of time? Why would he go home and fall asleep, only to wake up a few hours later to commit the same crime he could have pulled off much earlier? Steven's lawyer asked these questions again and again throughout the trial. How could Steven have known we would be in the basement that night? Did he come into our yard, dressed like Santa, with the intention of breaking in and harming one of us? Was he looking for Gretchen? Or was he trying only to scare us, but somehow things got out of hand? Maybe he panicked. Maybe he didn't mean to hurt Turtle. Maybe it was all a horrible accident.

I guess any of those scenarios is possible, but anybody who might know for sure isn't telling. In the meantime, the best we can do is to fill in the blanks with our imaginations. Twenty-four additional minutes bring us to the forty-eight-minute total, give or take, in which Steven's whereabouts aren't backed up by multiple eyewitnesses. Steven is the only one who knows, without any doubt, what he was doing in those moments. Here's something we *do* know for sure: if he used those forty-eight minutes to kidnap my sister, the act wasn't costing him any sleep.

♦ ♦ ♦

Partial Transcript of Police Interview with Clayton Barnes, Conducted January 4, 1986

Clayton Barnes: We were worked up from the call. That's why we didn't fall asleep as soon as we got back. Fire gets your adrenaline pumping, and then you have a hard time winding down. There was a movie that came on after—the one with the killer tomatoes. By then I was ready to hit the sack, but Jack said Helen would throw a shit-fit if he let me drive home, so I slept on the couch for a few hours.

Detective: Helen wouldn't have wanted you to drive?

CB: She's a real mother hen like that. Always worried about her boys. What did I care? I was sleeping real deep, too, until the cops come banging on the door while it was still dark outside. That's when all hell broke loose.

DET: How did Steven react when the police showed up?

CB: Well, he was scared. That's how it seemed to me. He reacted the way you or I would react if someone woke us up from a dead sleep to accuse us of kidnapping.

DET: Maybe he's a good actor.

CB: He's no Al Pacino. I'm telling ya, Stevie was there when we left for the call, and he was there when we got back, asleep in his bedroom. So what if he'd closed the door when he got up to piss? Now, don't tell Jack I said this, okay? That boy was a worthless sack of shit after his accident. He wasn't the kind of kid who gives his mom much reason to brag, but he didn't take that little girl. He didn't have time. I've thought about it over and over—I ain't the kind of person who lies, not for a friend, not for anybody, and besides, I've got three daughters of my own, and I know those people are suffering like you and I can't begin to imagine. If I could help ease their pain by telling you something that I'd seen or heard, I promise you, I'd do it. But like I said, Stevie never did much besides take up space after he flunked out of school, and that night wasn't any different. I saw him with my own eyes. We all did. The TV was on, all the lights in the downstairs were on, and there he was, sleeping like a baby a few feet away from us. Now, I've thought about it plenty, like I told you. What kind of person could fall asleep after they'd done such a thing?

DET: I can't imagine.

CB: He'd have to be some kind of monster, wouldn't you say?

DET: Maybe so.

CB: Stevie isn't a monster. He just isn't. No good? Sure. But not a monster. A person who could fall asleep after that doesn't have blood in their veins, you know? They have something else. Ice, or . . . something else. Pure, liquid hate. A person like that doesn't walk around all their lives without folks noticing there's something different about him. Evil like that can't hide in plain sight. It's not possible. What kind of a world would that be?

Forty-Eight Minutes of Doubt, pp. 233–34

chapter twenty-two

Summer 1996

Rinse and spit."

"There's blood in my mouth."

"That's a sign you need to floss more often." Gretchen twirls in her chair, trying to make herself dizzy. "This is a boring job," she says, standing up only to stumble against the edge of the sink in the little room, knocking my free toothbrush onto the floor. "I have to get my kicks where I can."

She's full of it; I floss every night before bed. As dental hygienists go, my sister obviously isn't among the elite few who can make a professional cleaning bearable. She rushed through her job on my mouth, complaining for a solid fifteen minutes about the pitiful levels of oral care that she has to deal with on a daily basis. "Do you know what I hear at least once a week, Sam? I'm not making this up, I swear. At least once a week, after I scrape someone's teeth, they look at what I've dug out and say, 'Is that popcorn? I don't even remember the last time I ate popcorn!' Once a week at *least*."

"I know. You say that all the time."

"Sorry. It's my only interesting work-related anecdote."

She's all smiles as she walks me back to the waiting room, where our mom is balancing her checkbook, doing subtraction on her fingers. My sister starts calling out random numbers, trying to mess up her math so that she has to start over. "Eleven. Forty-three. Twenty. Sixteen. Four. Eighty-eight."

"You're rotten," Mom says, dropping the ledger into her purse. "No cavities, right?"

"Right." I've never had a cavity in my life. No way do I need to floss more; I could probably stand to floss *less*.

"Do you want to come to lunch with us?" she asks Gretchen. "I was thinking we could try that new Mexican place by the mall."

My sister pretends to study her fingernails instead of looking at our mom. "No, thanks."

"Okay. Next time, then."

"Doesn't Sam have another appointment today?"

My mom glares at her. "Not until one thirty."

"What other appointment?" I ask.

"You didn't tell her?" My sister lays her southern accent on thicker than usual as she feigns confusion. "Why not, Momma?"

"Gretchen. This is uncalled for."

My sister yawns. "I need to get back to work. I hope you took a shower this morning, Sam." She gives me a smirk that makes my stomach drop.

"Why would you say that? Where are we going after lunch, Mom?"

Our mother ignores the question; instead of responding, she takes my arm and guides me toward the door. "We need to hurry if we want to have enough time for a decent lunch." She gives Gretchen one final try: "You're sure you won't come along? Last chance. I hear they have amazing guacamole."

"I'm not hungry, and I hate guacamole. I've hated guacamole my entire life. Don't you know that?"

"I'm sorry. I guess I'd forgotten."

"You're thinking of Hannah. Hannah loves guacamole."

Let's go. Please, let's just go, I think, but my mom's hand is frozen on the doorknob.

"You're right. It is Hannah."

"Wait. No. I'm wrong." Gretchen taps a finger to her lips in thought. "It was Turtle who loved guacamole. Not Hannah. Turtle. She used to eat it with a spoon." She smiles. "Remember that, Mom?"

I can tell how hard my mom's working to summon what's left of her training from her days as a beauty queen: how to stay composed and keep smiling when all she wants to do is scream, or hide, or slap Gretchen across the face.

"Make sure you eat something for lunch. You seem tired, sweetie. And you're getting too thin." She's not wrong. Gretchen has lost ten, maybe fifteen pounds since summer began. Combined with her new haircut, she's starting to look puny.

"I don't care how you think I look."

"Well, I'm sorry for caring about my own daughter. You need to take it a little easier. I don't understand why Abby can't hire a private nurse for her father. You're too kind to her, Gretchen. Don't you ever feel like she's taking advantage?"

"She's not taking advantage of me. I want to help."

"You look like you haven't had a good meal in ages. What are the two of you eating? I can't imagine either of you is much of a cook."

"Right, well, we all know you can't imagine Abby as much of anything." Gretchen's jaw goes *click-click-click* as she grinds her teeth together.

"I don't deserve this kind of treatment. Not from my own child." She pauses. "Especially not from you."

Even in her most tender moments, my mother has never been as nurturing as, say, Remy's mom. We don't have frequent heart-to-heart talks like I've heard of other mothers and daughters doing. It's not that there's anything *wrong* with her; it's more like I've made a deliberate effort to not need her too much, and the arrangement seems to be working fine for both of us. When I was younger, after Turtle disappeared, she did her best not to let me out of her sight for years unless I was nearby with another adult whom she trusted. But you'd be surprised how easy it is to spend every moment with a person without ever truly getting to know them. You might say she watched without seeing. Even back then, I got the sense that her need to keep me close wasn't so much diligent parenting as self-preservation.

"I know I should have told you about this, but I thought you'd be embarrassed." There's no missing the big white sign above the door, announcing what I'm in for: Dr. Glick, Ob-Gyn. My mom fills out the insurance forms before passing me the clipboard so I can fill in the more personal information: Are you sexually active? How many partners have you had in the past twelve months? Did you use protection? If so, what kind? Are you presently using any method of birth control? Have you ever given birth? Have you ever had an abortion? Is there any possibility you might be pregnant? What was the date of your last menstrual cycle? Do you drink? Do you smoke? Do you use recreational drugs? If so, circle all that apply.

I can't even look at her without wanting to scream. She pretends to be engrossed in a months-old issue of *TV Guide* while I fill out the form, but she's obviously stealing glances whenever she thinks I'm not paying attention. So I act as though I don't notice, and then I check off whatever responses will upset her most without being too obviously false. By the time the nurse calls my name, I'm a self-described bisexual who has engaged in unprotected intercourse with "more than ten but fewer than twenty" partners. I also admit a weakness for "very occasional" cocaine use; chronic, moderate pain during urination; and "frequent thoughts of sadness and despair."

Dr. Glick is youngish and handsome, and I can't think of anything more embarrassing than his examining my naked body while my feet are up in stirrups and my paper gown flops open in the front. I wait with my legs pressed together at the knees while he looks over my chart, wondering whether I should speak up before he orders a massive amount of blood work and antibiotics.

"You're seventeen, Samantha; is that correct?"

"Yes."

"And you filled this questionnaire out all by yourself?"

"With my mother sitting beside me, yes. She sort of, uh, surprised me with this appointment."

"Oh? How lovely of her." He looks from the chart to my face, then back to the chart. "So, I'm taking a wild guess here: Did you think you'd surprise her with your answers?"

"Something like that."

"I see." He crumples the paper into a ball and tosses it into the garbage can, but he's smiling. "Okay. Let's start over. Are you sexually active, Samantha?"

"No."

"Planning to become sexually active in the future?"

"At some point, I assume."

"Do you want to be on birth control?"

"No."

"Do you have any medical issues you'd like to discuss?"

"No."

"Then what are you doing here?"

I sigh, trying to come up with a decent answer. *Because my mother is a pain in the ass.*

"Because my mother is worried about me."

"Ah," he says, nodding in understanding. "As mothers are wont to be."

"I'm sorry for wasting your time."

* * *

In the car, my mom touches up her makeup in the rearview mirror while I sit stiff and silent beside her. I'm clutching a paper bag filled with free condom samples, which the nurse insisted I take "just in case."

"What do you have there?" she asks, talking out of the side of her mouth while she colors her lips with coppery liner.

"They're Girl Scout cookies, Mom. Dr. Glick had a few extra boxes lying around beside his speculum."

"That's very funny, Sam." I can't tell whether she's frowning at me or her own reflection. "Really, though, what did he give you?"

"They're condoms, Mom. Are you happy? Now I'm protected from all the terrible diseases I'm exposing myself to with all the unprotected sex I've been having with strangers."

"Sam, I was only trying to be cautious."

"I don't want to talk about it. Take me home."

My mom almost never fights with me. She fights with my dad and with Gretchen, and I'm sure she'll fight with Hannah once she's older, but almost never with me. I don't even remember the last time we argued. This is too much, though. A pelvic exam isn't the kind of thing you surprise someone with, especially not your seventeen-year-old daughter. The more I think about it, the angrier I get. "Do you think we should stop to see an ear-nose-and-throat specialist before we get home, Mom? What about a proctologist? That way you can make sure all my orifices have been sufficiently penetrated today."

She swerves the car off the road and into the nearest parking lot. "What the hell has gotten into you? I'm sorry for looking out for your health and safety. Actually, no, I'm not sorry. I'm your mother, Sam; it's my job. And if it makes you feel any better, Remy is going through the same thing today with Mike."

We're parked next to a Dumpster behind a building. A swarm of flies hovers in a thick cloud above the trash, their tiny wings beating rapturously against the July heat. When I close my eyes, I think I can smell the garbage fumes rippling past.

"I know what you're doing with him, Samantha. I wasn't born yesterday."

"Excuse me? What is it you think I'm doing, exactly?"

She rolls her eyes. "I don't expect you to tell me everything. I know you're old enough to make your own decisions. But if you're going to lie to me, then I don't—"

"I'm not lying!"

"Oh, no? What would you say if I told you that Susan found condoms in Remy's bedroom?"

"I'd say that Remy is being foolishly optimistic."

"I've seen the two of you together. You're with him *all the time.* And I'm not even angry—I'm just concerned, that's all! Can't a mother be concerned for her teenager?"

"But you don't have any reason to be concerned! I'm not doing anything wrong!"

"Like how you weren't doing anything wrong when you went to the Holiday Inn with Noah last year? You're *Samantha*," she says snidely, "not Gretchen. I expect more from you."

I can feel my heart pumping blood to every pressure point in my body. I can hear it rushing behind my ears.

My mom can tell she's pushed me a hair too far. She softens her tone and tries to move past it. "I shouldn't have said that about

Gretchen. I'm sorry. And I'm not trying to hurt you, Sam. I'm trying to be a good parent. It's my last chance."

"What about Hannah?"

"Don't drag Hannah into this. Hannah is still a baby. Don't you dare drag her into this mess."

"You think *I'm* the one dragging her into a mess?" I laugh in her face. "That's hilarious. You had Hannah to replace Turtle, and she doesn't even know it yet. You won't be able to hide it from her forever."

My mom's breath stutters in her throat as she starts to cry. She pushes her sunglasses onto the top of her head and dabs at the corners of her eyes, blinking rapidly, trying to divert the flow of tears away from her mascara. "I didn't think I had to worry about you. You've always been such a good girl. I don't know what I did wrong with Gretchen, I really don't. I did the best I could with what I had. That's all any parent can do, you know. We did our best, but she was wild, Sam, like an animal. Do you remember? Tell her she's grounded, and she would sneak out of the house. I'd have locked her in her room, but she would have climbed right out the window. We told her to stay away from that boy, and she only chased after him harder. She wasn't just a rebellious teenager, she was a destructive force. Nobody was safe. And then your little sister . . ."

"Mom, stop." I can't listen to her narrate the worst moments of our lives, not in a hot car beside a Dumpster with the insides of my nostrils tingling from the smell of all that decaying meat a few feet away. Every time she sucks in a breath, I imagine a curl of black flies and death tunneling down her windpipe, seeping into every pore of her body. I can't stand to see her like this, not because of something I've done. "If I do anything with Remy or anyone else, I'll be careful. I promise. Please, just calm down."

"Thank you." She is trying hard to compose herself, a skill that she's had plenty of practice sharpening over the years. She can go from smiling and happy to falling apart in a few seconds flat, and then back to cheerful just as quickly; she's like the Porsche of emotional meltdowns. It's sad to know that the ability has grown so refined, and it makes me suspect that she's never anywhere near as happy as she sometimes seems, as if it's just a face she's learned to maintain for as long as possible, until she loses her focus and it drops away, and she has to scramble to piece it back together again.

When she stood onstage at the Miss Pennsylvania pageant in the seventies, beaming at the crowd and waving like a pro, her smile stretching so wide that the gums showed on the sides of her mouth, I'm sure it never crossed her mind that her life would be anything other than enchanted. Back then, she never had to wrap her head around the fact that shitty things happen to good people all the time. Instead, she campaigned for her title on the platform that hard work and good deeds were sufficient tools to build a sweet life. I've seen the video clip: she stands in a purple sequined evening gown slit up to her thigh, her posture that of a lucky girl who moves confidently, almost giddily through her charmed life. "I believe that kindness can change the world. When you treat others with love, respect, and dignity, it multiplies and spreads."

It's easy to watch the pageant now and consider her words a load of pandering bullshit; the judges might not have cared about her message if her dress hadn't been so sexy or her face so lovely. But I believe she meant it. When she hired Lenny the landscaper

without bothering to inquire about the moral quality of his employees, she assumed they would all reciprocate with the same kindness she'd extended toward them. Sometimes kindness doesn't
beget anything but misery. My mother didn't have to learn that
until she was in her thirties; I've known it nearly all my life. I'm
not sure which of us is better off.

◆   ◆   ◆

The police and prosecution were quick to call the case a slam dunk. District Attorney Patrick Klein held a press conference immediately following Steven's indictment, during which he bragged that "I have zero doubt in my mind that we've got the right guy, and I'm going to do everything I can to make sure he can never hurt anybody again." If there had been any effort at all to investigate anyone else, his words put an end to it—but in fact there were plenty of other people who could have been involved that night.

Forty-Eight Minutes of Doubt, p. 51

chapter twenty-three

Summer 1996

A week has gone by since I showed Remy the picture of Mister Marbles in the woods behind my house during our birthday party. The photograph is tucked between the pages of my hardcover copy of *Wuthering Heights*.

It's nothing; I know it's nothing. It's the song that bothers me more than anything else. If I heard it only that one time, how do I remember all the words? And why would he sing it to us in the first place? He must have known it would scare us. As much as I try not to think about the photograph, just knowing it exists makes me feel uneasy. At least twice a day, I take it out for another look, hoping every time that it will be different somehow—maybe I'll realize the man isn't there at all, and it's just a double exposure or a trick of the light that looks at first glance like a person. It's silly, and I feel stupid even getting my hopes up; it's the same thing I do every time I read *Bridge to Terabithia* and hope for a different ending, even though I know what's going to happen.

I'm sitting on my bed, staring at the photo in my lap and willing it to change, when Gretchen strolls into my bedroom wearing only a bra and underwear.

"Oh—oh, hey, Sam. You're in here." Her hair is soaking wet, dripping water onto my floor. "I thought I heard you," she says, trying to play off the obvious fact that she was hoping to snoop around my empty room.

"What do you want?"

"Can I borrow some of your jewelry?"

"I guess so." I barely own any jewelry, and none of it seems like it would suit Gretchen's style. But it's not like I have any good reason to refuse her. "It's all in my jewelry box. There's not much, but you can take whatever you want."

Gretchen winces as she carefully creaks open the lid with her clean, delicate fingers. She leans over to peek at the plastic ballerina curled up inside, her pointed toes wedged into a metal spring, waiting to resume her endless pirouette to the metallic rendition of "Für Elise."

My sister starts poking at the contents, frowning. "Is this all you have?"

"I told you it wasn't much."

"This is all crap."

"Thanks, Gretchen."

"I know you have better stuff somewhere. Where's your hiding place?"

"My hiding place?"

"Where do you keep your weed and condoms?"

I bat my eyelashes at her. "With my hypodermic needles and pharmaceuticals, naturally."

"Naturally," she laughs. "How about the locket you found in Remy's basement?"

I reach into my shirt for the chain hanging around my neck. "This one?"

"Aha! Yes! Can I borrow it?"

I hold still while she leans over me to unclasp the necklace before I've even given her permission to take it. My palm trembles over the photograph resting faceup in my lap. I don't know why I care whether Gretchen sees the picture.

"Whatcha got there?" She swipes my hand away to get a closer look. "Ooh, is that me? Oh, my God. Look at my *hair*."

"It's from one of my birthday parties with Remy." I try to act nonchalant. "I found it in his basement."

"Lemme see." She snatches it away before I have a chance to stop her, holding it up to the light for a better look. I can't be sure, but I think I notice her gaze deliberately avoid Turtle's face.

"I *remember* this party. Wow."

"Gretchen?"

"Hmm?"

"Do you see the man in the woods?"

She takes a closer look at the photo. "Oh," she says, and I think I detect a hint of trepidation in her voice. "That's Frank Yarrow."

"Frank Yarrow?" My ears ring at the sound of his name. Frank Yarrow. I've heard it before.

"He worked for Abby's dad sometimes. I think he might have been homeless."

"Did you know him?"

She shakes her head. "No," she says flatly, "but I saw him around sometimes."

"Was he—was he nice?"

Gretchen won't look at me. "I don't know. It doesn't matter, Sam. He's dead now." Now that she has what she wanted—the locket, clutched in her fist—she's done with pleasantries.

"He's dead? When did he die?"

"A long time ago," she says, annoyed. "You were still a little girl." She pauses, one hand poised above my doorknob. "I think he was Amish. There was something wrong with him; he had some kind of mental disability."

"Remy and I saw him at the railroad tracks once. He was terrifying."

Gretchen turns to frown at me. Her short hair is beginning to dry into small, silky blond waves, delicate as fluff. Her pretty face has a sharp expression. "You couldn't remember him, Sam. He died when you were too young."

"We saw him," I insist. "He gave us marbles."

"You're wrong." There's something about the way she says it that keeps me from arguing any further. She isn't going to believe me. "Forget about him, Sam," she says, before she pulls my door closed. "He was nobody."

*   *   *

Later that night, Remy and I are on the seesaw at the playground across the street when a blue car pulls up outside Abby's house. We're hidden by darkness as we observe the scene, our bodies gliding slowly up and down through the cool night air. The driver, a man, walks around to the passenger side and opens the door for Gretchen. The two of them go into Abby's house, their arms around each other's waists the whole time, their heads close together. The car is still there in the morning. I don't see Gretchen for the rest of the weekend.

chapter twenty-four

Summer 1996

Over a few weeks last spring, I called Davis Gordon a number of times. I always did it from Noah's house so my parents wouldn't see it on our phone bill. Noah didn't know about it at first; nobody did. If his mom wasn't home, I would tell him I needed to use the bathroom, and then I'd sneak upstairs to use the fancy white phone on her nightstand.

I never knew exactly what I wanted to say to Davis. It didn't matter, because I always hung up shortly after he answered. I called him maybe seven or eight times in less than a month.

I made the phone calls around the same time I started spending most weekends at Noah's house. I was drunk on the thrill of being so close to him. I used to have to remind myself to breathe every time he touched me. I couldn't believe the energy I felt in his presence. I remember thinking it was no wonder love made people go crazy sometimes.

Noah figured things out easily enough: Davis's number was a long-distance call, and his name showed up with the charges on the phone bill. He didn't press me much to explain myself, which was good, because I couldn't have explained anyway. Even *I* didn't understand why I called.

A few weeks later, when I asked Noah for a ride to the annual Mid-Atlantic Conference of True Crime Writers and Investigative Journalists that was being held at a New Jersey convention center, he didn't hesitate. He still doesn't know the whole reason for our little escape. For him, I guess it was enough that he got to stay overnight in a hotel with me.

I almost didn't show up to meet Noah today. It's been weeks since we saw each other at the group meeting, and I've been trying to convince myself that he's forgotten all about our plans. Yet here I am, stepping off a filthy bus after riding for more than an hour into the city, outside the public library where he's waiting for me. He's perched on a cement wall with his legs hanging over the edge, his right sandal dangling from the tip of his big toe. He doesn't look any better than he did a few weeks ago at the meeting. His clothes look like they were slept in. His face—always smooth before—is peppered with the beginnings of a beard. Most guys can only pull off one look, but once I'm over the initial shock of seeing him so disheveled again, I realize that Noah has managed to shift his appearance from polished boy next door to tortured intellectual without it looking ridiculous. Remy, for example, could not pull off this kind of look. I feel guilty for comparing the two of them. Remy doesn't know I'm here. There didn't seem to be any point in telling him.

We find a small, unoccupied study room near the back of the library, behind the nonfiction books. The only sound is the buzzing of the fluorescent lights on the ceiling, their plastic shells littered with the dead bodies of flies and other insects. Noah sits with his arms slung over the back of his chair and his legs sticking way out, taking up almost half the room.

"I'm not going back to school in the fall." He's working on a Rubik's Cube that he's been holding, but I can't tell whether he's making any progress on it.

"You aren't?"

"No. Do you want to know why?"

"Not really."

"Sit down, Sam. You look nervous."

"I am nervous."

"Why?"

"Because my parents don't know I'm here, and if they did, they wouldn't be too happy about it."

"You tell them everything?" He winks at me. "Come on. Don't you want to have your own life? Your own secrets?"

"I've never really thought about it." I can't help but notice how his smell fills the whole room. He smells like sweat, like the out-doors. Remy always smells like deodorant. Sometimes he wears Old Spice cologne, which I'm not crazy about, but I'd never tell him that.

"I know that's not true." He leans closer to me. "I know you, Sam. You want to be so good, but it's hard. I wish you could have stayed with us. We would have had so much fun together." He pauses. "We still could, you know."

I fold my arms across my chest, trying to flatten my boobs and hide my cleavage. I can feel him staring at me. He knows what I'm doing, and why. I don't feel as safe as I'd like to in this room: the door is closed, the blinds pulled shut. On our way in, the only other people I noticed were the librarian at the front desk and an almost definitely homeless woman who was reading the comics section of the newspaper, giggling to herself over *The Family Circus* with the kind of laugh that instantly marks a person as mentally unbalanced.

"I don't have a lot of time, Noah. What do you want to talk about?"

He puts his hands on the table palms up, cupping the Rubik's Cube and staring at it as though it were a crystal ball. "What's the worst thing you've ever done?"

I can tell he's not kidding. "You think I'm going to tell you?"

"You act as if I'm a stranger, Sam." He tries to put his hand over mine, but I flinch and pull it away. "What's the matter with you? I thought we were friends. More than friends."

"We are."

"Then what's the problem?"

"I don't know."

A short silence falls between us.

"Listen to me. I did something awful, and I'm going to tell you about it." He grins. "Lucky you."

The room feels so cramped and clammy that I can taste the air. Above us, the dead bugs are baking in their lonely, fluorescent grave.

"You don't have to tell me."

"I want to. Before I do, though, I want you to know . . . you won't like me afterward."

"Great."

"I'm serious. There was a girl at school last year I never told you about."

He's right; the thought of Noah with another girl stings, even though I don't have any claim on him.

"Are you okay?" he asks. "I'm sorry. If there was anyone else I thought I could tell . . . I'm sorry. I should find a shrink. My mom is right."

"It's fine. Go ahead, tell me about this girl."

"Laura."

"Tell me about Laura, Noah."

chapter twenty-five

March 1996

The view from the window of room 108 at the Uniontown Holiday Inn is a brick wall.

"Did I ever tell you about the guy my mom almost married? The one who died?" Noah asks.

"There was a guy before she married your dad?"

"Yeah. Philip Possus. That was his real name. He's the whole reason she believes in shit like psychic vortices and ESP and the tarot."

"How did he die? Please don't turn the light on."

"We haven't been outside all day. I'll feel crazy if I don't see the sun. That's how Philip went crazy."

"He went so crazy that it killed him?"

"Yes. He and my mom got engaged young, at, like, seventeen. It doesn't actually matter how old they were. They went on a trip to New York City because my mom wanted to see the Rockettes perform, and after the show they went to a bar—even though they weren't old enough to drink yet, I guess—and two guys who were standing beside them got into a fight. Philip tried to butt in and break it up, and ended up getting his face rearranged.

"One of the punches knocked him out for thirty seconds, maybe a minute, according to my mother. She says that when he regained consciousness, Philip was crying and freaking out, asking questions about people she'd never heard of before. He told her it felt like he had lived through decades of a whole different life in that thirty seconds.

"Philip had all these new memories of growing up in Florida with different parents. He knew details—what their house looked like, the names and birthdays of the people he'd dreamed up; he remembered going to Disneyland with his parents, riding the tram, going through the haunted mansion . . . He'd never been to Florida in his life. He told my mom about meeting a different girl and falling in love with her. He remembered their wedding day and moving to Arizona with her and having three kids. He knew all their names and what they looked like. He mourned for those people in his dream as though they were as real as you or me.

"He couldn't get over it. He went to doctors and shrinks, trying to figure out how to move on, but nobody could help him. He finally broke off his engagement to my mom and disappeared to search for this other family that he insisted was real. He couldn't accept anything else."

"Did he ever find them?"

"No." Noah switches on the bedside lamp, and I cover my eyes until I'm used to the light. The brightness shifts the tone of the room. I need a shower.

"We have to leave early tomorrow morning. I don't know how long the rest of the drive will take, and it's a long trip home after that."

"It's less than two more hours. I have a map."

"Do you think my parents are worried about me?"

"Yes." Noah runs his hand along the curve of my body through the thin white sheet, bringing it to rest on my hip. "But they know you're okay. I'm sure they must know we're together somewhere. They're probably way more pissed at me. I'll take the blame, okay? I'll be your fall guy."

"You don't have to do that."

"I don't mind." His fingers press against the sharp edges of my hip bones, prodding me closer, until our bodies lock together. His mouth is on my neck. The warm air tickles my skin as he mutters, "You have enough to worry about already."

Is this how Gretchen felt with Steven? I wonder. Did her skin feel electric when he touched her? Did she think it was worth it at first—both of them risking so much potential trouble for the thrill? She had no way of knowing the eventual price our whole family would pay.

"I can't keep my hands off you," he says. He searches deeper beneath the sheet, his fingers as clumsy and frantic as animal paws. I realize it's possible—maybe even probable—that my reasons for this trip are only a parentheses in Noah's story line, which doesn't intersect with my own story as much as I've been telling myself it does. Am I being naive? Maybe he doesn't care why I asked him to bring me here, as long as he gets what he wants.

I resist when he tries to nudge me onto my back, sitting up and scooting away on the bed to hug my knees against my chest. "So what happened to Philip? He went crazy?"

Noah sighs, giving up for the moment. "I guess you could say that. My mother sure thought so. She lost touch with him for a few years after that—you can understand why—and then one day his mom called to tell her Philip was dead. He hit a semi head-on while he was driving the wrong way on the interstate. My mom thinks he did it on purpose. She thinks he was trying to find a way back to his other life."

"But it wasn't real."

"It was real to Philip, Sam. In the end, that was all that mattered."

chapter twenty-six

Summer 1996

Her name was Laura Merck. She was this quiet, sort of mousy-looking girl. She wasn't even that pretty, Sam. She wasn't anybody I would have noticed under any other circumstances. She wasn't like you." He pauses, waiting for me to react. I don't move. I don't even blink. My guts are still churning at the thought of Noah touching someone else.

"She was in my freshman comp class," he continues. "All freshmen have to take it, and she ended up sitting right behind me because of the way the seating chart had everyone arranged. Anyway, our teacher was this guy, this grad student who had, like, zero interest in explaining basic writing skills to us. It was clear from day one that he wasn't looking forward to spending the whole semester grading essays about whatever dry, boring shit usually gets covered in that kind of introductory class, making sure everyone knows how to write a coherent paragraph and use proper grammar and punctuation. The first thing he did was tell us that instead of focusing so much on mechanics and stuff, we were going to be doing more thoughtful kinds of writing. So the first assignment is to write an essay about ourselves called 'How I Got This Way.' Of course, you know, I wrote about what happened to Bethany when I was a child, because what else is there to explain about myself, right? You know what I'm talking about, Samantha. I know you do. It's like, sometimes I wonder whether I could even exist independently of her. As though I'm just a subplot in the Bethany Story, and if what happened to her hadn't happened, there wouldn't even be much of a reason for me to exist."

"That's ridiculous."

"No, it isn't!" Tiny, shiny beads of sweat gather on Noah's upper lip, so small I can barely see them. "When I was reading through the essay after I'd finished it to look for mistakes—because we were still getting graded on all that stuff—you know what I realized? I barely even got a mention in the whole thing. It wasn't about me at all. None of it is. All my life has been about Bethany. When people talk about me—and when they talk about you, too, I bet—they don't think about us without thinking about *them*. My sister, your sister. We aren't Noah and Samantha, full stop. Our names, at least our first ones, barely even matter. I might be Noah Taylor on paper, but to everyone who knows me I'll always be Bethany Taylor's little brother. Full stop."

His hands have the same faint yet constant tremble that I noticed a few weeks ago at the meeting. Despite this, they've been working the Rubik's Cube the whole time he's been talking to me, and now the yellow side is fully reassembled, which he somehow managed to pull off despite barely glancing at it over the past few minutes. Everything he's just said is true, of course, to varying degrees. But what's the point in talking about it? Nothing is going to change. Sitting here with him in this tiny, cramped room all afternoon, the two of us complaining about our shitty luck, feels like a level of wallowing that I'm not interested in exploring.

"Maybe it's just that you aren't a very good writer."

"I don't think so. I got an A on the assignment." His eyes have this tendency, whether he smiles or frowns or whatever, to slip into what seems to be their default expression, the look of a person who's just thought of something very clever. From all the pictures I've seen of Bethany Taylor over the years—and I've seen plenty—I recognize the expression as a trait shared by the siblings. They look alike in other ways, of course, as brothers and sisters do, but this gaze gives its wearer the look of a person who is both bright and wise. I know it's hard to imagine a twelve-year-old looking wise, but it's true: if Bethany were alive today, I'm betting she'd be a smart cookie. For just a second, the thought pops into my head that maybe Chester Stark chose Bethany because he was drawn to her gaze; there's something undeniably riveting about it. But before the idea is fully formed enough for me to properly consider it, I push it down inside me as far as it will go and do my best to ignore it.

"We paired off in class and exchanged essays. This girl, Laura, was my partner. She was so affected by what I'd written that it was as if she zeroed in on me and wouldn't let go. We started spending all this time together during the week. She was so interested in my fucked-up, tragic life; it was as though she wanted to save me. Some girls are like that, you know? She wanted to be a kindergarten teacher. She was what you'd call a nurturer, the kind of girl who'd make a really great mom. And even though she thought she knew me, she didn't know anything, not really. She didn't know who I was outside of this narrative I've built up over the years about Bethany and what it was like to grow up without her, not knowing where she was or what had happened to her. Laura thought she was getting, like, an exclusive peek into my soul or something. She believed it because I *let* her believe it, even though I knew it was all bullshit and that she didn't have the first fucking clue who I really was.

"So then one night after we'd gone to a party and were both a little drunk, we went back to my dorm room and had sex."

The word—*sex*—hits me like a smack across the face. The whole room ripples, and I find a well of hate inside me for this girl I've never even met.

If Noah notices, he doesn't show it. "I didn't usually go to parties," he continues. "You know that. I went home every weekend. But I didn't have a whole lot of money for gas, so I stayed that time, and Laura wanted me to take her to a party. She didn't go to them very much, either, and she definitely didn't drink; at least, I never saw her drink, or heard her talk about drinking, until that night. She was innocent like that. It wasn't that she looked down on people for partying; it was just that it had never been a part of her life, and when she got to college she had too much sense and self-respect to go crazy. She was probably the only freshman I knew who was genuinely excited to actually learn something in college, unlike the rest of us, who were all just psyched to get wasted and screw around for four years and hopefully graduate with a decent GPA and no

STDs. Her ears weren't even pierced. Anyway, we went to this party, and I think she had maybe three beers. I wasn't exactly keeping track, because I was drinking a lot more than she was, and the whole night was kind of a blurry mess. But I know for sure that she was definitely tipsy."

"And you had sex with her anyway," I say flatly.

His eyes widen. "It was her idea, Sam, I promise. I asked her, like, fifty times if she was sure she wanted to do it, and she kept insisting she was ready. She was a virgin, she said, and she wanted to lose her virginity to me. Don't look at me that way, Sam. She wanted to do it, and she wasn't so drunk that she wasn't making sense—I mean, I think she was of sound enough mind to consent, okay? So we did it, and I could tell it was way more emotional for her than it was for me. I know that's shitty, okay? I know I shouldn't have done it. But I wasn't really thinking with my brain, if you know what I mean. Don't look at me like that.

"After it was over, we were lying in my bed together and she said something about Bethany. I don't even remember exactly what it was—something about how it made her so happy to make me happy, because it broke her heart that I'd been sad for so long. She told me that she loved me, and that nothing made her happier than knowing she'd given a part of herself to me, because she thought maybe I could use that part of her to help fill the part of me that was empty. It was so sincere and kind that it was almost too much. There was something repulsive about it, because I didn't love her back. The feeling just wasn't there, not for me. So without really thinking about what I was doing—I told you, I was way more drunk than she was—I told her that she had it all wrong."

Noah leans against the table and grasps my forearm with a damp, cold hand. This time, I don't pull away. He tightens his grip enough to still his tremble. I know I shouldn't let him touch me, but it feels so good that I don't want him to stop. He looks like he's going to start crying. "It felt so good, Sam. Once I started talking, I can't even tell you how it felt. Better than anything. Better than sex with the most beautiful girl in the world. I didn't look at her, though, because it was like I *knew* if I saw her reaction, I wouldn't have the balls to keep explaining myself, and I *needed* to explain. Maybe I just needed to say it out loud. My roommate had hung up this huge poster of Jack Nicholson that covered nearly an entire wall—you know that scene from *The Shining* when he chops down the bathroom door with the axe and yells 'Heeeere's Johnny!'? It's a photo of that scene. Instead of looking at Laura, who was lying naked right next to me in bed, I looked at Jack. It felt easier. I explained that I didn't remember Bethany at all, because it's true: I don't have a *single* memory of her. I don't remember going to see *The Empire Strikes Back* at the drive-in the night she was abducted. I don't remember her voice, or her laugh, or any of the things I've gone my whole life pretending to miss so much. I mean, I've seen her on our old home movies and in a million photos, but I don't feel any emotional attachment to her. She's just a girl. She's nobody to me, really, but I went for so long acting as though she were everything. The truth is that I don't care that she's dead. I don't love her, and if I ever did, I don't remember. You know how I *do* feel about her, though?"

He stares at me, waiting for me to respond, and every second that goes by without an answer makes it clearer to both of us that I know exactly how he feels about Bethany, because it's the same way

I feel about Turtle sometimes, an honest and 100-percent-true feeling that is too terrible to acknowledge for more than a moment. Like any other thought too awful to hold on to for long enough to really examine its nuances, I push it down. I do it all the time. Every day.

"You hate her."

He nods. "Yes. I hate her for destroying my family, and for ruining my parents' lives. For being so fucking stupid that she followed a stranger to his car, at night, alone. I wish it had never happened, but not because I want my sister back. It's because I want my life back. Maybe my dad would still be alive. Maybe my mom wouldn't be such a pathetic mess. If Bethany hadn't disappeared, we would have had normal lives. And I hate her for that. I hate her so much, Sam."

"I know." Our heads are together above the desk, foreheads touching, arms slid around each other's shoulders. His hand is against the back of my neck, his fingers caught in a tangle of my sweaty hair. We can tell each other the truth, right here and now, but I feel like the opportunity would vanish if I pulled back or moved at all. "I hate her, too."

"You aren't talking about Bethany." His other hand cups my jaw.

"No."

"You can say it, Samantha. It's okay."

"I hate my sister. I hate Turtle."

"She ruined everything."

"She ruined everything." It feels like being in church. I'm a sinner at the altar, and he's the priest, guiding me to echo his words. But there is no rush of freedom that accompanies my statements; my voice is flat and unemotional compared to the fervor of

Noah's tone. He means all of it; I don't. Unlike Noah, who was too young for his brain to hold on to memories of the love and affection that he and Bethany must have shared, I remember loving Turtle all too well. I hate what happened to her, but she is not the one to blame. I hate her because her absence is a constant reminder of that night. I hate her because it's easier that way; by keeping the hate contained, by keeping it focused on an innocent four-year-old whom I will never see again, I can hope that it won't seep into the rest of my life.

The doorknob rattles. A narrowed pair of eyes tries to peek through the gaps in the closed venetian blinds covering the room's only window to the nonfiction section.

"Don't move. Stay here." He grasps a fistful of my hair, winding it around his damp fingers. Beads of sweat feel sticky between my breasts. His gaze is cast downward, watching as the sweat rolls down my cleavage and settles in the small rolls of flesh on my tummy. It's the kind of sweat that comes more from feeling than from an outside heat source; the room isn't all that warm. Depending on how well she can see through the blinds, the librarian probably thinks we're in here making out. She knocks insistently, five rapid taps of her knuckles against the wooden door. When Noah stands up without warning, the release of his hold on my neck and shoulders leaves me shivering.

He cracks the door a few inches. "We're using this room to study."

"Sir, this is a public facility. You can canoodle with your girl-friend somewhere else." She looks past him at me, just as I snort at her use of the word "canoodle."

"Is something funny, Miss?"

"You said 'canoodle,'" Noah tells her. "Nobody says that."

The moment he starts speaking to the librarian, Noah changes somehow: it's as though he's flipped a switch to reveal the charming, decent young man hidden beneath his scruffy face and rumpled clothes.

The woman is very old, so old that her spine has started to curve from the stress of so many years of working to keep her upright. Her glasses have one of those metal chains attached so that the wearer can let the glasses hang around their neck when they aren't using them to see. In contrast to her body, her voice is steady and firm but quiet—the voice of someone who's spent so much time in a library that she automatically keeps her speech within an acceptably low decibel range. "Unless you've reserved the room in advance, you can use it for only thirty minutes. You two have been in here for thirty-four minutes. Also, if you'd read the sign posted right outside the door, you would know that we do not allow patrons to lock themselves inside these rooms."

"You'd like us to canoodle somewhere else, then." He gives her an All-American grin, which she can't help but return. He's charmed her into submission.

"All I ask is that you don't lock the door. It's a violation of the fire code."

"Thank you. I'm really sorry, ma'am. We just wanted some privacy."

"I understand. I'm only doing my job." Now she's the one apologizing.

"Of course. We really are sorry." As he's closing the door, she pokes her head through the crack long enough to chirp in a new, much warmer voice, "Let me know if you need any reference materials!"

We listen, silent, as her footsteps grow distant; once she's gone, Noah locks the door again before resuming his seat beside me, sliding his hands back into place around my shoulders. The spell is broken, though. The fluorescent lights seem to buzz more loudly than before. The Rubik's Cube with its finished yellow side seems less impressive than it did a few minutes ago; anybody can finish *one* side. The smell of his sweat has lost its allure. Before, it smelled like what I'd guessed must be pure pheromones, hormonal magic. Now it just smells like sweat. I lean away to disentangle myself from his grasp, which feels cloying and needy as he tries to hold on.

"You didn't finish telling me about Laura."

He nods. "The end is the worst part."

"Just tell me, Noah."

"She got very upset. For a while, she tried to argue with me. She wanted me to say that I didn't mean any of it. But once it was out there, it was as if the words were hanging in the air, floating all around us. There was no taking them back, see, because it was obvious how happy I was to finally have said everything out loud. I'm not kidding—it felt better than the first time I ever got laid. Sorry. All I mean is that—"

"I know what you mean."

"Yeah, I know you do. But Laura didn't know, and she didn't understand at all. She got way more upset than I could have anticipated. She was crying, calling me a fucking liar and a monster, saying that I'd intentionally deceived her by using my dead sister to get pity and to make myself more interesting. She said I'd *stolen* her virginity; I think she called it 'emotional rape.' And even if I had wanted to explain myself, it wouldn't have worked. She didn't get it, and I knew she never would. Other girls—hell, other *people*—they aren't like you, Sam. They don't know how it feels. She kept telling me 'Everything about you is a lie,' and she was right."

"Did you tell her that?"

He seems surprised by the question. "No. Of course not."

"But she was right. According to you, that's exactly what your life has been. So then, what did you say to her? Did you tell her you were sorry?"

"No."

"Because you weren't."

"That's right."

"So what happened? She broke up with you? And you're telling me that's the worst thing you've ever done—lied to a girl so you could get laid? Honestly, Noah, that's not very impressive. If that's the worst thing you can come up with, I think it makes you a typical guy."

"She walked back to her dorm that night. Alone." He picks up the Rubik's Cube and holds it yellow side down in his palm, staring at the disorganized squares of red, blue, orange, green, and white. "She had asked me to walk with her. It was around two in the morning. It's a huge campus. During orientation, they spent, like, an hour of every day stressing the importance of using the buddy system when walking anywhere at night. She even said that to me: 'We're supposed to use the buddy system!' And I don't know;

the way she said it, so goddamn wholesome and upstanding, it was as if something shifted inside me, and I just wanted her to get the hell out of my room. I'd just had this major emotional break-through, and I thought I could lie there and sort of bask in it for the rest of the night, but she kept hounding me to walk her home. The more she bugged me, the more determined I was to make her go alone. She was crying when she finally left. It was bad. I didn't even walk her to the door of my *room*. I didn't even get out of bed, or give her a hug, or the fucking flashlight that was in my nightstand drawer, like, six inches from my hand."

"What happened to her?"

He doesn't say anything.

"What happened to her, Noah?"

"She got hurt. I don't know exactly what happened; I only know what I heard from other people and what I read in the school paper. She was walking home across the quad when she got the feeling someone was following her. She tried to run into the liberal arts building to get away, but the doors were locked because it was so late. So she ran around to the back of the building, where there's a set of outside stairs going down to the basement. It was dark, and she was scared . . . She tripped at the top. The stairs are the old, metal kind, all rusted and sharp." He winces at the memory. "The fall hurt her pretty bad. It knocked her out." He pauses. "It was a long weekend. It was two and a half days before somebody noticed her lying down there. She couldn't even scream for help because her ribs were broken. She almost died."

After hearing so many terrible stories at all the support group meetings I've attended over the years, after all the quiet afternoons and late nights spent alone with my imagination, in which those stories came to life and played out over and over again, no matter how hard I tried to block them out—it's hard to feel much of anything for this faceless stranger. It's the absence of emotion that frightens me more than anything. A girl at the bottom of some stairs—there are much worse things. A girl who *lives!* Other girls should be so lucky.

And this girl in particular—this girl who slept with Noah deserves all the pain in the world.

I can't mean that, can I?

"But she survived, Noah. Right? She recovered. At least she still has the rest of her life to live."

"She was in the hospital for, like, three weeks. I couldn't go visit her. That isn't true, actually; I *could* have gone, but I didn't want to. When she was finally released, she didn't come back to school. Her parents came and got all her stuff. She wouldn't go back to campus, not even for that."

"So what happened to her? Where did she go?"

"I have no idea." He turns the Rubik's Cube in his hand, staring at each side for a few seconds. "I can never solve more than one color. I know there has to be a way, but it seems impossible. So you know what I do sometimes, when I want to impress someone? I work on it for a little bit, until I've got one side all done. I act as if it's so easy, and then I pretend to lose interest in solving the rest. Like it's so simple for me that I can't be bothered to finish."

"Here," I say, taking it from his hand, "I'll show you how." He watches as I peel each colored sticker from its square, being careful not to tear any of them as I line them up along the edge of the table, until the yellow stickers are the only ones remaining on the cube. Then I rearrange the stickers in order by filling in one side at a time, from red to blue to orange to green to white.

"You know that's not how it's supposed to be done," Noah says.

"I know. But nobody can tell the difference, can they? Not if they didn't see me."

"But that's cheating, Samantha." He smiles. "I know you're not that kind of girl."

"I'm just trying to help you."

He grabs my hand. "Do you think it was my fault?"

"Yes."

"She hates me. Her family hates me. All her friends hate me. When they found out why she was walking home alone, they told everyone. People I don't even *know* have told me they hate me, and you're holding my hand. If I try to kiss you, I think you'll let me. Why would you do that? What's the matter with us, Sam?"

I've never bothered asking myself that question until now. "Maybe we're bad people. Or maybe we've just done terrible things."

"I've done terrible things. You haven't."

"Yes, I have."

"Nothing as bad as what I did to Laura."

"No, Noah." I lean forward and kiss him on the mouth. Just once. Then I move my lips close to his ear. The words sound like a whisper and feel like a howl: "What I did was so much worse."

• • •

In January 1986, there were nine convicted sex offenders on the Indiana County registry. Police were able to verify alibis for all but two of them. Darren Shepherd, age thirty-three, was on probation after serving thirteen months of a five-year prison sentence for pleading no contest to indecent sexual assault on a minor. His victim was his girlfriend's thirteen-year-old daughter. Darren couldn't prove he was home all night on New Year's Eve, but police ruled him out based on his looks alone. Darren was six and a half feet tall and weighed over three hundred pounds. He was also African American.

But the other man, Brett King, matched Steven's physical traits more closely. Like Steven, King was white and stood around five feet nine inches tall. Steven weighed one hundred forty-three pounds; King weighed one hundred fifty. He'd worked as a custodian at Mother of Sorrows Elementary School from 1978 until the spring of 1984, when a female third grader told the school nurse that King had snuck up on her in an empty classroom after recess one day. Before she had a chance to leave the room, he exposed himself to her. While King was in jail awaiting trial, three more students came forward with similar stories. He made parole after serving ninety days of a thirteen-month sentence and moved into a studio apartment above a bar in Shelocta called the Golden Pheasant, owned by his sister, Marcia.

King told police he'd been home alone all night on New Year's Eve, but Marcia was the only person who remembered seeing him that evening: "He came down around maybe 11:30. It wasn't too long before midnight. I saw him dropping quarters into the cigarette machine near the bathrooms."

King was forbidden to enter the bar during business hours. Too many locals knew what he'd done; Marcia was afraid she'd lose customers if anybody knew her brother was living above the bar.

"I saw him for only a minute from the back, but I know my own brother. He didn't stick around. He got his smokes and went back upstairs."

Turtle Myers had attended morning preschool at Mother of Sorrows on Tuesdays and Thursdays starting in September 1983. King claimed he didn't remember her.

Marcia didn't think her brother was capable of planning a crime. "They tested his IQ in prison. He's dumb as a box of rocks," she told me. King's IQ was tested twice in his adult life. He scored a 99 on his assessment in 1983. But on the earlier test, which he took in 1970 as part of a failed attempt to join the military, his score was 118, which is considered average. Nineteen points is a significant difference. It's not impossible that King intentionally did poorly on the test he took in prison, hoping it would make him seem more sympathetic.

And there's more: at around three in the morning on January 1, 1986, Jenny Hicks called the Indiana County emergency line to report a disoriented customer at the all-night diner where she worked as a waitress. She told the dispatcher that a man with blood on his face and clothing had stumbled inside and gone straight to the bathroom. "He left a few minutes ago, and now there's blood all over the sink and floor."

Jenny locked the bathroom door and waited for the police to respond. When nobody had shown up by five o'clock, which was the end of her shift, Jenny cleaned the bathroom and went home. Could that man have been Brett King? We'll probably never know. Jenny doesn't think so; she told me the man in her restaurant that night was definitely not Brett King *or* Steven Handley.

Police didn't follow up on her 9-1-1 call for another twelve hours. "I guess they had their hands full that day. They didn't even go to the restaurant right away—they came to my house. I asked the cop if he thought they'd test the bathroom for things like blood and fingerprints. He said it wouldn't matter since I'd already cleaned everything up with bleach.

"He said the guy was probably a drunk who'd been in a fight. I didn't understand how he could be so certain. I mean, the man I saw didn't have a bloody nose or a split lip. He didn't look like he'd been in a fistfight. He looked like he'd just murdered someone. That's the first thought that popped into my head, the minute I saw him: it looks like he just finished killing someone."

Forty-Eight Minutes of Doubt, pp. 183–84

chapter twenty-seven

Spring 1996

Davis Gordon is the keynote speaker at this year's Mid-Atlantic Conference of True Crime Writers and Investigative Journalists. When Noah and I finally reach the convention center, I have to buy a pass for the conference just to get inside the building. The pass costs me forty dollars, which is more money than I have in my wallet; I have to dig through Noah's car to come up with the last dollar in change.

Since he doesn't have a pass, Noah has to wait outside. I stand in line for almost an hour until I'm finally face-to-face with Davis.

"Samantha." He glances at a woman dressed all in black standing nearby. Maybe she's his publicist. She raises her eyebrows, and he tries to alert her to my presence without me noticing by tilting his head ever so slightly in my direction.

"I'm not going to make a scene, if that's what you're worried about." I look behind me, where there's still a long line of people waiting for Davis to sign their copies of his book. "I doubt your followers would tolerate it."

"Have you been calling my house?" he asks.

"*No.*" I pause. "Maybe."

"It's okay. I'd be happy to talk. But why did you keep hanging up?"

"I don't know."

"Is there something in particular on your mind?"

"Yes. No." I'm too nervous to think straight.

Davis considers me standing in front of him, obviously hurting and confused. Until the book came out, I had liked him so much. I can tell he wants to help me, but now that I'm here, it's clear this isn't the right time or place.

"I can't talk to you right now, Samantha. Can you wait until after the signing?" He looks at his watch. "I'll be done in an hour. We can get lunch. How does that sound?"

The woman in black appears at his side. "Everything okay here?" she says brightly, smiling at me with intense, unblinking eyes.

"Everything's fine," he tells her, not taking his eyes off me.

"Good." She looks down at my hands and sees that I'm not holding a book. "Did you want to have something signed?"

"No." I can't believe we came all this way, and he's telling me to leave.

"We need to keep the line moving."

"I can't stay for lunch. I have to go home," I say. I pause. "My parents don't know I'm here."

"I won't tell them. Are you sure you can't wait, though?"

"Yes, I'm sure."

"You can call me whenever you want, Sam." He smiles. "Don't hang up next time."

"Thanks."

I'm about to walk away, feeling defeated and ridiculous, when he reaches for a stack of bookmarks printed with the cover image from *Forty-Eight Minutes of Doubt*. "I can still give you an autograph."

"That's okay," I say, looking at the woman still hovering behind him, giving me a dirty look for holding up the line.

"Wait, Sam." He grabs my wrist and stares at me. "You really should take one."

I wait for him to scribble something on the blank side of the bookmark. When he's finished, he slides it picture side up across the table. I shove the bookmark into my purse and walk away without reading it. As soon as I'm out of the room, I duck into the first bathroom I see.

There's no autograph—just a message written in Davis's messy handwriting: *Ask Gretchen about Frank Yarrow.*

◆ ◆ ◆

"We were fighting because I'd said hello to a guy I knew at Ruby Tuesday's, Dan Shaffer. He was the manager there. I hadn't seen him in ages. We were in the high school marching band together. You get close to everyone in marching band, because you spend so much time together. Even though I graduated a few years ago, it would have been weird if I *hadn't* said anything to him.

"Levi was screaming at me in the car, and Tara was crying in the backseat, and it had started to rain. It was one of those quick, heavy summer storms. We were on the two-lane road that goes past the golf course. It was something like ninety degrees that day. When Levi pulled over and kicked me out, all I could think about was getting Tara from her car seat so he wouldn't drive away with her. I didn't think about my flip-flops on the floor of the front seat, or how they'd just put down a new layer of asphalt on the road. Then Levi drove away, and the rain had stopped, and I was holding Tara in my arms and crying. The soles of my feet were already getting blistered.

"Steven—people always called him Stevie back in high school—I knew him from band, too. He was in the concert band, not the marching band like me, but we all practiced together sometimes. I knew all about his accident at the prom, and what happened at Penn State, and how he was supposedly damaged goods. It was a big deal at the time; I was only a sophomore, so I wasn't at the prom that year, but everyone had heard about it. Stevie was one of those guys everyone liked: jocks, band geeks . . . So when he pulled off to the side of the road and told us to get in his truck, I didn't think twice about it. He looked the same as I remembered him from high school.

"I *was* terrified that Levi would come back and see us with him and think I had . . . Well, it's hard to say what Levi might have thought. I told Stevie to get us out of there. I was shaking. Tara was crying. Her diaper needed to be changed, but I'd left my bag in Levi's car. So Stevie stopped at Kroger for diapers and wipes on the way to my parents' house. He dropped us off, and that was it. I didn't see him after that, not until his face was all over the news.

"I wasn't afraid of him. Neither was Tara. She was only a toddler, but kids have a way of knowing when they shouldn't trust someone. I feel so stupid now when I think about getting into his truck like that, but don't you think I would have sensed it if he'd been planning to hurt us? I can tell when a person isn't . . . He didn't seem any different to me. All the stories I'd heard about Stevie and how much his accident screwed him up in the head didn't describe the man who drove us home that day. He didn't give me the same feeling I got around Levi. What else was I supposed to do, walk until my feet bled? We could have been hit by a car, or gotten heatstroke. Stevie was my angel that day."

Forty-Eight Minutes of Doubt, pp. 300–302

chapter twenty-eight

Summer 1996

I wake up covered in sweat from a dream in which I'm standing across the street, watching a fire tear through the houses on Point Pleasant. The Souzas' dogs are howling in a window, trapped, pawing at the glass.

It takes me a few seconds to realize that I'm in our living room, not my bedroom. I must have fallen asleep watching television. The running water I hear is coming from the kitchen faucet; in my dream, it was the sound of a gushing fire hydrant.

I recognize Gretchen's footsteps in the kitchen. She lets the faucet run for a long time while she splashes water onto her face.

She opens a nearby cabinet and fumbles in the dark for a glass to fill with water. Everybody else is asleep. It's the middle of the night.

"Hurry," someone whispers to Gretchen. It's Abby.

My sister starts to cry softly. "I don't think I can do it."

"Shh." Abby murmurs something I can't quite hear.

"I can't. I can't, I can't, I can't," Gretchen babbles, her voice growing dangerously loud. Our mom is a light sleeper.

"We're almost finished."

"I'm so scared."

"Don't be. I'm the one who should be scared."

Gretchen's voice grows raspy and frantic. "I won't let anything happen to you."

"It doesn't matter. Nothing can hurt me."

Gretchen gulps down water. She struggles to calm her breathing. The ice maker in our freezer rumbles to life, startling them.

"Let's go," Abby whispers. "We're going to wake someone up."

They don't move. Neither of them says a word for at least a minute. I peek over the edge of the sofa and see Abby leaning against the counter. Her arms are wrapped around Gretchen. My sister's face is buried in the space between Abby's neck and shoulder. Abby's eyes are closed. Her makeup is streaked with tears. She reaches up with a trembling hand to touch my sister's short hair.

"Shh," Abby says again, repeating the sound over and over into Gretchen's ear like a mother trying to calm her fussy child. Then she opens her eyes and looks straight at me. I expect her to yell or to walk over and smack me, but she doesn't react at all. She just closes her eyes, smoothing Gretchen's hair while my sister cries, and it occurs to me that Gretchen might not love any of us as much as she loves Abby.

After the two of them slip out the back door, I count to fifty in my head before slowly getting up and tiptoeing toward the kitchen.

Without turning on the light, I look around the room for any clue to what they might have been doing in here.

My mind understands before my eyes can fully recognize the sight. It swiftly knocks the wind out of me, as if I've been shoved into a deep, dark hole and I'm still falling. Nothing else in the room seems to exist: only the stuffed bear on the table. His eyes are flat and black against his white, furry face. His torn ear is mended with a thick scar of purple thread.

His name is Boris. He was Turtle's teddy bear, and he was in her arms when Steven took her away.

chapter twenty-nine

Summer 1996

The sun is finally rising. Light streams through the trees in the forest, casting shadows on the ground all around me. The playhouse in Remy's yard looks alive as the gaps and cracks in the old wooden planks seem to burst into brightness where the sunlight overflows.

I've been awake for hours, uncertain about what to do next. I don't know how Abby and Gretchen came into possession of Boris, but I have a pretty good idea.

On hot nights, Remy likes to sleep with his bedroom window open. I stand beneath it and softly call his name until he appears, still half-asleep. I'm holding Boris behind my back so Remy won't see him right away. "Let me in," I say in a stage whisper.

He disappears from the window, stumbling into the basement a minute later to unlock the sliding glass door.

"My parents are already up. You could have just knocked on the front door, you know." Now that we're up close and he's a little more awake, he notices that I'm still wearing the same clothes from yesterday. I'm sure I look awful, but I couldn't care less. After I found Boris, I took him up to my room to get a better look in private. I wasn't going to let my parents discover him in the kitchen like that; the shock might have killed my father. I sat in a corner and studied his fur, which has become more gray than white after so many years. I felt the weight of his stuffing and ran my finger along the tight machine stitches of his seam and then the wider, less precise purple stitches where Mrs. Souza reattached his ear. I was looking for anything at all that might suggest he was a replica, not the original Boris.

It is the same bear. I show him to Remy. "Do you remember this?"

Remy stares at Boris for a minute without comprehending, and then I see the recognition fill his eyes. He barely touches the curve of purple thread with one trembling finger. He seems afraid to actually feel the fabric, as though something awful could be transmitted by prolonged contact with this artifact of tragedy. "Where did you get this?" he breathes.

"From Gretchen and Abby. They came into the house in the middle of the night. I heard them talking in the kitchen. Gretchen was crying. Once they were gone, I found him sitting on the middle of our kitchen table."

Remy starts to cry. "But that's impossible."

Yet here we are. While I was waiting for the sun to rise this morning, Davis Gordon's telephone number popped into my head without any conscious attempt on my part to remember it. I won't call him today, though; I need to talk to Gretchen and Abby first, and then probably my parents.

"Why do you go to Helen Handley's house and shovel her snow, Remy?"

"What?" He wipes his eyes, smearing tears and snot all over his flushed face. "Are you kidding me? Where did Gretchen and Abby get this bear? That's the question you should be asking, Sam— where the hell did they get this?"

"I want to know why you shovel Helen's driveway."

"Because . . . I don't know, because it makes me feel better."

"Why does it make you feel better?"

"Why does it matter?"

He knows why it matters. He *must* know, even if he doesn't realize it yet.

"I went to see Davis," I blurt. "This spring, I had a boy drive me all the way to New Jersey. Davis was speaking at a conference in Newark. I saw him, Remy, and he told me something important."

Remy shakes his head, refusing to listen. "No. It's over. Davis wants to make money, that's all. He's trying to make something out of nothing."

"You know that isn't true." I pause, listening to the sounds coming from upstairs, waiting until I'm certain that Remy—and nobody else—can hear me.

"Why did you lie for me, Remy?"

The ceiling above our heads creaks with the weight of Susan's footsteps as she walks around the kitchen, getting breakfast ready for her family. I imagine her brewing some coffee while she watches the *Today* show on the small countertop TV in the kitchen, sipping Folgers from a cup that says "World's Best Mom," oblivious to the universe crumbling at the bottom of her basement stairs.

"No." He shakes his head furiously now, even reaching up to put his hands over his ears like a little boy. "I didn't lie! Why are you saying this to me? I didn't lie, Sam. I didn't. We saw him. We *saw* him," he insists. His face crumples into an expression that is part terror and part denial as he leans against the nearest wall for support. His knees buckle beneath him, and he slides all the way to the floor with his face buried in his arms, still shaking his head, refusing to confront the awful truth that has gone unspoken for so long. Until now.

I kneel down beside him and pull his head up, forcing him to look at me. "It wasn't him, Remy. It wasn't Steven."

His eyes are bursting with horror. "No. You're wrong." His head shakes harder—*no, no, no, no*—as though the motion might dissolve the facts if done with enough force.

"Maybe you didn't see him. You can tell me the truth. Were you even awake that night? Did you see anything at all? Or did you say it was him only because I did? It's okay if you were scared, Remy. We were only kids. We didn't know what we were doing. People will understand."

We are both crying now, huddled together on the floor with Boris between our bodies. Remy's dad opens the basement door and calls down the stairs to Remy. "What are you doing down there, kiddo? Breakfast is almost ready!"

"I'm just talking to Sam, Dad," Remy manages to reply.

"Hi, Sam!" Mike shouts. "Come on up and eat some breakfast while it's still hot, you two! Suzie made eggs."

"Maybe later," I shout back.

There's a pause. "Suit yourself." And he closes the basement door. We hear it creaking shut, but I don't hear the door latch.

Remy grasps my arm now, his eyes wide with sudden panic. "We have to get out of here. We can't let my parents see him." He means Boris.

"Let's go to Abby's house."

"*Shh.* They'll hear us," he says. "Oh, God—Sam, what are we supposed to do? We couldn't have been wrong. I saw him. I remember . . ."

"It was the man from the picture," I tell him. "The same man we saw at the railroad tracks. His name was Frank Yarrow."

"You're wrong."

"I'm not wrong. He worked for Abby's dad."

"You're wrong, Sam," he repeats. He seems so certain. How would he know anything about Frank? He barely remembered the day we saw him at the tracks. But then he backpedals, his face tight as he searches his mind for some semblance of certainty about anything at all, and comes up short. "I don't know," he admits. "I was awake that night, Sam. I thought it was Steven . . . I thought it must have been him. I'm so sorry."

"Shh." I wrap my arms all the way around him and hold on as tight as I can. "It wasn't your fault, Remy. I saw him. I knew it wasn't Steven. I'm sorry. Oh, my God, I'm so sorry. It's my fault she's dead." The words come out as gasps. "It's my fault."

chapter thirty

January 28, 1986

It was a Tuesday. My parents didn't send me to school that day. My mother was asleep, or at the very least in bed. For the next five years, she was either unconscious or so deep into a self-medicated stupor that she barely seemed to cast a shadow. My dad and I watched the space shuttle prelaunch coverage over a breakfast of stale Christmas cookies and tap water while Gretchen lay on the floor nearby, half-asleep under a quilt made from our mother's old pageant gowns.

I was eating the last pizzelle when Abby's dad came by to drop off a new dead bolt for our basement door. (By the end of the season, he had single-handedly replaced every lock in our house with superior ones from his hardware store. I figured it made him feel useful.)

"You two going to watch the *Challenger* launch? Darla bought me a forty-eight-inch television for Christmas. You oughta see the picture it gets." He noticed the tray of cookie crumbs sitting between us.

I think Ed and my dad could have been friends if my mom hadn't been so determined to snub Darla when Gretchen and Abby were small. It was all so stupid and petty.

"When was the last time you went outside, Sam?" he asked me. "This morning? Yesterday?"

I shook my head.

"Darla got up at five to start pork and sauerkraut in the Crock-Pot, and there's no way the three of us will finish it all. And it's a sunny day, believe it or not. Why don't you two come over?" He didn't mention Gretchen even though she was in the room, because her eyes were closed and she seemed to be sleeping. For some reason I thought she was pretending. I saw that her eyes were open as I headed out the door.

There were woolly bear caterpillars crawling up the walls in Ed Tickle's house. We'd seen them all over the place that fall. Supposedly it meant that the coming winter would be brutal. They mostly disappeared when the weather grew colder, but Darla and Ed couldn't get rid of them for some reason.

I counted eleven caterpillars inching up the walls of the Tickle living room. It seemed as though they were all trying to get to the same place.

"I can't stand to kill them," Darla told us apologetically, "so I go around the house once or twice a day and scoop them all into a bowl and dump it outside. Ed says it doesn't hurt them much when they freeze to death. It's like falling asleep."

The kitchen table was cluttered with paperwork and Mary Kay makeup samples. Ed brought us plates of pork and sauerkraut to eat while we watched his new TV. It was so big and deep that it took up more than half the room. A clock in the lower corner of the screen counted down to the launch, which was less than a minute away. My father and Ed were sitting together across the room. Ed held a bottle of champagne to open when the shuttle launched. I could hear my dad speaking in a whisper, telling Ed something about the search for Turtle.

". . . depends on the evidence they find, and how the weather is going."

Darla noticed me eavesdropping and turned up the volume on the TV. "Pay attention, you two," she told my dad and Ed. She beamed at me. "Can you believe this, Sam? You're about to witness history right here in our living room."

"Anyway," my father finished saying to Ed, "we're hoping the stars will align soon."

Through the Tickles' living room wall, which they shared with Mr. and Mrs. Souza next door, I could hear the old couple's German shepherds howling at something.

We watched the shuttle climbing toward space, leaving behind thick white ribbons of smoke to unravel in the atmosphere. Ed popped the cork on the champagne. While the bottle was still over-flowing with bubbles, he poured a little into three plastic cups, passed one to Darla, and raised his glass to toast with my dad. "To the stars aligning."

A caterpillar dropped from the ceiling and landed on my plate. I was watching it squirm around in my mashed potatoes when

Mrs. Souza began to holler at her husband in Portuguese next door. Their dogs started barking their heads off.

Darla covered her eyes and turned away from the TV screen, foamy champagne sloshing over the side of her cup and onto the carpet. "Turn it off, Ed."

He was still holding a mouthful of champagne. He stared at my father and swallowed. "Did that just happen? Oh, Jesus. Oh, my God."

"There's a caterpillar in my food."

My father and Ed looked at me, their expressions puzzled and horrified.

"The shuttle exploded, Sam." My dad looked like he was about to cry.

Abby hadn't been watching with us, but now she was standing in the doorway to the basement. She was breathless from running upstairs in such a hurry. She picked up my plate and took my hand, leading me into the kitchen.

"Is it true? Did it explode?"

"Yes," Abby said. She hooked her finger around the caterpillar on my plate. It was covered in buttery mashed potatoes, damp and wriggling in her palm. She wet a sponge and dabbed at the caterpillar's fur, but it wouldn't keep still long enough for her to get it clean.

"Let's go home, Sam." Behind me, my dad put his hands on my shoulders.

"Wait. Abby is saving the caterpillar."

"No, I'm not. It's too late." She dropped it into the sink and turned on the water, rinsing it down the drain. All that work to save it, and she just gave up. She flicked the disposal switch beside the sink, and I heard the blades spinning, grinding the caterpillar into pulp. That's when I started crying. I'd witnessed the deaths of seven people on live television minutes earlier and felt nothing, but when Abby killed the worm in my food I cried.

We thought Gretchen had been asleep the whole time we'd been gone, so we assumed she hadn't seen the explosion. When we got back to our house, my dad turned off the television and went upstairs to check on our mom. I stayed downstairs with Gretchen. I was trying to crawl under the blanket with her. Our faces were almost touching when she opened her eyes to stare at me.

"Did you see it?" she whispered.

"Yes."

"They're all dead."

"Abby killed a caterpillar." I started crying again. "She ground it up in the sink."

"Shh. Come here." My sister pulled me beneath the blanket and put her arm around my shoulders. Our house was so quiet that I could still hear the Souzas' dogs barking all the way over in their yard.

"She tries to save them," Gretchen said. "She kills them only if she knows they're going to die anyway." She held me so tightly that her fingernails dug into the flesh on my ribs. "She tries to save them," she repeated, "but she doesn't want them to suffer. Sometimes she has to kill them in order to help them, Sam. Sometimes it's the only thing to do."

chapter thirty-one

Summer 1996

Abby is unusually calm as she leads Remy and me into her living room. "Gretchen is upstairs," she says with her back to us. "She'll be down any minute." She pronounces each word so carefully that I feel certain she's on something: Xanax or Valium or Klonopin. I've seen enough people on heavy meds to recognize the signs.

The caterpillar infestation might be gone, but the Tickle house is still a cluttered mess, which doesn't surprise me at all. Neither Abby nor Gretchen has ever been the domestic type.

"Who do you have there?" Abby's lazy gaze settles on Boris, whom I've placed on the sofa between Remy and me. "Oh."

"We know what you and Gretchen did," Remy says to her. "Sam heard you both in the kitchen. Where did you get the bear, Abby?"

She doesn't answer the question, or even look him in the eye.

"Maybe we shouldn't have done it that way. But we're running out of time." She seems to be speaking more to herself than to either of us.

We hear the stairs creaking, and Gretchen walks into the room, stopping in the doorway when she sees us on the sofa.

"Is he still awake?" Abby asks. She means her father.

Gretchen nods. "He's having a lot of trouble breathing."

I look at Abby, expecting her to say something or to go upstairs to help Ed, but she doesn't seem the least bit concerned. She's still looking at Boris.

Remy gives me an uncomfortable glance. I know he doesn't want to be here; he wanted to skip the visit altogether and go straight to his parents, or the police, to admit what we'd done and show them the bear. He thinks we should let someone else figure things out from here, but I'm not so sure. It didn't go so well the last time. "Is your dad okay?" he asks Abby.

"He's suffering terribly." She pauses. "But he's still alive."

Gretchen stares at us. "You two shouldn't be here. Go home, Sam. Take the bear with you. Mom and Dad need to see him for themselves."

"Why?" I demand.

"Because it's the only way they'll listen."

"Where did you find him?"

"Don't worry about it. You'll know soon enough."

"We need to tell you something. It's important."

"Not now. You both need to leave." She tries to wipe something from her fingers with a dirty napkin that's been balled up in her fist and nearly shredded to damp bits.

"Come on," Remy says, tugging me up by the elbow. "I knew this was a bad idea."

"Wait a minute." Abby steps in front of him. "Where will you go now?"

"To the police."

"To tell them what?"

I glance at Remy. He shrugs. "Gretchen wants us to leave. We're going."

"If Gretchen doesn't want to know, you can tell me." Abby stands with her arms crossed, her face tight with impatience. She's sweaty and exhausted, not at all pleased to see us even though she's trying to convince us to stay.

"Tell me where you got the bear," I repeat.

She looks from me to Gretchen, then back to me. "You go first."

I'm not sure how to start. "I did something wrong the night Turtle got kidnapped. I lied about something."

"We both did," Remy adds.

My words are enough to crack through the hazy veneer of whatever drug is running through Abby's bloodstream. "What was the lie, Samantha?" She glances at Gretchen again, and the two of them exchange a series of quick, indecipherable thoughts with their eyes.

"I told the police I saw Steven take Turtle from the basement. I was so scared, and I knew everyone wanted an answer so badly." My mouth is so dry that I can't even force myself to swallow in the heavy silence that follows. I want Remy to say something, or at least to try to comfort me somehow, but he's too busy keeping himself calm to bother with anyone else. He's started crying again, and I can tell he's embarrassed to be so emotional in front of my sister and Abby, which is crazy.

"I saw a man dressed up in a Santa costume. That much is true. But it wasn't Steven." I pause again, managing to swallow once before I look Gretchen in the eyes. "I'm sure of it."

My sister can barely speak; her voice comes out as a hoarse whisper. "What makes you so certain it wasn't him?"

"His teeth." It's Remy who says it. "It was his teeth," he repeats. He seems as stunned as any of us by the revelation. "He had straight, perfect teeth. That's right—isn't it, Sam?"

I nod. Until this moment, I wasn't sure whether Remy had been awake that night, despite his insistence. Right from the beginning, I'd suspected he hadn't seen the man's face at all, and had only echoed my accusation of Steven because he trusted me.

"I had my eyes closed for most of it, but when he bent over to pick Turtle up off the floor . . . I knew something bad was happening, and I was too afraid to scream. I was afraid he'd kill us." Remy stares at the drab, gray carpet. He doesn't want to look any of us in the face. "I peeked out of one eye when he was leaning over beside me. His beard was hanging down below his mouth as though it didn't fit him right. The room was dark except for this tiny sliver of light across his face. He was opening and closing his mouth, wiggling his jaw while he adjusted the beard, and I saw all his teeth." His whole body trembles. "That's when I pissed my pants," he whispers.

Any traces of Abby's stupor are completely gone. "What about you, Sam? Did you see his face?"

"No," I admit, "not the whole thing. He was wearing the beard, and it was dark—but there were other things. There were little things about him that weren't like Steven."

"Like what?"

"He didn't walk the same way Steven did. And he seemed older somehow . . . and it was as if he breathed differently." I look help-lessly at Gretchen—my big sister!—whose palm is pressed against her stomach as though she might throw up any second.

"You could have helped him," she says. A look of puzzled hor-ror creeps onto her face. "Why did you lie to everyone, Sam? What's the matter with you?"

"I don't know! It was like . . . like Steven's name was just *there*, in my head. He was someone Mom and Dad hated. Dad had been getting into all those arguments with him and trying to get him in trouble, and when I said his name out loud, it felt like the whole world stopped moving. I can't explain it, Gretchen. I panicked. It just happened, and the minute I said it, I wanted to take it back. But I couldn't—I didn't. I was so scared, Gretchen," I say, crying. "And then everything started happening so fast. Steven got arrested, and it made *sense* that he'd done it. Everybody believed it. What was I supposed to do? The longer it went on like that, the harder it was to imagine telling anyone the truth. I kept telling myself I really *had* seen Steven. I told myself for so long that eventually I believed it, with all my heart. It was as if my memo-ries had managed to correct themselves so they would fit the narrative: when I thought about that night, I saw Steven's face in my mind. It was as real to me as anything else."

It's the honest-to-God truth. I believed it for years. We moved away, and Steven went to prison. Gretchen went to college. She dropped out and got married, and she seemed to be doing okay for a while. Our parents survived after Davis Gordon's book came out and broke their hearts all over again. Hannah was born. Life went on, as much as it could, and every new day took me farther and farther away from that night. The truth got smaller and smaller until it eventually vanished. At least I had thought so.

Until last winter, when Kate O'Neill disappeared from church. My synapses crackled with alarm when I saw her photograph on television. At first it was just a vague, unsettling feeling that I couldn't quite understand. My parents didn't watch the news much, and they went out of their way to avoid reports about Kate. But Noah's mom was obsessed with the story; I got all my updates from watching the news with Noah at his house.

We watched Kate's parents as they pleaded for their daughter's safe return. They shared a slew of details designed to make Kate's abductor realize that she was a real human being with feelings and thoughts—she was somebody's child, not an object to be destroyed and discarded.

Kate is counting the days until our church carnival this spring. She can't wait to eat funnel cake. It's her favorite treat.

Someone was paying attention to those details. He made sure Kate got her funnel cake. Then he killed her.

Who could do something so awful? Was he the same kind of person who would have made sure Turtle got the Space Barbie she wanted so badly because he felt sorry for everything he was about to take away from her?

It was a special kind of cruelty. It had been only a few weeks since the photograph of Turtle had shown up in our mailbox on Christmas morning, and it was as if her image on the glossy paper had sounded a single, sustained note of despair in my mind; now here was another one beside it. A few more and they'd make a melody.

"I went all the way to New Jersey this March to find Davis Gordon. Noah Taylor took me in his mom's car. Did you know I disappeared for two days like that?" I ask Gretchen. "Mom and Dad don't know the real reason. They don't know I saw Davis. They think I ran off with Noah to have sex at a hotel. Did they ever mention it?"

"No. We hardly ever talk about things like that."

"Davis told me to ask you about Frank Yarrow."

"I know," she says. She pauses. "I talk to Davis sometimes."

"Gretchen, I *did* ask you about Frank. Remember? I showed you the picture from the birthday party, and you told me to forget about it, and about him. You said he was nobody."

"I remember."

"But he wasn't nobody." I look at Abby. "He helped your dad build the playhouse, didn't he?"

"Yes," she says flatly. "Frank was Amish, so he knew all about woodworking and construction. My dad said he felt sorry for him. He gave him a job at the store, but only for things that didn't require him to interact with the public. He was too strange for that kind of thing. My dad said he would have made the customers uncomfortable."

"You told me he died a long time ago," I say to Gretchen. "Is that true?"

Abby picks up Boris and holds him against her chest. "Tell Sam where Frank lived, Gretchen."

She's silent for a moment before saying, "He lived in the house that caught on fire." My sister thinks I don't know what house she means. How could I possibly misunderstand? "The fire in the woods that Steven's dad and his friends got called to fight on New Year's."

•   •   •

"A few people on the jury said I didn't seem as if I took it seriously. They said it seemed like I didn't care. I *cared*. But I guess I wasn't taking it too seriously at first. I couldn't get over it happening at all, so I guess I thought everything would work out okay. I never killed anything on purpose in my whole life. Ask Gretchen—she'll tell you I was always gentle around those kids. Gretchen knows I couldn't do that, not ever, no matter what. She's lying if she says something different."

Forty-Eight Minutes of Doubt, p. 16

chapter thirty-two

Summer 1996

I thought I was having a heart attack," Gretchen tells us. "My chest hurt. It felt like someone was stabbing me with needles. My hands went numb . . . I was screaming, all by myself in the room. I thought I was going to die. I even thought about how I should just let it happen instead of going to the emergency room, because I'd probably end up showing them the letter and telling them the whole story. And I felt more afraid of that happening than I was of dying." She pauses to pass me the envelope.

The postmark is from October of last year. Inside is a letter from Davis Gordon explaining his new theory that Frank Yarrow was Turtle's killer. Davis is working on a sequel to *Forty-Eight Minutes of Doubt* that he hopes will lead to Steven's exoneration, and he believes Gretchen can help. He also suspects she might want to help.

His argument is convincing: Frank was born and raised Amish, but he was what they called a deserter. He'd been shunned by his family since choosing to leave the faith and its disciplined ways of life after he turned eighteen. He was in his midtwenties when Ed hired him to help build the playhouse. The two men grew close over the next few years. Frank was a little slow intellectually, especially when it came to social interactions. His life had been a struggle in the years since he left his family. When Ed met him, one day when Frank showed up at the hardware store to apply for a job, he was living without electricity in a one-room motor home in the middle of the woods. He didn't even own the thing; he'd found it abandoned one day and figured nobody would notice or care if he stayed for a while.

Frank never stayed in Shelocta for more than a few months at a time. He'd disappear—for days or weeks at a time, once for almost eighteen months—and resurface eventually at the hardware store, usually without any explanation. He lived on the outskirts of the real world: he didn't have a telephone or driver's license. Ed was his only friend.

Police hadn't investigated him because there'd been nothing to investigate. Frank had never been arrested. He didn't have a bank account; his address wasn't registered at the post office. Davis hadn't even known about him until after *Forty-Eight Minutes of Doubt* was on the shelves.

When Davis did finally start looking into Frank Yarrow, he didn't find much to go on. Not at first. Ed told Davis he believed Frank died in the fire that night, although he might not have been in the motor home at all when it burned down. He hadn't seen Frank since Christmas, but he defended his friend. He said Frank had been eccentric and maybe a little slower than most people, but he wasn't a killer. Frank was simple. He was as gentle as a kitten, according to Ed. But Ed didn't have a good explanation for why he'd never fully allowed Frank into his life. For example: Ed admitted he didn't want Frank spending time at the Tickle house, but he claimed there was no particular reason—he just hadn't thought it was a very good idea.

When Davis finally tracked down Frank's Amish relatives from his previous life—he'd come to Shelocta from a farm in Lancaster County, nearly two hundred miles away—they described him differently. With enough coaxing, Davis got them to admit that Frank had shamed his family somehow in the months before he decided to abandon them. There had been some kind of accusation—or maybe even accusations, plural—of inappropriate behavior. They wouldn't say what kind of inappropriate behavior it had been or give Davis any additional details; they didn't want any more trouble in their lives because of Frank. They didn't say that explicitly to Davis, but he got the sense anyway. It was enough to convince him that he was on the right track about Frank.

He believed Ed was, at best, in denial; at worst, Ed knew Frank was guilty but wouldn't admit it, even to help Steven get out of prison. Davis had already tried approaching Abby for more information, but she wouldn't speak to him; now he was appealing to Gretchen.

"At first I wouldn't help him. I pretended his theory was ridiculous, even though I had to admit that he made a pretty compelling argument."

"There was a pretty compelling argument for Steven, too," Abby points out.

"I know." She looks at her friend with such heartbroken compassion in her eyes. "But then somebody left the picture of Turtle in our mailbox on Christmas. That's when I knew Davis was telling the truth. Steven couldn't have sent the picture, not from prison. I thought it must have been Frank, and that he'd been involved somehow after all. Maybe he'd seen Steven dressed up like Santa Claus that night. Maybe Steven left his door unlocked while he was at Abby's, and Frank stole one of the costumes." She pauses. "Mike and I flew back to Texas after the holidays, and I was on my way here the next day. I needed to see Abby."

"But I thought you hadn't come back until after Ed had a stroke."

"I lied. I was here when it happened."

"Oh."

"I'm not getting divorced, Sam. I made up the whole story. Michael comes to visit me sometimes. He knows everything. I'm going home soon—back to Texas."

"But why did you have to keep it a secret?" Remy asks. "Why does it matter if anybody knows that your husband is in town, or that your marriage is fine?"

"Because I love Michael, and I want to protect him. I'm doing this on my own." She looks at Abby and quickly corrects herself. "We're doing this alone."

"But what are you doing, exactly? What are you protecting him from?"

"From me," she says simply. "I'm not here to help Abby take care of Ed, Samantha. I'm here to help her kill him."

• • •

Letter from Steven Handley to Gretchen Myers

Dear Gretchen,

   I don't know if you're reading these letters. You probably aren't. They're going to kill me soon, and I don't know how to stop them. I bet you wish you'd never met me. I wish I'd never met you, either. I know you don't love me, and I don't think I love anyone now. This place has a way of making people shrivel up and die way before they get around to actually killing us. If I ever get out of here, I'm going to spend as much time outside as I possibly can. I don't see much sunlight here. I think I miss the sunshine more than anything else.

   I guess you hate me for what you think I did, but I hope you know deep down that I didn't hurt Turtle. I think about her every day. There isn't much else to do here but think about stuff. I didn't do it. I know I could say it a million times a day and it wouldn't matter, but it's true. Did you know the truth doesn't matter? All that matters is what people want to believe.

Forty-Eight Minutes of Doubt, p. 312

chapter thirty-three

Summer 1996

I knew something wasn't right. The night it happened, my dad went out after midnight. Gretchen didn't see him, but I did. I heard his truck starting up in the driveway and I looked out my window, but I could barely see him because he didn't turn his head-lights on until he got all the way to the end of the street. I didn't think much about it at the time. People forget to turn their lights on, you know? But later on, I realized why he'd done it. He didn't want anybody to notice him leaving.

"I don't know how long he stayed out. We fell asleep, and I didn't wake up until Susan came to my door in the middle of the night to take Gretchen home. It was such pandemonium after that. My father wasn't the way he seemed to everyone else—he wasn't the kind of person I could just ask 'Why did you sneak out on New Year's, Dad?' He never would have told me anything anyway. He was a private person. He had a lot of secrets, and he didn't like any-body trying to figure them out, not even Darla. Frank was the only person he seemed close with, but he wouldn't let the rest of us get to know Frank at all. I mean, I knew him a little bit—he came into the house to use the bathroom a few times when they were build-ing the playhouse, and I'd see him at the store every once in a while—but I didn't know anything about him. He never talked. My dad said he was slow, and there was no reason for me to think otherwise.

"He was creepy." Abby shudders at the memory. "I never under-stood what my dad liked so much about Frank, or why he even cared about him at all. He'd dropped by our house a few days before Christmas that year to give us an ornament he made for our tree. It was his present for us. He'd made a little replica of the playhouse, carved out of wood. It must have taken forever. I remember thinking, *How could someone so dumb make something so beautiful?*

"But even then, with it being so close to Christmas and every-thing, I don't think he stayed at our house for more than three minutes that day. I don't think he said more than two sentences to any of us. Frank gave my dad the ornament, and my dad put it on the tree. Even though she didn't really know him, Darla tried to get him to stay after that—it was Christmas, after all. I remember how she offered him some food and everything—but he obviously didn't want to stick around.

"After Frank left the house that day, things got really awkward between my dad and Darla for a while. It was obvious that she thought there was something weird about Frank. I don't think he'd ever done anything specific to offend her—she'd barely ever seen him, even though he'd known my dad for years—but it was the idea of him that bugged her so much. She was jealous in a way, I guess, because my dad had this way of controlling everyone around him, of letting only certain people know certain things, and Darla felt like he never showed her enough of himself." Abby pauses. "Darla had her own problems. She always talked about how my father was so private, but there were things she could have known about if she'd wanted to know them. That was the thing about Darla: she was the kind of person who ignored whatever she didn't want to see. She was good at lying to herself. She had to be that kind of person, though—otherwise my dad wouldn't have kept her around for very long.

"Anyway, I knew something was off about that whole night, and I knew it had something to do with Turtle. There was my dad leaving so quietly, without his lights on, and then Frank's motor home burned down the same night. I knew it couldn't have been just a big coincidence. I think Darla knew, too, because she was different after that. She stayed with us for only a few more years, and I could feel her pulling away from me the whole time, as if she knew she was going to leave me eventually. Or as if she knew she was going to leave *us*, I guess I should say.

"We were drinking together one night, just the two of us. She was drunk as hell, and somehow I got up the courage to ask her about Frank and the night Turtle disappeared. She told me she thought that Frank had kidnapped Turtle, and that my dad knew about it. She thought my father had killed Frank so he wouldn't be able to hurt anybody else.

"I was at school the next day when Darla disappeared. I was

taking some classes at the community college. I was going to transfer after one more semester and go to nursing school. I always wanted to be a nurse. Did you know that?" she asks Remy and me.

We shake our heads.

"That was a dumb question. Of course you didn't know. I didn't talk about it much, not even with Gretchen. I thought if I told too many people or got my hopes up, it would definitely never happen. I used to do okay in school, you know, but my dad didn't want me going away to college. He wouldn't even let me move out after I graduated from high school. He liked to be in control. All the time."

Abby lights a cigarette and starts pacing back and forth across the living room, smoking while she talks. "I came home from class—I'd been in a biology lab all morning—and she was gone. She didn't even take all her stuff—just a few suitcases. She left a whole lot more behind than she took with her: all her Mary Kay supplies, most of her jewelry . . . It was as though she'd left in a big hurry."

"How do you know she actually left on her own?" Remy asks. "Maybe something happened to her."

"Maybe," Abby says. She doesn't elaborate. "My dad was a mess, though. So was I, if I'm being honest. Darla was the closest thing I ever had to a mother, you know. She'd been around since I was four, and she was always nice to me, even when I didn't deserve it."

Abby starts to cry. "I don't know if I *ever* deserved it, to be honest with you. I was a horrible kid. You can't even imagine the things I used to do. It's a miracle I'm still alive. My teenage years must have been hell for her. My dad sure as heck never paid much attention to me, not once I started getting older, but I always had Darla, even if she wasn't Mother of the Year. She wasn't perfect, but she was all I had, and it was better than nothing. Some of us have to take what we can get, wherever we can get it. Not every girl has parents who love her the way parents are supposed to love their kids. I miss her every day. I wish she'd call or write me a letter— anything at all. I'd just like to know that she's okay, wherever she is.

"So after she left," Abby continues, "my dad told me to box up the rest of her stuff and either throw it away or take it to Goodwill. He didn't care which, he said; he just told me to get rid of it. But I couldn't do it. Not with everything. I put some of her things in a box and took it up to the attic. I'd never even been up there before; I'd never had any reason. It's just a bunch of beams and insulation. But my father used to go up sometimes, and I didn't want him to know that I'd kept any of her stuff. He would have been furious with me. So I was walking around on the beams, trying to find someplace to tuck the box away where he wouldn't see it, and I saw this little rectangle cut into the drywall. I can't believe I even noticed it. I could barely make out the lines; they were almost impossible to see, and they really just looked like part of the drywall more than anything else—like a seam or something.

"I kind of tapped it a few times to see if it was loose, and it was. Once I'd pried it away, I looked through the hole, and I could see into the Souzas' attic.

"The holes went all the way across. There was another one on the opposite wall, leading to your attic"—she nods at Remy—"and one more going to yours," she says, looking at me and Gretchen.

My sister has obviously heard the whole story before. She listens quietly, her face stony and blank.

"I kept trying to convince myself there must be a good reason for them. I didn't want to think my dad had anything to do with it; I was hoping he didn't even know about them. So I put them all back into place, and then I hid Darla's stuff. I was about to leave—and that's when I saw the backpack." She swallows. "It was Frank's backpack. He was always carrying it around with him. I unzipped it to look inside, and I found Turtle's bear."

It feels as though all the air has been sucked from the room. I can barely breathe.

"So what did you do after that?" Remy glances toward the stairs as if he's afraid Ed can hear us. "Did you confront your dad? Did you ask him why he had Frank's book bag?"

"No. I didn't say anything."

"But you must have done something, right?"

"There were other things in the backpack. It wasn't just the bear. There were things that made me think my dad might have been the one who hurt Turtle."

"What kind of things?" Remy's the one asking questions now; I don't think I could speak even if I tried. My mouth feels as dry as sandpaper.

"There were pictures of her sleeping. Dozens of them. I guess he'd been sneaking into your house at night through your attic."

I feel like I'm going to throw up.

"He's a bad person." Abby wipes her eyes. "But he's my dad," she whispers, her whole body trembling. "How could I tell anyone? He's my *daddy*."

I remember Ed Tickle slipping handfuls of Altoid mints to Turtle whenever he saw her. The same Ed Tickle who built the playhouse in Remy's yard. I remember how he helped us look for my sister, passing out fliers and joining the search parties as they assembled into a single line at the edge of the woods. They lined up shoulder to shoulder to trek through the forest, one measured step at a time, so they wouldn't miss an inch of ground.

"But why was everything in Frank's backpack?" Remy's knuckles are white, his fingers squeezing my hand.

"I think," Abby begins, "that Frank was in the playhouse on New Year's Eve. It wouldn't have been the first time. He used to sleep there sometimes. I guess it was nicer than his motor home. I only know because Darla told me the night before she left.

"I think my father saw Steven in his costume and had an idea. I think he dressed up—there's a Santa suit in our attic—and kidnapped Turtle from your basement, and I think Frank saw him do it. Maybe Frank tried to stop him, and my dad had to kill him." She swallows. "I think the backpack is a souvenir. Just like the bear.

"When Gretchen got the letter from Davis a few months ago, she came to see me, to confront me about what I knew and when I'd known it. I told her everything. Then we waited until my dad left for work the next day, and I showed her the attic. I showed her the backpack."

Abby is trembling; she looks as if she might fall over any second. "Go get it," she tells Gretchen.

My sister walks to the kitchen and opens one of the cabinets. She pulls the backpack down from a high shelf, brings it into the living room, and hands it to me.

"Look inside," Abby says.

As I unzip it, she continues speaking. "I kept thinking about how my dad had been in such a good mood around Christmas last year. Now I knew why."

The first thing I see in the backpack is a wrinkled brown paper bag filled with something soft. I'm too afraid to look inside on my own, so I turn it over and dump the contents onto the rug.

It's hair. Piles and piles of long, red hair.

"It's Kate O'Neill's hair," Gretchen says. She stares at me. "And when she looked again at the photos of Turtle sleeping, Abby realized one of them was missing."

Ed Tickle abducted Kate O'Neill. Her family lived about ninety minutes south of us in Virginia. He stopped by to drop off Turtle's picture, either on his way there or back, even though it was a huge risk. Because it was *worth it* to him. Because he's the monster in this story; not Steven Handley or Frank Yarrow.

"We waited until the weekend, and then we poisoned his soup," Gretchen tells me softly. "But he didn't die."

She looks at each of us, one at a time, before her gaze comes to rest on my face. "He's up there right now, Sam. Breathing. He's in a lot of pain. He's hurting real bad." Her eyes start to well up and spill over. "We have to finish it soon. You can help us, Sam."

chapter thirty-four

When Remy and I leave Abby's house, Gretchen comes along with us. She brings the backpack. The three of us drive to the police station, where we sit in a bare, chilly room and tell our story to Officer Bert. He's the same policeman who listened as we said Steven Handley's name over hot chocolate in my kitchen a decade ago. We tell him about Abby's dad. We show him the backpack, and the red hair stuffed into the brown paper bag.

By the time police get to Point Pleasant, Ed Tickle is dead. The official cause of death is asphyxiation. He choked on his own vomit in his sleep.

This is how the story ends for him: his own daughter wouldn't pay for his funeral. He's buried in a cemetery a hundred miles from here, among the bodies of other men and women who went to their graves without ceremony—wards of the state who died alone in prison; nameless vagrants who will forever be known as John or Jane Doe; and people like Ed, whose families had no interest, for whatever reason, in purchasing a casket or gravestone or even saying a final prayer for their dead relatives. His grave, I'm told, is marked only by strictly functional coordinates etched into a small metal placeholder. If someone wants to dig up the land to make room for a strip mall in a hundred years, they won't get much resistance from any surviving relatives.

This is how the story ends for Steven: two days before Turtle's funeral, he walks out of the state penitentiary as a free man and feels the sunlight on his face, unobstructed by prison bars or guards or barbed wire fencing, for the first time in over a decade.

This is how the story ends for Gretchen: she goes back to Texas, where Mike Culangelo has been waiting for her all summer. She doesn't call or write.

Here is how the story ends for Abby Tickle: she is gone by the time the police get to her house and discover Ed's body in his room. Since then, plenty of well-meaning strangers have called in supposed sightings of Abby to the local police, none of which have turned out to be useful. People claim they've spotted her in coffee shops and strip malls from West Virginia to San Antonio. A local librarian swears Abby served her a beer at a bar in Cancun. They're all wrong, probably.

Here are some facts for you, along with some lies. You tell me what's true. Put the pieces together and see if they fit.

In the early morning on New Year's Day, 1986, two eyewitnesses saw Steven Handley kidnap Turtle Myers from her basement while her parents celebrated above them.

Betsy "Grandma Bitty" Mitchell died in her sleep after a miserable decline into paranoid dementia. The first sign that something was wrong came when the otherwise rational woman grew convinced that someone was sneaking into her bedroom at night and spying on her as she slept. Her family knew she was imagining things: they always locked their doors at night, and Betsy's bedroom was on the second floor. How could a person get in and out without there being any signs of a break-in? It would have been impossible.

Turtle Myers died ten years ago; her remains have never been found. Some people think there's a chance she's still out there, alive, maybe with Darla. Nobody knows what happened to her, either; nobody even knows her real last name.

Before we left Abby's house, Remy and I followed her and Gretchen upstairs into Ed Tickle's bedroom. He was alive, but barely. His face and clothing were caked in vomit from the poison that had been building up in his body all summer.

We watched Abby force his mouth open and tilt a cup of undiluted antifreeze down his throat. When he tried to resist, Gretchen helped Abby hold his head steady. Once he'd swallowed the last of it, Abby held her father's mouth shut while we waited for the poison to do its job. We watched him gag on his vomit when it came rushing up his throat, but we didn't help him. We watched his face turn blue and the skin beneath his eyelids swell with fluid. His mouth was messy with throw-up and spit, and his lips were purple.

We watched him die, and then we waited with his body for an hour in order to give Abby a head start.

Jane is fifteen. She lives with her mother, who sells Mary Kay and loves her only daughter more than anything in the world. Sometimes Jane dreams about a different life, with a different family. In the dreams, everybody calls her Turtle, or sometimes Tabitha. Some mornings after she wakes up, it takes her a while to figure out which life is real and which one is a dream. Sometimes she wonders whether they are both equally false. If she wakes in the middle of the night and goes down the hall to her mother's room, her mother turns on the light and gets her a glass of water. She tells Jane that she worries too much. *Don't let your dreams scare you*, she says. *Everything is fine. I'll never let anybody hurt you. Tomorrow will be a better day.*

Wouldn't that be nice?

acknowledgments

This was a difficult book to write. I never could have done it without the support, ingenuity, and general *goodness* of so many people. I don't know how or why I've been so lucky, but please know that I feel enormous gratitude and love for you all.

Emily Easton: The first time I met you in the flesh, we were at a dinner for the Walker/Bloomsbury folks to kick off the NCTE conference in Orlando. It was my first conference as a published author. I was terrified. Your kindness put me at ease that evening. When you became my editor, I was, once again, terrified by your knowledge and assuredness. I wouldn't take back a second of the time we spent working together. I learned a *lot* from you. Thank you for being tough on me! Thank you for pushing me, even when I resisted! Thank you for your confidence in my work! I'm a better writer because of it.

Laura Whitaker: You're a fabulous editor. I love working with you so much; I hope I didn't make you too crazy as deadline after deadline passed with each draft "basically finished" on my end, while I imagine you were ready to track me down and physically force me to wrap it up more than once. Your "put-the-skin-on-the-exposed-flesh-and-bone" analogy became my mantra during the last few months of revision. Thank you for putting so much time and energy into this inherited project.

Andrea Somberg: You've been my agent for, what, ten years? I'm still going to keep thanking you in every book, since none of them would have seen the light of day without your hard work.

All my dear friends: Mary Warwick, Penny (Sasha) Dawn, Alisa Shetter-Zisman, Jennifer Merck, Amanda Warman, Sameer Naseem, Mallory Warman, Scott and Patty Warman, Cheryl and Dennis Kenna. My late grandparents, Oliver and Mary Alice Kern: I miss you both very much. My daughters, Estella and Esme . . . I adore every last one of you, with all my heart.

Thanks also to Lisa Bevington, for your inspirational thoughts on the mass delusion that afflicts all children: Belief in Santa Claus.

Catherine M. LoChiatto

j e s s i c a   w a r m a n is the author of *Breathless, Where the Truth Lies, Between, Beautiful Lies,* and *The Last Good Day of the Year,* which have received seven starred reviews altogether. *Between* was published in a total of twelve countries around the world. Jessica has an MA in creative writing and lives in Texas.

www.jessicawarman.com

@jkwarman

Don't miss more stunning thrillers from
Jessica Warman

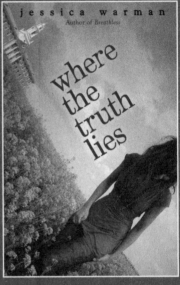